THE 13TH PROPHECY

The fifth book in the best selling
Demon Kissed Series

www.DemonKissed.com

Join over 45,000 fans on facebook!
www.facebook.com/DemonKissed

THE 13TH PROPHECY

H.M. WARD

Laree Bailey Press

Copyright © 2012 by H. M. Ward

Laree Bailey Press, 4431 Loop 322, Abilene, TX 79602

Printed in the United States of America
First Printing: March 2012
10 9 8 7 6 5 4 3 2 1

Library of Congress Cataloging-in-Publication Data

Ward, H.M.
The 13th Prophecy / H.M. Ward—1st ed.
 p. cm.
ISBN 978-0615598468

Bringing these characters to life
Has been an amazing experience.
Thank you to my friends and family
Who supported me while chasing my dreams.
And thank you to the awesome fans who loved
Demon Kissed from the very beginning!

Demon Kissed

H.M. WARD

PAINTING OF IVY TAYLOR

THE 13TH PROPHECY

CHAPTER ONE

The shadows surrounding the Pool of Lost Souls were different. They weren't just inky splotches of darkness—they appeared to be alive. The crevices on the stone walls of the massive cavern formed eyes that were hollow and dark. They seemed to shift as I moved, watching me. Waiting. This place filled me with dread, more so than the golden grave of the Lorren. Both locations were massive tombs, but this one—I don't know—there was something more ominous about it.

Something that made me want to run and never come back.

I glared at Eric, who was walking a few paces in front of me. His shoulders were squared as he walked along the edge of the Pool. Determination made his gait rigid, but I knew he was the reason why I felt the dread coursing through my body.

"Cut it out," I snapped. Since I pulled Collin through the mirror and said the Demon Princess' spell, my ability to numb my senses turned spastic. The sensations crept up on me like a breeze at my back. There was nothing I could do to eradicate the problem. There was no logical reason why I could feel again. The only correlation was Eric. It only seemed to happen around the fallen angel. As he walked on in front of me, with tension lining his tightly corded muscles, I couldn't comprehend why he'd choose to use bloodlust now to cause the remnants of my emotions to go haywire. The timing seemed off. It wasn't like he was reveling in my fear. He appeared to ignore it. It was strange. At times, a sudden flash of fear would crash thought my body like an icy hand squeezing my heart.

Eric turned his stoic gaze in my direction. Speaking over his shoulder he replied, "Some things are beyond my control." He didn't smirk. There was no pleasure in his expression. Whatever was happening, he didn't seem to be controlling it. Maybe the encounter at the mirror messed with him, too? I didn't know.

The skin on the back of my neck prickled. Annoyed at him, I smoothed away the gooseflesh with my hand saying, "Whatever, Eric."

In front of us, the blue waters went on forever, filling massive sections of the cavern that were completely lost in shadow. A choking sensation crept up my throat as I gazed at a shallow cove. The sand was crushed to powder and rock walls surrounded three sides. If the sun was suspended above, it would've looked like a beach.

Clearing my throat, I forced the accumulating tension back down. Somewhere in the back of my mind I wondered if I'd ever feel pleasure or pain on my own, without it being induced by blood. My chance of survival, however, was so remote that it wasn't worth thinking about.

Eric moved in front of me. His shoulders were broad, his muscles ripped tight. His head didn't swing side to side like he thought we were being watched, but I knew he sensed it too. We had to stay, because there was no other option. It wasn't like we could avoid this. Coming here was a necessity, a necessity that I created.

Eric cleared his throat. His light hair hung over golden eyes that narrowed to thin slits. He had been in a weird mood. This place bothered him, too. As we neared the crystal clear water, he stopped. Pain flashed behind his eyes, so quickly that I wasn't sure if I'd seen it.

He glanced over his shoulder and back at me. His voice was deep and soft, as if he knew we were being watched. "We shouldn't be here," he said. His gaze studied my face for a second, then returned to the surface of the water. He stared blankly, but I knew better than to think he wasn't paying attention. Eric didn't space out and get lost in his thoughts. He was the master of deception. If he was stone still, there was a reason for it.

But, since he wasn't sharing what that reason was, I pushed past him. I stopped when my shoe was less than an inch from the water within the Pool. Last time, the depths tried to kill us. Last time Eric and I stood here, we were mad at each other for different reasons. He was someone else then. So was I.

I cleared my throat, pushing the memories aside. I agreed with him. We shouldn't be here. It was the height of stupidity, but it was completely necessary and he knew it. "You know we have to do this. There isn't any other way to find that damn rock."

We needed Satan's Stone, but Eric couldn't remember much about it. Actually, he couldn't remember anything about the stone. That information was stored in his soul with no way to call the information to his mind. He was able to glean some memories from me, but that was only residue—traces of the energy from his soul, that was in my body. A demon kiss only supplies the Valefar with energy. The rest of the soul is thrown away and ends up in The Pool of Lost Souls. If we wanted the memories of angelic Eric using the stone, they would be found here.

We'd spoken with Lorren about how to get the information from his soul. Souls were difficult to understand. They contained energy that kept the body alive. It was this energy that fed the Valefar. After that, little was known about what they were or how they changed. It was clear that drained souls were prisoners in the Pool. Kreturus trapped them there, but none of us knew exactly why or how. That presented problems with extracting information from a soul. The best we came up with was, 'ask it.' If that didn't work, we'd wing it.

The thought of involving Eric more made me queasy. Every time I did something else, he seemed to get worse. I thought it was me. I thought I was the one who freed the dormant evil that rested within Eric, and awakened it. Eric was on his own crash course and I was on mine. I glanced at the Pool. Eric's soul was trapped in the crystal depths and would remain there for eternity.

I glanced around looking for the source of the eyes I felt on me. But there was nothing. No one sat across the water. There was nothing masked in the shadows. There was only the sound of the constant drip, drip, drip of water, and the hollow noise that fills massive empty spaces with silent echoes.

The last time one of us touched the water, it awakened the Guardian. Those who touched the water were pulled into its dark depths and drowned. But now that the Guardian was dead, was it still a risk? I didn't know and neither did Eric. It was possible that the Pool would still destroy anyone who touched it. There was only one way to find out. Brushing my hair back, I twisted it over my shoulder to get it out of the way, and crouched down next to the water. When I reached out to touch the surface of the Pool, Eric's fingers wrapped around my wrist. He'd knelt next to me.

The pressure on my wrist increased before he flung my hand back at me, slamming it into my chest, "No," he glared, practically growling. "It's my soul. I'm the one who'll try and call it. There's no point in both of us dying today." I didn't protest. We both knew the Pool could kill us. There was no time for disagreements. No time to consider if Kreturus threw something else within the waters, or what to do if Eric was killed.

Without another word, Eric slid his hand beneath the surface of the water. Stepping back, I watched an odd expression slide over his face as his lashes lowered. Eric watched the calm water lapping against his skin, forming ripples around his submerged hand. The tension that lined his shoulders eased, and he almost seemed peaceful.

But I knew now that Eric would never have peace. It was his price for using the stone. It made me angry and bitter. Time wouldn't heal his wounds. Rather, it seemed to make more, allowing them to fester inside of him. Without Al to guide him, Eric seemed lost. He'd spoken to Lorren a little bit, but both of them were so broken from using the stone, that they weren't much help to each other.

I fixed my gaze on the water, expecting it to wrap around Eric's arms and pull him under, but the Pool remained fluid. The water continued to lap the shore, moving normally against Eric's wrist. And that's when we saw it. A pale figure emerged from the depths of the Pool, and floated toward us—a figure that I recognized. I knew that the soul moving toward us was the Eric I killed. It was the Eric who saved me so many times. This was what was left of him—a silent soul, bound to the Pool.

My body tensed as Eric's frozen soul rose out of the water, higher and higher. He strode toward us with that familiar gate of his, each foot pressing down on the cool liquid beneath as if it were solid rock. Wide-eyed he stared at us, saying nothing. As the soul moved toward us, Eric remained at my feet with his eyes pressed closed. I watched him for a moment, considering whether or not I should say anything. Would the soul slip back into the water if I alerted Eric? I didn't know. So I waited until his soul was a stone's throw away.

Leaning forward, I tapped Eric's shoulder, and said, "Look." I'd bent down slightly, and leaned over his shoulder. Lifting my arm, I pointed toward the spot where his soul stood—pale and shimmering, a translucent blue sheen surrounding his ghostly form.

Eric had been crouching, lost in thought. When he opened his eyes, he was startled to see a mirror image of himself standing so close. If he reached out, he could touch the most precious thing he ever owned. My eyes darted between the two. I didn't know how Eric would react—either one of them. But neither one of them moved. They both stared at each other.

My heart jumped into my throat as I heard a sound. A small noise carried across the water. Eric and I both stared and then looked at each other. Something was across the lake, sitting in the darkness, watching. We didn't have time for this. We didn't have time to deal with a stalker. We had to get the information and get out. As it was, I had no idea where Kreturus went after I nearly killed him. I seriously doubted that he'd

~ 8 ~

spare my life if he found me down here. I tried to kill him. I enraged an ancient demon and was messing with his lost souls.

I swallowed hard and lifted my hand from his shoulder. "Eric. Ask him. Ask him where the stone is."

Eric's soul turned his head slowly toward me. His eyes were wide, but instead of orbs of gold—they were Caribbean blue. My breath caught in my throat. The soul contained all of Eric's softness. The kindness, the things that tempered his rage and thirst for vengeance were all contained in the being in front of us. That meant the boy sitting next to me was pure evil—and I made him that way. I made him …

Eric reached his long fingers out toward his soul. Eric's soul mirrored the gesture, lifting his pale hand. Their fingers lined up perfectly, like a mirror was wedged between them.

"Where did I hide the other half of Satan's Stone?" he asked. "I don't remember, but I know you do. Can you tell me?" Eric's voice didn't shake, but it didn't sound normal either. He didn't control himself in that second, and his emotions hit me like a brick.

My eyes darted between them as my heart pounded in my chest, sensing the anxiety and hopelessness that was within Eric. I edged closer to the two, my face turning to Eric's soul to see what he would say.

A familiar voice rang out behind me, making my heart leap into my throat. "The dead can't speak."

CHAPTER TWO

Collin stood in the shadows. His hair was matted to his scalp. Grime and blood were smeared across his face. But his eyes—they were bright blue, richer than I'd ever seen them. He stepped toward us.

Eric's arm flew up in front of me in a protective stance as he pulled me away from Collin. He whispered in my ear, "Effonate." It wasn't a request. I tried to pull away, but Eric wouldn't release me. I could overpower him, but his blood was messing with my brain. I couldn't think.

Twisting my shoulders, I said, "No. Wait. He's..." but I didn't get to finish.

The same noise I heard before echoed over the water, louder this time. All three of us turned toward the source of the sound. Something was coming. And I had no doubt who sent it after me—Kreturus. We had to finish this and leave now. But I knew Eric wouldn't trust Collin blindly. He needed proof. Something definitive and final that would allow us to know if this was the boy I loved or the monster who tried to kill me. Collin watched us, his eyes sliding over Eric's arm around my waist.

I cleared my throat, speaking before Eric had a chance to ask him. "Prove it," I said. "Prove that you're Collin and not Kreturus. Quickly."

Palms up, Collin smiled and stepped toward us. But Eric's grip around my waist tightened as he pulled me back, stepping into the water. The frozen Pool soaked through the bottoms of my shoes. A shiver crawled up my spine. Eric's soul stood next to us, watching.

Collin's smile faded. His eyes met mine as he spoke, "There's no way to prove that to you, but something happened. After you left, Kreturus tried to reclaim me, but he couldn't. Your spell did something to him. I don't know what, but he couldn't re-enter me. Ivy..." his eyes were wide, brilliant blue, and

~ 12 ~

pleading—begging me to believe him, "you severed my blood bargain." His lips remained parted as the last words fell to the ground in a deafening thud.

"But... That's not possible." My voice was weak, not even a whisper. Eric's grip around me tightened and I glanced over my shoulder at him. I wanted affirmation. I needed him to tell me if it was possible. I didn't think a blood bargain could be broken.

Eric glared at Collin, snapping, "You can't believe him, Ivy." His grip around my chest tightened, smashing my torso flat like an oversized seat-belt.

"And she can believe you?" Collin retorted, stepping closer to us.

Eric was breathing hard. I could feel his chest rise and fall against my back. His muscles tensed, ready to fight, "She..." Eric began, but he never got to answer. The faint sound that had traveled across the surface of the water was suddenly louder. Much louder. And it rushed at us in a deafening gust.

Collin's eyes widened as his jaw dropped, slowly turning toward the sound. Tension rippled the muscles in his arms. He stepped toward us, wrapping his fingers around my forearm. "He knows you're here." I looked up at him. No icy hot flash traveled through his touch. The bond was broken. "Kreturus sent something. We need to leave now - before it gets here."

I shook free of Eric and Collin, turning toward the direction of the sound. The blood lust altering my thoughts faded without Eric's touch. I could think. Across the waters of the Pool of Lost Souls there was a massive opening in the cavern wall. Behind it was nothing but endless blackness. Shadows thicker than tar dampened all the noises that flooded from that cave—except this one. This sound was a cross between a roar and a screech, and as it got closer there was no doubt in my mind that it belonged to something hideously large.

But we couldn't leave. Not yet. We couldn't walk away empty handed. Kreturus knew we were here. It was possible he'd destroy Eric's soul, and then we'd never find the stone. We had to get the stone. We'd all die without it. I wasn't leaving without getting that information. I'd rather die trying. The pit of my stomach twisted as I turned back toward Eric's soul. "If he can't speak, then we need to take his memories."

Eric's mouth hung open. He didn't follow my thoughts at first. Or maybe he did, but he was too desperate to protest what I was going to do. It felt like I was like desecrating his grave, messing with his soul, but there were no other options. His soul was stuck in the Pool. The only way to take it with us was to shove it back into Eric.

Instead of refuting me, Eric nodded and asked, "How?"

I didn't answer. Instead, I closed my eyes and focused on my power. It was coiled tightly, deep within me. Lifting my hand toward Eric's soul, I opened my eyes. The ghostlike boy reached for my hand. At the same time his fingers slid into my palm, a rush of wind blasted me in the face from the screaming cavern across the water. Kreturus' beast was coming.

The gale was so strong that Eric and Collin were pushed away from me. Power anchored me in place, and before Eric was out of my reach, my other hand grabbed him by the wrist. My hair whipped around my shoulders, as I locked eyes with Eric. *Trust me*, was the only thing I thought. If he messed with me while I was trying to do this, I had no idea what would happen. Eric nodded once, quickly. His eyes darted across the water, watching the massive black hole, waiting for the creature to appear.

Collin stumbled behind me, and lowered himself to the ground so the force of the wind wouldn't knock him off his feet. His arms covered his face, keeping the sand from pelting his eyes. I wanted to know if he was the boy and not the demon, but there was no time left. I supposed we would find out shortly. If Collin helped the beast, then he was still bound to Kreturus. If he helped us, he was free.

~ 15 ~

Pressing my eyes closed, I felt power snake from my stomach, uncoiling, and sliding into my chest as I remained still. Collin shouted as something screeched out of the opening across the Pool. Eric's eyes went wide as he stared slack-jawed at the beast. Its wings were spread wide, and the wind rippled over the edge of its enormous black feathers. Its head was angular with two small eyes that burned like fire. Scales mixed with feathers, covering its grotesque body. Its underbelly was almost human, with strong muscles and taught arms with fingers balled into fists. It looked like a demon, a human, and a bird all in one. The beast cried again, and the cavern shook with its screech.

Warmth trailed from my ears and trickled down my neck. I glanced at Eric and saw him touch the trail of blood that flowed from his ear with his free hand. When he turned his palm to confirm that blood was flowing from his ears, he said, "We have to fight it! Ivy, stop!" He tried to pull his hand out of mine, but I wouldn't let him. The power that I'd used would claim the pain price any second and I wasn't doing this for nothing.

The hideous creature barreled at us from across the water. It's wings were spread wide as it moved across the surface of the water. Another cry emanated from its beak, echoing across the water. The sound bounced off the walls making it sound worse. Eric pressed his hand to his ears, trying to protect them from the sound. But I wouldn't release his other hand. The trickle under that ear increased. It was possible this beast could kill with it's scream.

Without another thought, I felt the dark magic begin. Everything happened in a matter of seconds, but during those seconds, time seemed frozen—stuck. Staring down a frightening beast with outstretched talons and a death cry can do that. The magic fused Eric's grip to mine. Our palms glowed dark purple and black. It looked as if streams of smoke billowed out between our hands, swirling upward under a black light.

With each second, my grip grew hotter and hotter. Eric's face turned white as the beast grew closer and closer. It would reach us any second. If its maw could draw blood with a screech, I didn't want to think about what its beak could do. I closed my eyes, blocking everything out. I didn't hear the screams. I ignored the rushing wind that was powerful enough to knock me over. But I stood, with my feet fixed in the bottom of the Pool of Lost Souls where my power grounded me. If I didn't finish this fast enough, that thing was going to kill all of us.

Concentrating on the grip of Eric's soul, I felt it meld to my hand. And then Eric's soul began to fade as it was absorbed into my body. The spell I used transferred energy from one form to another, using a conduit. I was the conduit. Eric's soul was the energy. It was a guess. I didn't know if it was working or if I was destroying his soul. The palm gripping Eric's hand burned like it was in a raging fire, the other turned cold—like I was holding the hand of the dead. And I was. The coldness soon faded and I felt the soul being absorbed into my body. It moved through me quickly and snaked into Eric's body through our woven together fingers, and up his arm.

Eric screamed as if the two were alien to each other when I forced them to fuse. His arm jerked, trying to end the transfer. But I wouldn't release him. We needed the stone. We had to have it. Eric stopped fighting, and his grip went slack. His face contorted with pain as he pressed his eyes closed and forced his body to relax. That was when I felt it. The magic completed itself. Eric's soul was in his body. My hand dropped to my side, exhausted.

Eric fell to the ground, his arms pushing him upright as he tried to stand, but the magic weakened him. His arms gave way and he crashed into the shallow water at the edge of the Pool. His eyes closed, and I wondered if I killed him. But there was no time to consider anything. When I looked up, the beast was about to crash into me. Dropping to my knees, I tried to avoid his hands, but he grabbed me. Cold flesh burned into my arms, as the beast plucked me from the shore. Its grip on my arms tightened as it turned sharply.

Just as we turned, the pain price for merging Eric's soul back into his body pounded into me. Suddenly, there was no air. It felt as if it had been ripped from my lungs in one merciless gush. My jaw opened to scream, but nothing came out. The pain price stole my voice, my breath, and if it didn't stop—my life. My hands frantically tried to grasp my throat, as if that would help. But the beast's grip on my arms didn't falter. Pressing my eyes closed, I tried to suppress the panic that was lacing up my spine and squeezing every last bit of air from my body like a steel corset. The force that was crushing me didn't ease, but continued to grow. A sharp snapping sound came from my chest as it filled with fire. And then it happened again. Rib after rib cracked, like my bones were made of toothpicks. Pop. Snap. Fire. Burning flames poured through my chest in an unrelenting wave.

I pressed my eyes shut, trying to endure the pain, when the beast was hit from the side. It screeched as its body was sent off kilter, slamming into the cavern wall. The burning cold hands that clutched my arms went slack. Wind rushed against my face as I opened my eyes. I was falling toward the Pool. My hair streaked around my face in a wild tangle. I barely pressed my lips closed as I crashed into the Pool of Lost Souls and sank beneath the surface. I continued to tumble downward, out of control as the frigid gel-like water penetrated every inch of my body. The pain price continued as I drifted down, deeper and deeper, into the Pool. When my body finally collided against the bottom, my fingers frantically grasped at the silt.

The pain price stopped as abruptly as it started. I forced my eyes open. Something to my left gleamed, though it was mostly covered with mud. Recognition flashed. It was a tooth—a silver tooth. Reaching out, I grabbed it and shoved it in my belt. Launching myself off the Pool floor, I swam back to the surface. My lungs burned as I kicked wildly. Now they were really starved for air. I couldn't tell how far away the surface of the Pool was. It was so dark. I just kicked my feet as fast as I could, hoping that my face would break through the surface any second. But it didn't.

With each passing second, nothing changed. I kicked, stretching my arms, and thrusting the thick water back with my cupped hands, but the surface seemed just as far away. My lungs felt like they were on fire. The ceaseless burning made me want to open my mouth and gasp. That's when things got weird. At first I thought it was from the lack of air. I heard voices crying in the darkness like lost children. Going against every urge I had, I stopped struggling and remained still. I didn't swim, or kick. I waited. I waited to hear it again.

Holding my breath, I watched as a girl formed in front of me. Her body was small and lean. Blue hair floated around her face. "Please save us. Please. You're the one. You must be..." She wore a pinafore. It moved under the water, like a piece of paper caught in a stream. Desperation was as visible on her face as it was in her voice.

I stared at her, thinking I must have opened my mouth and died. I must have drowned. The dead weren't supposed to be able to speak. They shouldn't have been able to talk—but I heard her. Fear entered my mind. There were things I wanted to do—things I'd left undone. Collin. Regret smashed into me, nearly making me open my mouth and scream. The girl must have recognized the look on my face. She reached up, keeping me from opening my mouth, and pressed two fingers to my lips. A burst of fresh air rushed into my lungs. Coughing, and slightly shocked, I looked at her with wide-eyes. Just when I thought I had a good grip on things, it turned out I didn't.

I thought I drowned, but couldn't make sense of what was happening, "Did I die?" was all I managed to ask.

Smiling, she shook her head sadly, "No, you're still alive. Keep breathing. The magic will keep you alive.

There is nothing down here that can hurt you. Not anymore. Not since he left."

Her little fingers stayed pressed to my lips. I breathed again, slower this time. When I exhaled little bubbles rushed out. I watched them rise and fade in the darkness. Looking back at her, I asked, "You mean the Guardian?"

She nodded, "He controlled us. We were forced to destroy anything that touched the water, constantly adding more souls who could never escape. The Pool is magic—dark magic. Although the Guardian is gone, we still cannot leave." Her head tilted sadly to the side, "But, you can save us. You can free us." Her fingers remained pressed to my lips and I continued to breathe. My hair floated around me as I watched her glowing face. "We are neither dead nor living. Kreturus drains our power for his own use. Destroy the Pool and you'll lessen his power. You'll make him weaker."

The little ghost girl watched me as I asked, "I thought this place was filled with the dead. How...?" My mouth moved but I didn't know what to ask.

Another girl, an older girl, appeared. My heart lurched. It was the soul of my sister—Apryl. "We're not what you think we are. We're souls with no bodies. There is no form to cling to. No comfort. No warmth. We're trapped in an eternal grave that cultivates us for our power. A soul contains endless power as long as it's separated from flesh. The living are weaker. They die when he uses their power. But we do not. And until now, no one has been able to penetrate the waters and live. And yet, here's my little sister." She smiled and my gut twisted with remorse. She saw it flash across my face as she floated closer to me. Her hair billowed around her face, but lacked the normal color of a fiery sunset. Instead it was a cold and pale greenish blue like everyone else trapped down here. "You've already mourned me. There is no saving us. Not one of us can walk the world again. We're stuck here, Ivy. There is no rest, no peace for us as long as we are trapped here. Do you know what that's like? To die a violent death, and know you're trapped forever, only to be used again and again? We've made him invincible. But you can undo him." She pointed at the sliver tooth in my belt. When I saw it on the bottom of the Pool, I didn't know why I picked it up. It was spontaneous. Now I wondered if they compelled me to do it. I could feel their desperation all around me. Her thin fingers pointed at the tooth. "You can alter this. If you add your power to the fang and stab the surface of the Pool, you'll free all of us."

She watched me, never blinking, waiting for an answer. If I made it to the surface alive, I didn't know what I would find. The beast was up there. Suddenly, it didn't matter. I could do this—if it was what they wanted. And any help I could get in defeating Kreturus was help I'd take. But it felt like I was destroying them—all of them.

I found my voice, "Are you sure this is what you want? All of you?" I looked around now seeing hundreds of faces nodding. They encircled me. The sorrow in their eyes was fathomless. I stared at my sister. Was she a shadow? A ghost? What was a soul anyway? "Where will you go? And how do I add my power to the fang?"

Apryl smiled at me. "You'll know. Stab the Pool, little sister. The rest will be revealed over time..." And she faded into the darkness.

I glanced around and all the faces surrounding me were swallowed by shadows, until only the little girl who pressed her two fingers to my mouth remained. I smiled at her, swallowing hard, I said, "I'll do it. Help me get to the surface." I had no idea how long I'd been under, but when I emerged, I didn't expect to see what I saw.

The beast was half crippled with one of its wings hanging at an odd angle down its scaly back. It stood on hind legs where its talons gouged the rock in long, deep scrapes. Collin stood in front of a lifeless Eric, still sprawled on the shore. He'd been fighting the beast, waiting for Eric to wake up. A smile formed on my lips. Collin was fighting the creature. That meant he was free—the blood bargain was really broken. Somehow my botched spell freed him from Kreturus. And he needed help. Collin couldn't hold that thing off forever. But first things first.

I looked down at the Guardian's tooth in my hand. The beast didn't notice that I'd returned from the depths. It screeched at Collin as its claws and beak tried to snap him in half. The side of Collin's head was covered in blood. He fell to his knees. Sweat covered his body. Ignoring the massive amount of blood that trailed behind Collin, I lifted my hands and felt the air move around me.

In my mind, I repeated: Destroy the Pool. Destroy the Pool. It would alter Kreturus' power. It would make it easier to win. But there was so much blood... I averted my eyes, ignoring Collin's bleeding form. Focus! But I couldn't. I had to help him.

As I called my power, it snaked from my belly and curled into my palms like a sleeping cat. The pain price could kill me. I had no idea how much power it would take. And it was too soon after using my powers from before. Doing something of this magnitude back to back was suicide, but I had no choice. I could see the desperation on Collin's face. I couldn't ignore it. He needed my help. Altering my intended spell, I held my hands palms up, toward the roof of the cave. Magic snaked from my fingers into a thick shadow. The inky blackness crept toward the creature and wrapped around its neck, squeezing. The beast continued to fight as I continued to strangle it. Its massive jaws snapped once at Collin's shoulder, tearing its beak through his soft flesh. Then he swiped twice with his claws. One swipe missed, but the other made contact with Collin's chest and knocked him to the ground.

My jaw locked as tension lined my chest. The animal should have fallen already, but it continued to fight, ignoring me. Rage flashed through me, fueling my hatred. Another swipe would kill Collin. I couldn't allow that. My fingers clamped tighter and I tugged the shadows - hard. The sudden yank caught the creature's attention. A blood red eye zeroed in on me and it turned. And then charged. My hands pulled tighter and harder as the beast barreled down at me, shortening the slack in the black rope. I didn't flinch as its massive bladed beak came within inches of my face. With a twist of my wrist, I yanked the dark rope to the side - hard. A loud crack echoed through the cavern as the rope tightened, turning to steel in my hands, and shattering the bones of the beast's neck. The creature's eyes became hollow, no longer seeing. The beast's body crashed onto the ground at my feet, its neck snapped.

Releasing the steel rope, I sank to my knees as the pain price hit. The surge of agony forced me forward and I fell into the shallow waters of the Pool of Lost

Souls. Pushing myself up to my knees, I lifted the silvery tooth from my pocket. When Apryl's soul told me to add my power, I wasn't sure what she meant. But in that moment, I knew. My power was within me, beating in my heart, and coursing through my body—my blood. Taking my comb from my hair, I cut my palm. Blood flowed from the center of my hand, covering the silvery fang. I raised it over my head, watching my blood drip off the fang and into the clear water. The red drop dissolved, disappearing from sight instantly. A wild scream tore from my throat, as the pain price rippled through my body and new powers were unleashed.

I thrust down the bloody tooth in one hard strike. The tooth hit the surface of the water. My arms jarred on impact like I'd struck a solid surface. Red lines—my blood—spidered out from the point where the fang sat wedged in the water like it was ice. The scarlet veins spread across the surface of the blue waters, widening and lengthening as they spread. And then the Pool exploded like a pane of glass. Shards flew through the air in a blinding shimmering mess.

I covered my face with my arms, falling to the ground, no longer able to watch. As the pain price ripped through me, demanding my full attention, my body writhed without my consent. I curled into a ball, waiting for it to pass, but it lasted longer and hit me harder. Each successive use of dark magic cost more. And more. The venom in my chest burned. Clenching my teeth, I waited.

Eric remained motionless a few feet from me. Collin moved slowly toward me, holding his hand on his bloody side. I was barely aware of the souls screaming as they raced past us, emerging from the shattered surface of the lake. The souls shot between the shards with ease, climbing higher and higher, until their ghostly bodies dissolved into tiny specks of pure white light.

CHAPTER THREE

"Ivy," Collin's fingers pushed a curl away from my face. My eyes flicked opened. Every inch of my body felt like it'd been broken. "Are you all right?" I nodded faintly, trying to push the screaming pain coursing through my body to the back of my mind. A smile spread across Collin's bloodied lips. Sapphire blue eyes looked down at me. "You're a bad lair." His gaze darted over to the remains of the beast, and then back to my face. He hesitated to touch me, like I might still be unsure about him.

He knelt next to me, and continued, "The Pool of Lost Souls was one of Kreturus' main power supplies—and from the looks of it, you completely destroyed it and killed the messenger he sent to grab you. As badass as that was, we can't stay here." My eyes slid across his face, searching for him—for the Collin I knew. A crooked smile lined his lips as he offered me his hand. I took it and he helped me sit up. The cavern spun as I reached for my head. "There's a reason why I didn't just effonate you out of here. It seems we have another problem…" His voice trailed off as he glanced over my shoulder.

Eric stood there, golden eyes wide as he looked around the cavern. The more he craned his neck to take in his surroundings the more tense his arms and back became. I turned to Collin and asked quietly, "Why is he staring like he doesn't know where he is?"

I rose and walked toward Eric, reaching for him slowly. He seemed lost. Like he wasn't sure what happened or how he got here. His fingers clenched into fists. I understood why Collin didn't just take me and leave. He knew I needed Eric. Stepping closer, Eric startled and spun on his heel. His hands were in fists, close to his body. Defending himself.

I put up my hands, palms facing him, "Easy, Eric. Don't you … " but my voice died in my throat. The skin above his brow was smooth. Where was his mark? His scar? My voice was stuck in the back of my throat, trying to speak, but nothing came out. I stared wide-eyed, blinking slowly as Eric gazed at me. His hands slowly lowered to his sides, but the tension came back as soon as Collin stepped toward me.

Collin whispered in my ear, "I thought he was dead, but he woke up a second before you and started to move around. I'm not sure he remembers anything, but the look on his face says he does. I think he's just got holes in his memory, and is trying to fit the pieces back together. Having your soul back can do that. It'll pass. But that," Collin nodded, "that is permanent." He saw it too. No mark. Collin paused for a second, his eyes watching Eric. "Whatever you did to him worked better than what Kreturus did to me, but it seems to have had an unpredicted outcome."

Eric stared at both of us, recognition forming in his eyes. His gaze narrowed in first on Collin and then when it slid to me, scorn flashed brightly behind his eyes. He swallowed hard and redirected his gaze toward Collin, arms folded across his chest. Eric's voice sounded like the scornful Valefar version, "What? What now?" He shook his head, demanding an answer.

I stepped in front of him and reached for his hair. I had to be sure that the mark hadn't moved. I had to see for myself. As my fingers grazed his hair, Eric's hand shot out. His fingers wrapped tightly around my wrist, stopping me from touching him. It was completely beyond my comprehension as to how this could have happened. It wasn't possible. I couldn't be seeing what was so plainly clear. Eric's hair was filled with dirt and blood, clinging to his head. Smears of mud clung to his face. He'd tried to wipe it away. But it wasn't the blood, dirt, or wounds that made me falter. His fingers pressed into my arm as he shook it and threw it away from him. The jolt helped me find my voice. Locking onto his golden eyes, I said, "Your mark is gone." There was no trace of his Valefar scar. There was no lingering Martis mark in its place. There was nothing. I couldn't stop staring. My mouth hung open, completely shocked.

Eric pressed his fingers to his head. His eyebrows pinched together as if he didn't believe me. But the shock that was so clearly plastered across my face made it impossible to ignore. Eric turned toward the Pool. He fell to his knees and glanced at his reflection. His voice came out in a shallow puff of air, "Well, what the fuck does that mean?"

Eric's eyes were wide. For a split second, I could see fear behind them, fear which was quickly masked with anger. He practically snarled at me, but I didn't understand what happened. Souls couldn't merge with a body, not if the soul was good—which Eric's was—and the body was corrupt. The two became separate, acquiring different characteristics that made them impossible to fuse. That was what happened to Collin. That was why his soul was damaged and miniscule.

Kreturus destroyed it, twisting it, trying to force it into a body that had done heinous things. Confusion lined my face. There were only two logical reasons—I was able to do what Kreturus couldn't—or Eric never drained a soul from a mortal.

I turned to Collin with my mouth hanging open, and my brows at different shocked heights, asking the questions that were running through my mind. "How could this be? He was a Valefar. He had to kill to survive. That wasn't optional, was it?" Collin shook his head. I stared at Eric as his irritation grew as he listened, gazing in the water at his smooth skin. "I didn't think his soul would even go back into his body after what he'd done, but the two bonded like drops of water."

Collin stepped toward Eric. The movement made Eric stop staring at his reflection and jump to his feet. It didn't matter what he was—he didn't trust Collin. Collin glanced at Eric and then back at me. "It shouldn't have. Something's wrong here. It appears that he's no longer claimed by anyone. That's what the mark and scars are—a claim of ownership. You broke my blood bargain with Kreturus, but my scar is still on my head. It changed, but it's not gone. This is suspicious." Collin touched his chin with his fingers and circled Eric. Eric remained silent, as tension built within every muscle of his body. Eric's eyes narrowed into slits, watching. His fingers curled into fists at his sides. "The only way for his body to accept his soul would be if he failed to perform his basic Valefar right." Collin folded his arms. A surprised expression moved across his face. He asked Eric, "How'd you survive if you didn't kill? That's the only way for a Valefar to live. We have to demon kiss a victim, and steal their soul. If we don't, we die. So how'd you avoid it?"

Shock slammed into me again. Eric was an evil bastard. I made him that way. He killed lots of people. He did. He had to. But, as I stared at him slack-jawed, I wasn't so sure. Was it even possible? Shaking my head, I stepped between them and said, "It doesn't matter. We have to leave. Now." A frantic feeling was creeping up my spine.

Collin nodded, "I didn't take you before because you seemed hell-bent on having him with you. If he's mortal, he can't effonate with us. And it'd be suicide to try to walk him out of here. The portal is on the other side of the Pool. The Pool spans through half the Underworld. As soon as Kreturus realizes his beast is late, he'll send another—if he doesn't come himself."

I turned to Eric. His body was still rigid. "Can you effonate? Do you feel any of the power you had before? Any of mine?" Collin's lips parted as if he was going to say something, but he snapped his jaw shut instead.

A smug smile crossed Eric's face, a smile that made me think the next words out of his mouth were less than truthful. He looked down at me, shaking his head. "No. It's gone." His eyes never left mine. We couldn't leave him.

Collin reached into his pocket and was about to cut his hand with his black blade when I stopped him. Resting my hand across his, I looked into his eyes. "No. Eric has to realize that he's an ally. He can't do that if he's blood-bound to you." Collin's jaw twitched. He looked past me, at Eric. "I'll take him with me." I turned toward Eric, but Collin grabbed my arm.

"I can't let you do that! You're too weak." He looked down into my eyes, pleading with me, "Don't do this. There are safer ways..." He stroked his thumb along my cheek. I wanted to take his hands and press them to my cheeks, my lips...

Eric moved toward me. He was standing behind my shoulder by the time Collin stopped speaking. The two of them had always hated each other. And I didn't have time for a debate, or jealousy, or anything at the moment. Eric slid his arm behind my back, and Collin tensed. Eric said, "I'll walk out of here before I let one of you feed me blood."

I didn't shake Eric off. I slid my arms around Eric's waist, and pulled him against me. His muscles were tightly wound. The tension rolling off his body was scary—especially if he was human—which I didn't entirely believe. With a deep breath, I said to Collin, "We'll meet up with you. Go to the place where I first met you. Okay?" Heat snaked from my stomach, slowly filling my limbs. Fire coursed through my veins as I waited for Collin to reply. He met my eyes for a moment, and nodded. Then Eric and I were engulfed in a surge of heat and the world blazed around us.

CHAPTER FOUR

This wasn't the first time I effonated with Eric. His body was pressed against mine tightly. I could feel the curve of his chest beneath my cheek, and his hands pressed firmly to my back. Heat surrounded us, making it impossible to speak. Normally, the pain would have made me cry out, but I locked my jaw and focused on where I was taking us. I didn't say the exact location, because it was possible that Kreturus heard us. I hoped the place was still standing. I hoped I remembered correctly—that the school basement was an unused bomb shelter. It had the faded gold fallout shelter sign on the rear exit that went into the school parking lot. If it really was a bomb shelter, we should be safe there—at least for a little while.

The drain of effonating with Eric began to take its toll and we weren't there yet. The flames felt like they were ripping through my throat and cracking it apart in a fiery blaze. My body tensed under Eric's arms as I tried to swallow the pain. Effonating two people hurt like hell because it was double the pain price. His fingers pressed into my back. I could feel ten points of contact infuse my body with a burst of cool water. His lips pressed to my forehead and the pain abated.

I didn't have time to wonder what he did or how he did it. If I didn't focus, I'd kill both of us. Whatever Eric did, made it possible for me to control the effonation again. I pressed my eyes closed, trying to see the dark corner of the stage, the spot behind the curtain where I first met Collin. As soon as I remembered the cinderblock walls, the burgundy velvet curtain tucked in the corner, and the catwalk that was overhead, we were there. The space appeared as if a dream materialized before my eyes.

Eric and I released each other and gasped. Collin wasn't here yet. I leaned against the cold wall, sucking in deep breaths of air. The large deep red curtain still hung across the wooden stage. We were in the shadow of the right wing, hidden between the curtain and the wall. The black curtains hung in tatters between the door to the basement and where we stood. It looked like they burned in random places. They resembled Swiss-cheese more than curtains.

Eric stood across from me, unfazed. Shadows fell across his eyes, making him look more dangerous. I panted, trying to resume a normal rate of breathing. I walked toward him, looking up at him. Eric stood a head taller than me. His hair was a mess, and dangling in his eyes. Blood and dirt clung to his arms, marring the smooth surface of his skin. Eric stared at me, blank-faced, as I asked, "How'd you do that?"

What did I do to him this time? What was he? There was no way he was a mortal, not if he could help control the effonation. A mortal might not even survive it. I reached for his hand, and he let me take it this time. He watched as I turned his palm over and traced the lines with my finger. Staring at his palm, I felt his warm hand in mine. What did I do to him? What was he? A demon with a soul? A fucked up angel? I didn't know. My finger glided across the surface of his hand. I looked up into his face. He looked like the same messed up version of Eric that I made in the Lorren. He was acting the same. But he was different somehow. After he was silent, and made no move to respond, I said, "You're not going to tell me, are you?"

Eric watched me. His eyes darted between my face and my grip on his hand. Finally, he replied, "I realize that you think I know everything, but I don't know what happened with this. My mark's gone. I can lie, so I've not reverted to my previous angelic form. And yet, I still have some power." He shrugged looking down at me. "But I don't know whose power it is, or why it worked. Maybe it's some of your power. Maybe it's something new. You changed me. Again.

"And when you asked me if I could effonate before, there was no way I could harness the power to start it. But now?" He shrugged. "I might be able to. It's hard to tell. Maybe slamming my soul back into my body didn't mix well. How the hell should I know?" I stared at him, willing him to give more of an explanation. But Eric shook his head, saying, "What do you want from me, Ivy? I couldn't effonate before, but with you—after it started—I could lend to it ... and remove some of the pain you felt." He tilted his head, his eyes searching my face. Pain had fascinated him, especially my pain. His action didn't jive with crazy evil Eric, but the placid expression on his face did.

"So, you're not hellbent on torturing me anymore?" I asked.

A wicked smile twisted his lips, "I didn't say that. Make no mistake—nothing has changed. I still want to watch you cower as I tear you apart. Pain and pleasure,

Ivy. Your pain is my pleasure. However, I'm not stupid enough to allow it to destroy us both. I can siphon pain off, if I choose to do so. And at that moment, I would have reveled in watching you cry out as you burned, but I wasn't going to go down with you." He jerked my hand to his chest, placing it over his heart. "Feel that?" His heart was racing. I swallowed hard, staring at his eyes, leaning in closer. Bloodlust was overpowering me. My mind was growing hazy, my eyes unfocused. I nodded slowly. "That's what you do to me … Every time I see you, my pulse shoots through the roof at the thought of watching you suffer for everything you've done to me."

My throat was tight. It felt like I could barely breathe. The dried blood on Eric's face smelled so good. I couldn't pull away. It didn't matter that he was crazy. I leaned into him harder, pushing my body against his, leaning on my tip toes. He watched me with delight, as I flicked my tongue across his cheek. I pressed my eyes closed, savoring the taste of him in my mouth as he laughed. "Do you want more, little slave?" A beautiful smile lined his lips. The blood I'd tasted held little power. I wasn't sure why I did it. Why I didn't try to control the urge.

I shoved away from him, fighting the haze from being too close to him when Collin appeared next to us. We broke apart like we'd been caught doing something we shouldn't have been doing. I had difficulty hiding my hatred for Eric. The way he used me and manipulated me, without fear, made me nuts. He didn't think I'd fight back. He should be afraid of me. I was stronger than him! And yet, he dared to do this to me over and over! And knowing Collin was coming right behind us. He made me lick dried blood! Disgust rushed through me. Eric had a cocky smile on his face. He lifted his eyebrows once, as he folded his arms over his chest to taunt me. My fists balled at my sides as I glared at him.

Collin sucked in a gasp of air, and coughed. He glanced at us, knowing something happened. Whether he saw it or not, I didn't know. And I didn't want to admit I'd swallowed Eric's blood. Or that I was addicted to it. The more demon blood I had in me, the more I became like them. The demons. I was losing myself. I could feel myself being drowned out by his blood, being forced to be something I was not. The worst part was, I felt nothing looking at Collin. He was so close, but he might as well have been a lamp pole. I felt nothing around him. Eric used his blood to play on my emotions. That was the only time I felt anything.

Collin looked at me. I smiled at him, trying to ignore Eric. Collin said, "I remember meeting you here—how you didn't even give me the time of day." He smiled, remembering me blowing him off. He looked around at the rest of the theater, moving toward the center of the stage. Turning back to me, he said, "We're lucky this was still here. Most of the places we used to go are gone."

"Thanks to you." Eric was still leaning against the wall. His arms were folded over his chest as he glared at Collin. Glancing at me, he added, "You can't seriously think he's coming with us?" He spoke as if he forbade it, as if he could tell me what to do. Anger coursed inside of me, but I didn't get a word in.

Collin laughed and turned around, walking back toward Eric. Eric remained where he was, his confident slump unfazed by Collin's approach. "You can't think I'd let her wander off with you. Last time I saw you, you shredded a pack of demons and turned their scales into confetti." More things Eric wasn't supposed to be able to do.

Eric pushed off the wall, standing eye to eye with Collin. "I wouldn't bring up that day if I were you. Possessed by a demon or not, you're the one who killed the Guardian and opened the floodgates of Hell. It was your hand that destroyed her life—her world." Eric tilted his head to the side, gesturing toward me. He made it clear that Collin fucked up my life. A smile slowly slid across Eric's lips. "That day things changed, and I ended up fighting for the other side. Her side. I protected her. You did not."

Collin gnashed his teeth. His fists were balled at his sides. The muscles in his arms were corded tight, ready to fight. "I had no choice that day or any other before it," he growled. "But you did. How did you survive if you didn't kill mortals? You should have been weak, but you weren't. What did you do?"

Eric was staring at Collin. His body looked like it would explode. He breathed through his teeth, ready to attack. But when Collin said the last question, Eric's eyes flicked to my face. It was a split second that wasn't intentional. But I saw it. Me. I was the answer to that question. He wasn't weak because of me. He didn't have to kill because of me.

Rage exploded in my mind. And I shoved myself between them and slammed my fists into Eric's chest. His fingers crushed into my wrists after the first blow, grabbing my hands hard. "Me. It was me! Wasn't it? You used my soul. You used my body to sustain yourself!" I looked up into his face and knew my words were true. I knew that I guessed right. Eric's face made no movement to show remorse. There was no apology in his eyes. If anything, there was laughter—a slight arrogance that he was able to take from me for so long. Collin moved to help me, but I twisted out of his grip on my own. And then I shoved him, yelling, "You didn't kill anyone, because you took everything you had to have to survive from me. That's why I felt weak when you searched my memories. You were stealing my soul!"

Anger coursed through me and connected in a sudden jolt. I felt it flare up my arms. I smacked my palms into Eric's chest again, but this time the force was loaded with power. It sent him flying through the stone wall that separated the stage from the seating area below. The cinderblock cracked as he flew backward into the carnage that was left of the auditorium. Half the roof had been ripped off, revealing the wintery sky. Eric landed hard, ripping out a row of chairs as he slid across the floor. The power of my hit surprised me, but I didn't stop. He couldn't keep doing shit like this. And stealing my soul! What the fuck?

I sprang through the hole in the wall and went after Eric, before Collin could stop me. Eric wasn't mortal. I didn't know what he was, but I kept making him worse. More vile. More deplorable. And the whole time he'd been draining me, he'd been making me weaker. Making me more likely to fail. Before Eric could get up, I slammed my fist into his stomach and pinned him to the pile of rubble, kneeling hard on his stomach.

"You know you liked it," he hissed as my fist flew. The punch connected with his face and I heard bones crack. Blood poured from his nose and dripped down his chin.

The rage that fueled me allowed me full access to my emotions. And the crimson trail that was on his lip made my back go rigid as the scent of his blood slammed into me. I didn't expect it. And from the look on his face, neither did Eric. The scent of his blood filled my mind, freezing me in place. It was too much. There was too much raw emotion within me. I wanted a taste. A drop. I had to have it. I leaned forward and licked the trail of blood, pressing my eyes closed as I did it.

Before I had more than a tiny taste, Collin grabbed me by the waist and yanked me off of Eric. I went slack in his arms, instantly regretting what I'd done. Eric made me so mad. I just wanted to best him. I wanted to win and show him that he shouldn't screw with me. And now my message was blurred with blood. My throat tightened as Collin gently lowered me to the floor. Eric's blood burned inside of me, like a warmth that I was missing. It sealed out the coldness, and connected me to him in a way that I didn't want.

"Enough!" Collin yelled, as he pulled me back. Shock was in his voice. He scolded me, not saying anything about the blood. Not saying anything about the shame plastered across my face. "You have to stop. Ivy, you know about *Akayleah*. You know you can't let it control you." I breathed hard, fighting the instincts that were warring inside of me. One wanted to rip

Eric's clothes off and lick the blood from his lips—the other instinct just wanted to rip him apart. *Akeyleah* and bloodlust warring within me.

My voice cracked, "Collin, I … " I wanted to explain. I felt the need to tell him what Eric did to me. Why I acted like that, but he turned on Eric before I got out another word.

Collin's eyes rimmed. He looked at Eric as he pulled himself up and wiped the blood from his face. Collin approached him, saying, "And you..." Eric's eyes darted toward Collin, narrowing. "You have two seconds to explain before I kill you. I don't care why she wants to protect you. Not after this. You've been giving her blood! Convince me that you didn't weaken her. That you weren't feeding off of her soul..." Collin moved toward Eric. With each step, my heart lurched inside my chest. "Convince me or I'll kill you myself." Collin drew his blade. The jagged black edge pointed toward Eric's gut.

Eric glanced at the blade and back at Collin's face. "I held my own when you had Kreturus' power. What makes you think you could possibly kill me now?"

"Wrong answer," Collin hissed and moved his arm to land the blade in Eric's stomach.

Before I knew what happened, I was between the two of them, blocking Collin's blade. "You can't," I breathed. "I need the stone. He knows where it is."

This was the second opportunity Eric had to run and save himself, but he didn't leave. The scent of his blood filled my head, as Collin forced me behind him.

"He's using you, Ivy. His blood is still filled with demon blood. I can smell it. And I know you want it." Collin's eyes were pooling blood red. He spoke to Eric, "I let you live last time. Make no mistake about it. But this time, this time you aren't leaving this place alive." Collin's threat didn't make Eric move. Instead it appeared to enrage him.

Eric pushed me aside and walked up to Collin. They stood eye to eye. "Valefar need souls to feed off of to survive. When was the last time you ate?" Collin's anger streamed across his face, but Eric cut him off. "Yeah, well, I didn't eat much either. But, unlike you, I could control myself. It was a benefit of being Ivy-made. She made me what I am! I wasn't like the rest of the Valefar. I only took what I needed. I needed her pain, her blood. And yes, I did take some of Ivy's soul." He glared at me with vicious eyes. Eric's jaw clenched as he tore his gaze away. "It was mine to take. She owed me a debt she couldn't pay. Sound familiar?" he spat the question at Collin.

Collin shoved Eric and moved toward him. Eric remained eerily calm and took the hit without backing down. Collin screamed, "Ivy owes you nothing! You have no blood bargain with her! You have no claim to her soul!"

Eric laughed, causing the pit of my stomach to drop. It was cold and callused. It was the laughter of the crazy Eric that hated every ounce of me. "I have every right to her soul. She took mine. She damned me. It was her action and hers alone that made me what I am. I am hers more than you'll ever be." Eric's golden eyes narrowed on mine. We locked gazes and he wouldn't let me look away. "She owes me. It goes beyond a blood bargain. She owns me and I own her." He laughed. "Look at her face. You can see it in her eyes. That's why she didn't kill me. That's why she let me do it. She knew. She felt it, and allowed me to take her power and use it. As long as it suited her … She condemned herself to this fate. It was her doing, not mine."

Collin turned, searching my face. His eyes met mine. It was as if he saw something within me. Something that said Eric was right. Eric had a claim on me. A claim I didn't understand and couldn't deny. There was no way to explain it. We were connected somehow, and it was more than blood and lust. There was something else tying us together. From the look on Eric's face, I suspected he knew what it was. But I didn't. And neither did Collin.

Eric's voice was quiet, menacing, as he said to Collin, "If you challenge me, if you force me to fight, I'll use her power. I'll drain her completely. Then the two of you will be screwed. Kreturus will capture her. She'll go down without a fight and you'll be Kreturus' slaves for eternity."

As Eric spoke, I stood there with my jaw hanging open. He was threatening to use my power against me? Was he that twisted? I didn't believe it. I finally found my voice, challenging him, "And what happens to you, then? You think Kreturus won't destroy you?"

A smile tugged the corners of his lips. Golden eyes met mine as he answered, "I don't care what he does." Eric's voice slid down my spine like a piece of ice. My gaze locked on his face. Eric moved toward me. He glanced at Collin once to make sure he didn't move, that Collin wouldn't stop him. Collin tensed, but remained still, beside me. "The only thing I do care about is making your life as painful as possible." Eric smiled, the corner of his lips pulling up as he whispered the words in my face.

I tensed, desire shooting through me. Eric's eyes slid over my body and I let him. I let his gaze linger on my curves. I'd let him do anything he wanted to me. And I didn't understand. It made no sense. I should destroy him, but I couldn't do anything except look away. I turned from Eric, not concerned that he was at my back. Any other enemy behind me would be a mistake, but not with Eric. When he killed me, he'd want to see the light fade from my eyes, face to face.

I shook my head, stopping in my tracks and turned back to Eric. I walked to the former angel. "The only reason you can claim anything from me is because I let you. It's because I'm not completely evil, and you are. Eric, every time your life changes, you're filled with hatred. Al paired us together because we are the same. Anger was shaping us into what we would become. When you lost Lydia, Al was there. She warned you. I know you remember. I know those memories are in your mind. I know you can see Lydia's eyes, and hear the screams rip out of her throat as she was slaughtered. Anger made you what you are. Rage shaped what you became and Al was right—we are the same."

Eric's expression appeared to be indifferent as I spoke. His slumped shoulders and I-don't-give-a-rat's-ass glare would have made me question the point of saying this to him. But I knew he heard me. There were moments when Eric was soft, when he seemed more like the person he had been. And now that he had his soul back, he could reclaim that person—if he chose to.

I swallowed hard, refusing to look away from his eyes as I bared my deepest fears and darkest thoughts, "I was in full crash and burn mode when we met. I watched you and your perfect life—your perfect notes, your perfectly pressed shirts, and your perfectly white sneakers—and I envied you. You said I didn't see you, that I didn't notice, but I did. It was painful to look at you. It was agony to hear your chipper voice when my world was falling apart. Your smiling face brought me nothing but pain. It reminded me that life didn't make sense. Bad things happened to good people.

"Anger clouded your judgment. Even then. It took you lifetimes to abate your lust for vengeance. And it never healed you. You were never the same. You wore a mask, a fake facade to hold yourself together. And I sat next to you, every day doing the same damn thing." I laughed, pointing my finger into his chest, looking up into his face. "You and I were so much alike." I pressed my lips together and shook my head. "But not anymore... I'm done with this. I'm doing what I think is right, and to hell with everyone else. Including you!"

Eric's gaze was locked on my glistening eyes. His expression didn't change while I spoke. I had no idea what he thought. He just continued to stare, taking in my words one at a time until I fell silent. Eric turned his back and walked away. He reached for the metal door to the basement, and tugged it open, not stopping or waiting.

He spoke over his shoulder, as he disappeared into the stairwell, "The price of using the stone was higher than you think."

CHAPTER FIVE

Collin cleared his throat. Concern etched his face, forming a deep crease between his brows. "We shouldn't stay in the open." I didn't move to follow Eric. I couldn't stand the thought of being in the same room with him. Collin wrapped his arms around me. I could hear his heart beating beneath his chest. The embrace should have made me feel better. It should have made me feel safe, protected, and warm or maybe even loved. But it was nothing more than pressure on my arms.

I stared at the metal door leading to the basement, dreading confinement with Eric. I needed to rest. The Sapphire Serum in my chest was taking its toll. I spoke into Collin's chest, too distraught to look into his face. The emotions lingered from tasting Eric's blood. "I don't know what to do with him, Collin. He could have left. He could have killed me." I paused, shaking my head softly. "When we effonated here, I lost control and started to burn. He took all of my pain away and lent me his power. It's things like that that make me uncertain. I can't tell if he's trying to help me or kill me. And there's been more than one time that his life was in danger, and he stayed. Anyone else would have run. What is he, Collin? What have I done?"

Collin's fingers were under my chin, tilting my face up to meet his. "I don't know what he is. And I don't know if it's because you made him that way. He was an angel before he was anything else. It influences him, but I don't know how. All I know is that I can say with confidence that I understand demons, and whatever Eric is, he isn't acting like one. His cruelty seems to be a need, not a want. Demons destroy for fun. That isn't what he's doing. And whatever he's doing to you—it pains you—but it seems to help you. Am I wrong? 'Cause that sounds insane." Collin looked into my eyes. His lips remained parted, breathing gently, but I knew this troubled him. And that was okay, because it scared the hell out of me.

Licking my lips, I nodded, "It seems to help. It seems to do something that I can't explain." Looking into his face, I saw that he already knew what I'd admitted. "That's why you haven't killed him, isn't it?" I didn't doubt he could. And I wondered why Collin held such a tight leash on his power.

He pulled me close, and smoothed the hair on the back of my head. "I'd do anything for you. Anything to save you from pain. But with this—it's different. I don't know why or how. But I trust you. I know you'll tell me if things get out of hand. And I'll help you deal with it, no matter how bloody it gets." He kissed the crown of my head, as I nodded. We remained still, feeling the winter wind blowing through the roof. Collin's heart beat steadily in his chest, as his arms held me tight.

Lying on the leather couch, I rested with my head in Collin's lap. I wondered about the kiss. I didn't feel the compulsion to steal his soul when his lips pressed against me. Nothing stirred inside me, demanding me to take it. I wondered where it went, or if it would return.

He insisted on stroking my hair and watching me sleep. Both of them saw how drained I was and knew I needed rest. But sleep meant being vulnerable to Locoicia. She could pull me through her black mirror while I rested. That was why Collin wanted to hold me. The reasoning was that he could stop her before she pulled me into the glass. And to tell you the truth, I was glad Collin was there, that he insisted on watching over me. Although his touch registered as nothing more than pressure on my skin, I still wanted him near me. It reminded me that I was alive, and not the cold heartless bastard that was watching me from across the room. Eric.

As I lay there, Eric's words echoed through my mind. The price of him using Satan's Stone was higher than I thought. Eric's price was more than a constant state of change. But I couldn't find any commonality to see what it was. I was aware of only one loss that did anything to him, and that was Lydia. He didn't even seem to grieve Al's death. But with Eric there was no way to know for sure. He kept everything hidden so deeply that it was impossible to tell what he was thinking with anything. Except when it came to me. He hated me with a passion. Sometimes the thought of facing Kreturus was less frightening than facing Eric.

Collin's fingers pressed against my scalp, tangling in my curls as he stroked my head gently. He'd remained quiet for a long time. Uncertainty lined the curve of his mouth. Worry still pinched his brow as he gazed down at me. His voice was soft when he spoke. "I didn't think you'd forgive me... For what I'd done." Eric sat across from us, lying on a couch with his eyes closed, although I doubted he was asleep. I didn't expect Collin to discuss it in front of him, but there might not be another time. His fingers traced the line of my cheek.

I pressed my hand to his, feeling the curve of his hand in my palm. I wished that I could feel the sensations that used to shoot through me when I touched him, but there was nothing. I released his hand, and looked up at him, "It wasn't you." My voice was soft, as if that could keep Eric from hearing our words. Once, there had been no need for words. Once, we were so close that our minds spoke for us. But not now. Never again.

"That's easy to say, but when you see me doing things..." his voice trailed off. His blue eyes were strained with anxiety. "When we leave here and you see what I've done—it was my hand that did it. It was my doing that freed Kreturus from his prison. I'm to blame for all of it, because I'm the one who started it."

I twisted in his lap, and sat up. Staring into his face, I asked, "What do you mean?"

Collin pushed his dark hair out of his face. His eyes darted to Eric and back to me. "I wish we could talk the way we used to." He tucked a stray curl behind my

~ 57 ~

ear. He pressed his lips together, pushing them into a thin pink line. "Kreturus escaped because I went looking for him. I found him, I made a bargain, and I lost. It allowed him to use me to come to the surface. And I couldn't talk about it. I couldn't warn you away or tell you what I was doing.

"It became harder and harder to try and keep you two apart. He would come up looking for you. He'd search my mind, trying to find memories that would lead him to you. I couldn't hide them anymore. The day you pulled me through the demon glass, Kreturus decided he would kill you if you didn't submit to him. He was going to make me the one to do it. If you'd hesitated when I fell through the mirror, I would have killed you. There wasn't a choice. And it's weird now..." he paused, looking over my shoulder at the wall. His face relaxed as if he were somewhere wonderful and not locked in a musty old basement filled with flats and old props. "Because I have a choice. He can't call me back. Kreturus can't make me do anything," he took my hands in his, rubbing the back of my hand with his thumb, "and I owe it all to you. You broke my blood bargain. I never thought I'd be free again. But I am." He leaned closer to me, his lips about to touch mine when Eric spoke.

"If you want to hook up with the person who freed you from your bargain, you're trying to fuck the wrong girl." Eric turned his head toward us, his golden eyes glaring. My jaw dropped, but he didn't let me speak. Tension shot through Collin's body as he pulled away from me, but I grabbed his arm before he could cross the room to Eric. "It was the Demon Princess. It was her spell. Ivy just fucked it up by leaving out an important fact." Eric turned his head away from us and covered his eyes with his arm—like he was bored.

I grabbed a candlestick holder from the table next to me and hurled it at Eric. "You're such an ass."

Eric's hand shot up and plucked the object from the air before it hit him in the side of the face. "What's your point?" He sat up, neither frowning nor smiling. His eyes had that look that made me want to cower. It was as if he were hungry and I was food.

I swallowed, ignoring the sensation creeping up my throat. It pissed me off that I couldn't feel Collin's touch, but Eric could still evoke a response from me. It was the lingering effects of his blood. "My point is that he's talking to me, not you! And I didn't screw up her spell. I said it perfectly. I did everything she said. I paid dearly for it, Eric. And if I hadn't done what I promised, the blood bargain would have taken effect and killed me. So, what happened?" Eric was silent. He turned away with a confident expression in his eyes. He knew too much. I could see it on his face, and he wasn't going to tell me. I huffed, "You know. How could you possibly know?" How could he possibly know why the spell didn't work. He was full of crap. There was no way it was possible.

"Ask Locoicia next time you see her," was all he said. Eric moved away from us, to the back of the basement, as far away from us as possible.

Collin watched him. He no longer had the Neanderthal reaction to pound Eric whenever he said something horrible. Instead, he listened and watched. People who were silent when they should be screaming are more dangerous. Good thing Collin was on my side. Eric was something I couldn't explain. A horrific act tied us together. And now, now I wasn't even sure what he was. Was he mortal? Could he die? He seemed to still have some of my power or demon blood. But I wasn't certain how much that was affecting him.

Collin broke the gush of thoughts that was flooding my mind. He pulled me back into his arms, and I slouched against his chest. The world was turning to Hell above me, and I couldn't do anything about it because I was weak. I was weak because part of my soul was inside of Collin. And Eric had taken some. *Fucking Eric.*

Collin wrapped his arms around me, and the tension faded from my shoulders. He whispered softly into my ear, "He knows something we don't." I nodded. That much was certain. But what, I didn't know.

CHAPTER SIX

Collin stayed by me, watching Eric, although I knew Eric wouldn't harm me. Not if he couldn't enjoy watching the pain in my eyes. Attacking me in my sleep wasn't his style. It was possible that the only reason he was helping me find the stone was morbid curiosity. That, and he thought I held the ward that kept him safe. Lorren hadn't said anything as far as I could tell, and I didn't bring it up again. If he figured it out, I wasn't sure what he'd do.

Collin's fingers stroked my brow as I drifted in and out of a light sleep. He didn't think it was safe to allow me to completely drift off for fear Locoicia would grab me and suck me into her demon glass. Instead of getting a good deep rest, I got enough to not fall over. I'd have to face her at some point anyway. It would be better if it were at a time I chose, which would be never. If I knew how she pulled me through the glass, I'd stop her. But I wasn't sure. It had to be one of the spells she taught me, or a concoction of them, but I wasn't sure which ones.

When I couldn't lie there anymore, I sat up. Collin's hand was on my back. I leaned into him for a moment, inhaling his scent. There was no reaction. No feeling of affection. No desire for things that would normally make me blush in the light of day.

As if he knew what I was thinking, Collin pressed a kiss to my temple and brushed my hair over my shoulder. "If you can still feel anything," he glanced across the room into the dark void where Eric sat, "for anyone, then there's a chance you'll recover from what she did to you. It's not over until the end. And I won't leave you, not when you face Kreturus. Not ever. Okay?" His words made me want to melt into him. As he spoke, my gaze locked on his deep blue eyes. Their gaze had made every part of me feel alive and safe not so long ago. Could I really feel him again? Could the disconnect between my mind and my emotions rejoined? I didn't know. I wasn't even certain that was the problem. And the numbness that kept me from Collin was a necessary evil to not feel pain. Otherwise the dark magic would claim its pain price and destroy me. I wouldn't be able to bear the pain.

For once, Eric waited for a lull to speak. He rose in the darkness and paced toward us. He stopped, standing above us, his arms folded across his chest. My heart raced, picking up the pace to match Eric's. Eric said, "We need to get going. I know where the stone is, but you'll have to kill a few Martis to get it." I looked up at him, my brows pinched together. "Don't look at me like that. What'd you expect? That it would be in a lock box under my bed?" He snorted, shaking his head. "Of course you did..."

I cut him off, "You hid your book in a wall." As if doing one cliché thing meant that he would do two. Collin lifted his hand from my back after pressing it to my shoulder, reminding me to keep my temper in check. I felt his eyes on the side of my face, causing my stomach to twist.

Eric's gaze darted between Collin's hand, and my face. Eric's expression was neutral. As always. "It was a book no one could read, except me. It was hardly valuable to anyone else. But Satan's Stone—anyone could find it. If they killed you and took the second half, they could use it."

Collin spoke, "Is that your plan?" Eric's attention shifted to Collin. "To kill Ivy and use the Stone yourself? Absorb her power and take over?"

Eric's mouth curved into a smile. He laughed. "You're very astute, but a child compared to me. Did Ivy not tell you? I already used the Stone. It cannot be used twice by the same person. Nor would I want to. I'm still paying the price from the last time I used it." He paused, his eyes shifting between Collin and me. "That's what you would do? You'd befriend her to gain her trust, then kill her and take her power."

Collin shot out of his seat. He was nose to nose with Eric. Every muscle in his neck popped as he held his arms and flexing fingers tensely at his sides. "Don't you dare try to fill her mind with distrust. Not now. Not after everything she's been through. My reasons for being cruel to her are transparent, while yours aren't. Why are you here, Eric? If it's not power, then what?"

Eric remained unphased, and shoved his hands in his pockets. He replied, "I like her company," and tried to shoulder past Collin.

I sat from the couch watching. Collin wasn't after my power. I knew he wasn't. He could have taken it several times, but he didn't. Eric's words were carefully crafted lies to make me... hate him. He said one thing—a horribly nasty thing—and then did something else. His actions typically didn't match his mouth. Ah, I started to understand. Was it possible that Eric was here, and it was not by choice? Was it possible that he was hanging around me for another reason—a reason that had to do with the stone? I rose before Collin had a chance to respond, and walked over to Eric. Looking up at him, I asked, "We're bound together, aren't we? It's something to do with the curse, isn't it? The cost from when you used the stone?" A triumphant smug smile formed on my face, and melted away just as quickly.

Eric's eyes melted, and the soft-hearted boy I'd known was staring back at me. It was as if a veil had been lifted and I could gaze into his soul. His eyes widened and I knew I could see him in that moment. Truly see what drove him to do and say the things he did. Nothing was hidden. A knot formed in my throat and I slid my foot back, backing away from him. Pressing my fingers over my mouth, I openly gaped at him as shock washed over me.

Eric's reaction was that of a cornered animal. The veil he hid behind slammed back down. It was masking something. Something important about the curse—about his curse from using the stone. Before I recovered from the shock, his hands reached for my neck. Eric threw me across the room. My back slammed into the concrete wall with a thump. Before I could slide to the floor his fingers were pressing against my throat.

Collin moved behind him, ready to attack, but I held up my hand. Collin stopped. There was something there, within Eric. More than it seemed. And I'd just seen something that for whatever reason, Eric kept hidden. But I didn't understand why. Why hide it? Why was he so threatened by me?

Collin's blue eyes were filling with fire. His body shook with rage as he watched Eric hurt me, and for some reason I told Collin to stop. And he obeyed. I needed time to discover what I thought I saw within Eric. And making him release me would reveal nothing.

I wrapped my fingers around Eric's wrists, trying to breathe. "Was that intentional?" I asked, wriggling beneath his grip. He was still so strong. I tried to make sense of what I'd seen, but the only thing I knew for certain was that it was a secret—something Eric didn't want me to know. When Eric didn't speak, I added, "Did you mean to show me that? Cause I'm guessing it was an accident. Since you seem rather pissed off and all … " The expression on his face gave one answer, and his eyes gave another.

He snarled in my face, "Never speak of it. Ever." His grip loosened and I fell to the floor, coughing. He shouldered past Collin and bounded up the metal staircase two at a time. When his foot hit the top step of the landing he said, "If the stone is where I left it, I'll be back." The metal door slammed behind him.

CHAPTER SEVEN

Collin was eerily quiet. His neck snapped back toward me when Eric crashed through the metal doors above. He pulled me up into his arms, as if he needed to protect me from the deranged angel. He pressed me tightly against his body, and then pulled back to look at my neck. But I just stood there, unable to believe what I'd seen. Eric. Soft, meek, kind Eric was still there. He was hidden by cruelty and pain, and all too happy to inflict it on others—except me. With me it was different. I could see it. He would slash Collin and revel in it. The pain he caused me was different somehow, but I didn't know why. The only thing that I could see was that the agony of his life twisted him into a monster. And now he was a monster with a soul. And what I'd just seen—I wasn't supposed to. If Collin had noticed, he wouldn't be concerned about me. For some reason, I was the only one who saw. And Eric didn't want me to.

I pushed my hair out of my face, and assured Collin that I was fine. "He won't hurt me, Collin." I tried to brush it off, and act like it didn't affect me, but he wouldn't let me.

"He just threw you into a wall and tried to strangle you." There was tension in his voice as he fought to speak at a normal tone and not scream in my face. It was Eric he hated, not me. "I don't think you quite get what's going on here." He looked down at me, concerned.

I turned away from him. The things that swam in front of my eyes, the revelation of Eric's cruelty still crystal clear in my mind. I didn't fully understand what I'd seen, but I was certain it was real. Otherwise Eric wouldn't have stormed off. But speaking of things, things tied to dark magic was foolish. It was possible speaking of it would only make it worse—make the curse strengthen. I didn't want that. At one time, I would have wished Eric every happiness in the world—but now. I felt so torn. Half of me wanted to kill him. The other half just wanted to submit to ease his pain. Pain I knew I was contributing to. Not from turning him Valefar. No, it went deeper than that and Eric knew it. Close proximity and luck enabled me to see the entirety of his curse. It wasn't as clear as Lorren had thought. Eric was right—his curse for using the stone was much greater than anyone thought.

I cleared my throat and said, "Let me rephrase then. He won't kill me. He has to act like that. He's hiding something. He's not quite human. I'm not sure what he is, but I know he won't kill me. He needs me. And, at some point I'm going to have to give him some of my power."

Collin's eyes widened, and jaw locked as he stared at me with disbelief. His arms folded tightly across his chest, showcasing every ripped muscle, tense behind a flimsy black tee shirt. When Collin finally spoke, he lowered his head, pressing his eyes closed. "What did you see... ?"

I saw Eric. I saw what he was. What I made him. I placed my hand on Collin's forearm and looked into his perfect face. "I can't tell you. That won't do anything. It might even make it worse. It's the curse. It's affecting things—things he does. I can't say more than that, but I need him here. Without him, I don't think we can overthrow Kreturus. Please understand." I waited, but

Collin's face didn't burst into a smile. He glared at me like I was the most stubborn, stupid person alive. Maybe I was. But it was my fate, my destiny and they were both part of it. I pressed my lips together and explained the one thing I could—the one thing that I knew he wouldn't refute. "The prophecy says I need both of you, or I'll die. Collin, please. I know you realize it. And I know you want to protect me, but..."

He exhaled loudly, and shoved his hands into his hair as he turned away from me. "Gah. You drive me completely crazy." He laughed harshly, releasing some of the tension that was strung in his body. "You want me to let this guy beat you, steal your power, possibly take more of your soul—and trust him not to kill you?" He turned back to face me as he spoke. By the time he finished, I could see the panic in his eyes. He realized what I was asking him to do, if the event arose. And I was certain it would.

"Yes, that's what I'm asking, as crazy as that sounds. Collin, Eric can use my power. It has to be why he's here. He's used the stone, so he can't steal it and use it again. And..." Collin started to say something, but I cut him off, "I know you don't want it. No one in their right mind would want to use the stone after meeting people who have." I laughed nervously. "And they were angels, Collin. Angels. Lorren and Eric's lives got ripped to pieces. They're suspended in constant agony for using the Stone. And here I am acting like I can do it and pay the price." I shook my head. At best it was suicide. And at worst... Oh, God, I didn't want to think about what the worst could be. I doubted Lorren or Eric could have ever dreamed up their curse. And here I was, getting in line to use the Stone for a third time. I didn't want to. I looked up at Collin, "What choice do I have?"

Collin's gaze rested on my face for a moment, before he reached for me and cradled me in his arms. "You always have a choice," he smiled against the top of my head, "you're the only person who doesn't see it."

I pulled away from him, shocked, "You think joining Kreturus is a choice? Are you insane? You were forced to be his slave for eternity. How can you say that?"

He reached for my face, brushing his thumb along my cheek. He leaned closer and looked down into my eyes. "Many people don't have the heart it takes to do what's right. Most people wouldn't knowingly sacrifice themselves to save someone else. And yet, here you stand, not even considering another option." He glanced away, breaking our gaze. When he finally spoke again, he asked, "So, your powers revealed something about him—something that I couldn't see?" I nodded. "Hmm. And I'm supposed to let him beat you and not do anything?" I nodded again. He laughed and shook his head. With a heavy sigh, he finally answered, "That's why you don't, fight back. That's why you let him treat you that way, isn't it?" I nodded once. It was a fact. A fact that I would change if I could. But at this stage in life, accepting it was all I could do. Collin was silent for a long time. His heart beat rhythmically in his chest.

With a deep breath, he finally said, "I don't understand, but I trust you. I trust this is important for a reason I can't comprehend. I can't say I won't do anything if he hurts you..." I started to protest, but Collin put a finger on my lip to silence me, "But I promise that I'll do the best I can. That's all I can offer."

A moment passed. And then two. Collin's gaze fixated on my mouth. My lips parted slightly, as a breath slipped out of my body. His hands moved around my waist, sliding to the small of my back as he pulled me to him. The hollow place inside my chest felt like it was going to explode. I should feel something. Some lust. Some anger. Some need to feel his hands on me—but there was nothing. Just a hollow ache telling me that part of me was dead, forever missing.

Before I could stop him, Collin pressed his lips to mine. Lorren said I wouldn't be able to kiss him again without taking my soul back, but nothing happened. That part of me seemed dormant, dead like every other desire within me. So, I allowed it and let the kiss linger wishing I could feel something. My fingers moved over toned muscles and up the curve of his arm to Collin's neck.

I pressed my lips against his, opening my mouth for him to taste me. And he did. I should have swooned. I should have melted. But I didn't. My fingers tangled in his silky hair as he kissed me. My eyes were closed tight, wishing I could feel something—anything. It was so lonely, all the time. Being denied touch, the emotions and sensations that went with it, was cruel. And yet, I'd chosen this. I'd chosen to not feel his hands on my body or taste his lips when they touched mine. I'd killed the bond between us, deafening it until it was so weak and muted that it no longer existed. Collin was my soul mate, but I felt nothing at all.

When I couldn't take it another second, I broke away from him. I wiped the kiss from my mouth with the back of my hand. I didn't know what to do—how to fix it. Desperation covered my thoughts, making them frantic. If I could feel him again, if for only a second, it would make me stronger. Happy. Content. My life went to Hell. Literally. There was nothing left of my previous life. There was no comfort. There was no moment of solace. Nothing to shield me from constant pain. But it didn't have to be that way. There was one thing that made me feel. One action that could make me sense Collin again—the way I used to. I gazed at Collin with my lips parted, breathing hard.

A single thought manifested in my mind. A reason, a small ray of hope that grew larger and louder as his caress fell on my numb body. It would work. It had to work. But I didn't think he would do it. And I didn't know if I should ask. I stared at Collin blankly, wishing things were different. Wishing things were the way they had once been when we sat in this space and laughed when he touched me and my body ignited. Things were so simple then. Anything was possible. But now …

He was breathing heavily, as he watched me. Collin finally said, "Tell me what you're thinking. The bond is completely broken. I can't sense you at all anymore. and the look on your face is worrying me." He shoved his hair back, and stood opposite me. Waiting. Waiting for an answer to a question I was afraid to ask.

If I asked, and he said yes—oh, God, I wanted to his feel his touch again, but it came at a price. A price that I didn't know if I could pay. And for what? For pleasure? For a few seconds of lust burning through my body? Was it worth it? Should I ask? I didn't realize that I was twisting my fingers until Collin took them in his hands.

He looked down at me. A small smile tugged at his lips. "Your eyes are rimming. What do you want, Ivy?" He whispered my name and I could feel my reply try to pour into my mouth, but I locked my jaw, refusing to ask. His hand brushed my cheek as he threaded his fingers through my hair. I tried to turn away, but he didn't let me. "Tell me."

I looked at the floor and the square gray tiles, trying to untie the knot in my tongue. "It's greedy. I don't need it, and shouldn't even think about it, never mind ask you." I tried to pull away again, but he yanked my waist tighter, pulling me flush against his body.

He brushed a kiss to my cheek, and whispered in my ear, "I'll give you anything I can. If it gives you a moments peace—a second of happiness, it's yours. All you have to do is tell me what you want. Tell me, Ivy. What is it?"

I pressed my eyes closed as my lips parted. I didn't want to say it. I didn't want to hear his rebuke. But the words had formed, and I couldn't stop them. It was a part of me that was stripped away and I wanted it back. Desperation made me want it. The kiss he just brushed against my skin sealed my desire to have it.

The words came out in a rush of air, "Your blood. I want your blood. I want to be able to feel you, respond to your touch. I want to want you again—the way I did before." Shame washed over me for revealing how much I wanted him, but I couldn't stop speaking. "A drop of blood could fix it. I'd be able to feel more than pressure on my skin when you touch me. I'd feel you. I'd be yours again..." My voice trailed off. My face was hot as embarrassment washed over me. I knew my eyes were rimmed, and I couldn't hide it. I looked away, trying to pull away from him.

Collin lifted my chin with his finger and looked into my eyes. A smile warmed his expression when he saw my face. "That was hard for you to say, wasn't it?" I nodded. He slowly pressed a kiss to my head, right on top of my mark. His lips slid against me and my heart rang with hollowness. I was dead inside. The Demon Princess made sure of it. Collin pulled away and looked at me. "I've wanted you for so long. I had no idea how or when you'd want me, or if you ever would. And here we are now, and I got my wish, but you can't feel any of it. Nothing at all?" He searched my eyes. I shook my head. "Ivy, you make me feel so much. I can't deny you that, but something about it seems wrong. Like I'd be forcing you. Like there won't be any way to know if you truly want the things you say, or if it's the blood talking."

I knew that would be his answer. My stomach sank. The pressure of his hands on me faded and was replaced by cold air. He stared at me, waiting for me to speak, but I said nothing. I could barely say it once. Offering to be his blood slave was idiotic.

I turned away from him, toward the stairs. I didn't know where I was going or what I was thinking at that moment. I just needed a minute, and some cold air on my face to wake me up from my delusions. I'd never feel anything again, except Eric when he screwed with my mind. There was no future for Collin and me. There wasn't even a last sensual embrace. It was already too late.

When my hand touched the metal railing, Collin spoke from behind me. "Ivy. I'm yours. In every way. I'll always be yours. But I want you to do it..." When I turned back, he held out his brimstone knife in one hand, extending it toward me. The expression on his face was unreadable. My foot stopped on the bottom step and didn't move. I blinked. Did he say yes? Collin didn't move. His gaze wasn't timid and didn't break when I stared at him, openmouthed in shock. "I can give you this. Come here... "

I slowly turned and padded back toward him. The knife lay in the palm of his hand. He watched me in a way that made my stomach clench as I stopped in front of him. I lifted the blade, and gripped it in my hand. Collin lifted his hand, palm up. I took his hand in mine, and couldn't stop staring at him. I wanted this so badly. My hand started to shake. Collin steadied it with his other hand. His fingers laced over mine, as I held onto the blade.

"Only a tiny bit. Only a drop," he warned. Collin was watching me, taking in my shaking hand and the way I bit my bottom lip when I was nervous. There was an intensity in his gaze that made this seem more sensual than I thought. The act itself meant something to him.

I nodded, unable to speak. Raising the jagged blade to his middle finger, I pressed into his flesh until a stream of red welled up into a drop. He didn't flinch when the blade cut his skin. I watched as his flesh healed instantly under the drop, preventing me from overindulging should I be unable to control myself. The thought made me feel vulnerable in a way that I didn't expect. Because that's what I was doing—giving Collin control over my body. Allowing him to access the remnants of my emotions the way Eric did. I watched the scarlet orb resting on his finger for a moment. Collin sucked in a deep breath as I raised the precious ruby drop to my lips. When I turned his palm, the blood ran down his hand like a crimson streamer. I quickly licked the trail, ending with the tip of his finger.

Collin's voice was like a sensual stroke down my body, "God, Ivy—that was sexy."

Sensations flooded my mouth as his voice swam in my head. His blood slid down my throat, sweet and hot.

It awakened the part of me that had been numb. I'd felt nothing for him. It had pained me so deeply to see him and not feel anything, but I never spoke of it. There was nothing to do about it. But this. This allowed me to feel everything.

As his blood slipped down my throat my body came alive. Every inch of me was hyper-aware of Collin. It made me respond to his scent, his touch. His blood burned through my body, igniting desires that had been disconnected. The sensation scared me. It was overwhelming and took control of me, so that I had no say in what I was saying or doing. The feelings propelled me to throw my arms around his neck and press my lips to his. And this time, this kiss exploded and I felt everything. The hollow place inside of me filled with lust, bursting and filling within me until there wasn't a single place on my body that I didn't want him to touch.

Collin's fingers tugged my hair gently as he deepened the kiss. Butterflies exploded in my stomach as he lowered me to the couch and pressed his body on top of mine. Each kiss, every time his lips touched me was ecstasy. I needed him. I wanted him, and I pulled him down hard on top of me, nearly tearing his shirt off in the process. Collin straddled me and smiled, but a line of worry was creased between his brows.

I reached for his face, and stroked the backs of my fingers across his smooth cheek. "I wanted you so much for so long." My voice was barely a breath, "You're not doing anything wrong, Collin. I love you. I want to show you. Please... let me show you." I ran my hands down his sides to his hips, and tried very hard to not move and wait for him to answer. My lips parted as I slid my tongue along my teeth, watching him. Taking in every movement. Long dark lashes surrounded his impossibly midnight-blue eyes as he gazed at me. The worry line smoothed and he lowered his body to mine, pressing kisses against me until I couldn't take it anymore.

His lips covered my body after he tossed my shirt to the floor. My hips moved against him as my fingers clawed his back. His weight pressed me into the couch. As his kisses slid over my body, the heat of his breath made me writhe beneath him. Collin said my name softly in my ear, and his lips pressed a gentle kiss to my neck. Without meaning to, my nails cut into his back. The scent of his blood filled the air, and assaulted me. Wildly, I flipped us over, so I was on top, but Collin realized what happened.

He pushed me off of him, with more force than I expected and said, "No more, Ivy." I felt the jolt of the command and didn't fight him. But, the scent of his blood made me so high-strung that it was agony to be still and wait for his skin to heal, but we did. As I lay in front of him, Collin breathed deeply, watching me—his eyes sliding over my body. It was so hot. I could barely breathe.

He whispered, "Close your eyes." As I lowered my lashes, I saw his lips press into the curve at my waist. Slowly, his kisses covered my body. It was all I could do to be still and keep my eyes closed. Every sensation struck through me like lightening, setting me on fire. He moved us slowly, and lay back, leaving me straddling his hips.

Then, Collin's arms wrapped around me and pulled me down on top of him. His shirt was gone, as were the rest of our clothes. While he'd kissed me, they'd been removed, one piece at a time. Until it was just me and him. A moan escaped my lips. My mind was wandering ahead, thinking about feeling him inside of me. I wanted to taste his mouth when I did it. I wanted to kiss him and hold him.

But Collin's voice cut through the lust and glued me in place, "Be still. Don't move." My hips didn't move, although they were burning. I could feel him below me, and he was so close. I didn't want to stop, but Collin's voice slowed me. His hands tangled in my hair as he pressed a kiss to my lip, and sat up again. Collin smiled, as he played with a curl that covered my breast. My long hair wildly fell around my shoulders.

The back of his hand slid across my breast making me suck in a breath. My control was faltering. Then I saw his face, and heard his voice, "Can I look at you, Ivy? Can you be still for just one more second so I can see how beautiful you are?"

He asked me. He could have commanded it and I wouldn't have had a choice. But he asked. I nodded slowly. The room was so hot. My head felt like it was floating. I wanted to give him anything and everything.

As Collin's eyes slid over my naked body a blush covered me. I'd never done this before. And the look on his face, the depth of his eyes made me wish I'd found him sooner. Collin caressed me with his eyes, and then slowly traced his finger along the curves of my body making me moan and beg for more. When he traced every inch, and caressed every soft curve, he flipped us over.

Collin pressed a kiss to my mouth. A smile lined his lips as I felt his hard body on top of mine. "Show me you love me, Ivy. Show me the way you've wanted to, the things you dreamed about, I want to give you those things. Tell me what you want." His voice was intoxicating. His words shot straight to my core and lit me on fire.

My heart raced as I thrust my hands into his hair, pulling him closer. His skin slid on top of me, as his lips drew closer, I said, "I want you." My eyes were hot, rimmed violet. I was unable to hide anything. Every thought, every desire I ever had for him came pouring to the front of my mind as our bodies became one, moving together.

In those few moments, time stopped. My life wasn't the destroyed Hell it had become. There were no demons, no angels, and no prophecies. There was nothing that could tear us apart. He was everything I wanted. Feeling his hands on my body, the way I'd let some other random guys touch me before—it was so much more. The feelings shot through me, taking me higher and higher. I loved him. I could admit it. And he loved me, and was free to do so. There were no bonds separating us. No bargains claiming him. It was perfect.

When Collin finally sated my lust, I laid in his arms. His hands were just below my breast, stroking my smooth skin. Collin spoke softly, sending a current of emotion through my body. "I saw your dreams. The things you thought of... of me. And you. All this time, I had no idea you wanted me so much, Ivy. Even that day on the beach..." his voice trailed off surprised.

I turned and looked up at him, "I've always loved you. I just couldn't admit it. I was afraid of..." My voice trailed off. Fear had dictated my relationship with him. It blinded me. And I felt it now, tying my tongue, preventing me from speaking.

~ 85 ~

"Afraid of what?" His hand stroked my hair. The rise and fall of his chest was intoxicating. I could lay in his arms forever. But I didn't want to answer. I didn't want to shatter the moment with fear. When I didn't answer, he added, "I find it interesting that your bloodlust seems selective."

I snorted a laugh, "What? What are you talking about?" I turned to look up at him.

"I can compel you to take your clothes off, but I can't get you to answer a question. A question that I already saw the answer to in your mind..." He pressed a kiss to the top of my head, smiling as he spoke.

I averted my eyes, feeling shy, "Then why are you asking?"

"Because, I need to hear it from you. It's different. Willingly giving something to someone is different than taking it. Those memories were stolen. Things that rushed forth that I wasn't supposed to see. Things I wasn't supposed to know..." his voice trailed off. The blood bond allowed him to see into my mind for only a second. And he'd seen some of my most intimate thoughts—secrets—about how I felt about him. And us.

Silence followed. He didn't demand I tell him. And it wasn't Collin that I didn't want to admit it to—it was me. I couldn't say the words, because then I'd have to accept them. But there was no turning back. There was no tomorrow for all I knew, so I wasn't going to waste today.

Shoving my fear aside, I took a deep breath and said, "I was afraid of acting on it. I told you once before—there's no such thing as true love. I believed it. I believed it so deeply that it masked what was in front of my eyes. That day on the beach. That night when you found me, and I had no idea how or why—I was just so grateful that it was you." I gazed down at his arms around me, his long tapered fingers holding me firmly to him. "I recognized the attraction, as we sat in the sand watching the sun set. That's what I kept telling myself. That I wanted you because you were hot. And that was it. But it wasn't. That wasn't the reason."

I pressed my lips together hard. Collin's hand stroked the side of my face as his arms tightened, hugging me harder. I started telling him. I had to finish. I had to say it. "Death screwed me up. Losing my sister, well, that year was unbearable. The thought of losing you was too much. I couldn't do it. I couldn't risk loving you, because I might lose you. And I couldn't take another loss. It would have destroyed me. So, I never allowed the thought to surface again, but you did things—said things—that made me smile and the thoughts, the affection for you, popped up again anyway." I smiled, averting my gaze from his. "Denial goes a long way..."

He pressed a kiss onto the top of my head. "If the bond weren't broken, I'd tell you to look into the memory of that day on the beach." He smiled. "You'd see everything. You'd see how much I adored you, and how desperately I wanted to ease your pain. You were everything to me. I wish I could show you..."

I turned in his arms and looked into his sparkling sapphire eyes. Smiling I said, "I love you, Collin Smith." My throat tightened as I looked at him. One moment of bliss. One moment of knowing that I was truly loved, came and went. And that drop of blood was more powerful than I'd known.

CHAPTER EIGHT

Eric took his time getting back. I rested my head on Collin's lap after we were both clothed again. His warm hands stroked my hair gently across my forehead. A blush would rise in my cheeks if I thought about what we did. His fingers traced the curve of my cheek as he smiled down at me.

After much comfortable silence he said, "Close your eyes. Rest. When Eric gets back, it'll be time to fight. If he gets back." The thought had crossed my mind as well. Sorta-mortal Eric ran off into the middle of a battle zone. I was certain things worsened since the last time we were above ground, but I had no desire to look and see how much. It would make it impossible to rest. Fury raged through me just thinking about it.

"He'll be back," I replied softly. There were things about Eric that I knew. Secret things. Eric wasn't leaving.

Collin's palm stroked the hair away from my face as he looked down at me. "There's no way to be certain of him, Ivy. I can tell there's more to it. More you aren't telling me. Just watching the two of you, I can see it. But I don't know what it is." His words were troubled, not jealous. He wanted to protect me from pain and hurt. And Eric was pain and hurt.

Tilting my chin up, I said, "You don't need to worry about him." I didn't affirm his suspicion. Although I was surprised he hadn't seen it, or heard me speak to Eric when—whatever that was—happened. A chill ran through me. Fatigue gnawed at my bones. I felt every inch of my body, being so near to Collin. It was something I hadn't thought of. I assumed the bloodlust would subdue. I thought I could push it away and call it back when I wanted it. But the emotions remained on the surface, sliding across my face as my brow pinched together.

"Maybe not, but you're worried. About something." His hand slid over my brow again in a gentle stroke. My eyes closed and opened as his hand touched me, soothing me.

I glanced up at him, "The thirteenth prophecy. I wonder if it says what the price will be for using the stone. I close my eyes and see your face painted on the canvas. It's like an omen—a morbid omen—telling me to make sure you're safe. But how could I possibly do that?" I laughed sadly. "Whenever I'm not talking, the price of the stone wanders through my mind. Lorren's price was horrible. He's encased in a tomb of beauty, forced to listen to the screams of the dying as they become part of his labyrinth. Eric is so much worse."

My hand drifted to my throat as my voice caught. I looked away, lost in thought—lost in nightmares that never ended, "I can't even describe how terrifying it would be to live his life. To never have peace. To constantly be out of control, falling farther and farther away from the ideals that once formed who you were." My mouth hung open. I was at a loss for words. Gazing up, I added, "I'm not that strong. I couldn't pay that price. You're my peace. You always have been. I can't lose you."

Collin shifted, lifting me up and wrapping his arms around me. When he pulled away, he kept his hands on my arms and squeezed. Hard. "Listen to me. I've done everything I could think of to stop this, and it's only caused you more pain. I can accept that I'm not the one to stop it. But," he brushed the stray curl out of my dark eyes, "the same thought swam through my mind. I would use the stone for you, but I think that will only make things worse. Every prophecy, every scroll, every painting has you at the center of this. Ivy, you're strong enough to deal with whatever the stone throws at you."

When I looked down, his hand tucked under my chin and lifted my face to meet his eyes. "You killed a Dreanok—that thing at the Pool—without a second thought. You let the most powerful demon, besides Kreturus, screw with your mind. And you survived. Locoicia is evil beyond comprehension. The fact that you even survived her lessons is a testament to your strength. You are strong. You'll do what's right when the time comes, because that's who you are. And I'll be there by your side."

Hope swelled within me. It was an emotion, crushed flat with all the others from the Demon Princess' training. But in Collin's arms I felt it crack open inside of me and spill into every last inch of my body. Hope holds power. Power that someone tried to take from me. Collin's blood gave it back. I wrapped my arms around his neck, and buried my face in his chest. Collin's hands rubbed my back, and then tightened the embrace.

He whispered in my ear, "I'll always be there for you."

CHAPTER NINE

As I rested in Collin's lap, my mind finally slowed enough to have some sense of peace so I could rest. I felt safe and warm in his arms. He was right, when Eric returned; it'd be time to fight. So I did the best I could and shoved every thought out of my head. Soon the silence rang in my ears and the only sound I was aware of was the beating of my heart.

That's when it happened. I knew it was coming, but it still startled me. My mind swam between the place where sleep and wake are easily confused. The black mirror appeared in front of me, as the school basement and Collin faded from existence. Instead of waiting for her to suck me through the glass, I lifted my hand and pressed through.

One of my boot heels clacked on the stone floor. Then the other. As I emerged from the mirror, Locoicia was standing in front of me. Amethyst eyes blazed beneath a black hood, hiding her face. The supple fabric flowed to the floor. A black gloved hand snatched my wrist and yanked me forward into the room. Away from the mirror—the only way to escape.

She chuckled, "Little One. So nice for you to visit." Her voice was overly sweet. I stood in front of her, not willing to be bullied by her. Her presence still scared me more than I wanted to admit. Because there was something alluring about her too. Her power, maybe? The way she wielded it. The confidence in her choices. I rarely felt that way. Most of my decisions were an accident made on the fly.

When I didn't respond, her arms folded across her chest. The long dark sleeves of her gown revealed leather gloves that went from her fingertips to elbows. She leaned closer to my face. A prick of fear ran down my spine. Her voice was deep and deadly. "Did you forget to tell me something? Hmm?" Her warm breath washed across my face.

I tensed, but refused to move. I wasn't going to back down. If I lost this argument, I lost everything. I didn't know who decided if a blood bargain defaulted, but I didn't want to be the one at fault. It wasn't my fault. "I didn't forget anything," I snapped. "I said the spell perfectly. I didn't stop when I saw the victim that was sucked through the glass, either." I glared at her. "You should have told me that. It was withholding information that could have jeopardized the spell. Instead you allowed me to believe he might be in possession of a human—some random Valefar. Not..." I bit off my words, not wanting to say his name in the off chance she didn't know. But the look on her face said otherwise.

"You didn't need to know," she retorted sharply. "You said so yourself, you continued the spell, which means that bit of information was not imperative. And yet, there was something left out. Some difference that caused the spell to go awry." Her fingers tapped on her arms, waiting for me to volunteer what happened. I had to fight to not clench my fingers into fists. Collin's effect on me was slipping in, making it harder to focus.

I pushed the feelings back, forcing them down before Locoicia tried to rip them out of me. "It was your spell. It didn't work. He didn't die."

She sucked in a breath, filling the bodice of her gown and released it slowly. She was livid. Her eerie eyes fixated on me. "Tell me what happened. Exactly. Leave no part out."

I considered walking away, but I couldn't. I had to know the blood bargain was broken. It seemed like it was, but I wasn't certain. I restated the events of the night as callously as possible, omitting Eric completely, and erasing Collin's name from the story. I felt protective of them—both of them. When I finished, she turned away with her spine ramrod straight, and she rushed to the shelf holding the chalices. She reached for the goblet that held our blood. When she lowered it in front of her, the tension in her shoulders faded. There was an audible sigh of relief. But I didn't know what she was looking at. What had changed? I rushed to the cup, expecting her to hide it from me. Instead she set it on the table and extended her arm, directing me to come closer.

"See for yourself," she stated, and moved away.

Caution tensed my muscles as I neared the table. When I peered over the rim of the chalice, my heart caught in my throat. I tried to make no noise, no expressions, but the Demon Princess was too astute to neglect to notice the smallest change. Words tumbled out, "It looks the same." I glanced up at her, waiting for an explanation.

Her red lips twisted into a cruel smile as she pressed her fingers together. "Yes, it does. That means the bargain is still in effect. If there was a breech on one side, the chalice would have killed you when you glanced into it." I glanced at her. Evil witch. She allowed me to near the thing so it would kill me. My jaw clenched. She continued, "There is one way to determine the outcome of the bargain." My gaze locked onto her horrid eyes. Her deep voice made my skin crawl, "We each take a sip."

"I'm not drinking your blood!" She reached for the cup, but I jerked it away from her grasp. I cradled the cup against my body, so she couldn't take it without risking spilling the contents. Since she was so careful with it, I assumed she didn't want to spill it. Locoicia's lips pressed into a thin red line. I scolded, "Do you think I'm stupid? That I don't know what that would do to me?" I had an idea, but the knowledge that the Demon Princess bestowed upon me didn't cover in detail what would happen if I drank the contents of the chalice when a blood bargain had gone awry.

"You're a stupid girl," she snapped, reaching for the precious goblet, but I twisted away—careful not to spill its contents. Fury exploded the next time she spoke, "There's no such thing as a two-directional blood bond! It has to be one-sided to implore powers of servitude over another. And since both our blood is in there—that can't happen!" I knew that part. That was what she'd taught me, but I had a hunch that altering the bargain wasn't in my favor. And I was already screwed every which way. I didn't see how she could make it worse, but I wasn't willing to take the chance. A new blood bargain would not fix the old one. It would only complicate it, and make it worse.

The Demon Princess didn't reach for the chalice again. Instead, she held out her hand, as if demanding something from a naughty child. My brow wrinkled in response. There was no time to think. What was better? The unknown, or drinking her blood? Determination strengthened my resolve. I reached my arm forward, carefully moving the full goblet to her... when I abruptly tilted it, spilling the contents on the floor. Locoicia frantically tried to grab the chalice before it hit the floor, trying to save any of the cups contents, but it was too late. The cup clattered against the stone as our blood formed a scarlet puddle on the stone.

She stood there for a moment. Frozen. Her arms were tense, slightly away from her sides. I watched the blood seep between the crevices in the floor, filling each space between the stones like little red rivers. Without a word, her hand shot out and reached for my neck. I twisted out of her grip, and uttered a spell that slammed her to the floor and held her in place. If she got free, she'd kill me.

I kicked the goblet that lay next to her head. It clattered across the floor, away from her face. "There is no bargain. It's gone."

Locoicia's hood fell away as she turned her face, fighting to free herself from my spell. Flame-filled violet eyes were swimming with rage. Dark hair fell across her face, obscuring it from me. But there was skin. Flesh. How could that be? She was a demon. I knelt next to her, feeling my power draining by the second and brushed the hair away from her face. Shock coursed through me as I stumbled back. Alabaster skin lined high cheekbones. Hair brown as chocolate flowed in long curly locks and spilled onto the floor. The shape of her lips, chin, and the set of her eyes... My hand slapped over my mouth. There was one place, one spot on her cheek that was covered in black scales. I didn't know what I was seeing. I didn't know why she looked like me, and I didn't have time to find out.

The Demon Princess snarled, fighting against the spell that pressed her face to the floor, "You fool! Spilling the cup doesn't end anything! It forces the bargain to remain, unaltered. It needed to be changed!" she hissed.

I rose, looking down at her and said with complete certainty, "No it didn't. I will kill Kreturus. I will fulfill my end of the bargain. I won't default because you twisted my words. It's set in stone, now. And, if you failed to teach me everything—I mean every little thing there was—you default. And I win." The pain price was about to slam into me. I wasn't sure if I could hold onto the enchantment holding her in place.

Moving rapidly toward the mirror, she called out behind me, "You're a clever girl. A cold-hearted clever girl. How do you intend to protect young Collin Smith when you kill the Demon King? Their fates are intertwined. You need me. You need my skill and the way I use my magic, not just my wisdom, if you wish to save him." I stopped, and turned slowly. Her body was pressed to the floor as if an anvil was holding her in place. Her words unnerved me terribly, making me pause to listen to her. Seeing her face was like looking in a mirror at an evil version of me. Locoicia spoke as I stared at our matching faces. "I'll help you save him. There are ways to defy his destiny." Her words grew more confident and less panicked as she spoke. I paused, staring at her. I knew she was lying, but I couldn't walk away. I couldn't miss the chance to save Collin. It was something I didn't want to think about. I didn't know what to do. I'd hoped the prophecy was wrong—that he would live. But hope was a foolish thing to hang all my hope on. I knew it. And so did Locoicia.

She'd lash out at me if I released her, and yet … Looking back at the glass, I couldn't leave. She said the only thing that could have made me pause. And it was too tempting to walk away from. I'd have to take her wrath if I freed her, and I wasn't sure I wanted to. But there was no other choice. She was right. I didn't have her mind. I knew all of the spells and incantations, but I still hadn't thought of anything to do to save Collin. Staring at her prone form, I made my decision. Uttering a word, I released her from the spell. She gasped, rolling to her side.

The pain price slammed into at the same time as she spoke her incantation. I was able to block it partially, but the pain coursed through me too hard—too sudden. My body bent in half trying to cope. Her laughter swam in the air as she pelted me with horrific spells. My skin ripped open in long thin lines that turned black. I focused, trying to force the pain away—but Collin was holding me. Nothing disconnected. I could feel everything with more vigor than I would have before I was numbed. A scream erupted from my throat as she towered over me, uttering another curse from her lips. I fell to my side, lying in my own blood. I couldn't focus long enough to block her. I couldn't force the pain away. Spell after spell beat me until I lay there, half dead, and barely breathing. My eyes stared blankly at the ceiling. Locoicia put her boot under my shoulder and rolled me toward the mirror. One more kick and I'd fall through.

"Wait," I said weakly. "Tell me... how to save Collin."

She laughed so hard and so long that I knew what she was going to say before she said it. "There is no spell that can save him, no magic that can undo the damage you've brought on Collin and yourself. You are a stupid, naive, fool. You'll kill Kreturus for me and, when you can't deliver an angel to me, you'll default on our bargain. I don't know if you realize this dear, but angels can't get to this glass to come to me. It's part of the Underworld." Her face—an exact copy of my face—leaned closer, whispering in my ear. "And then, when you kill Kreturus and default on our bargain, I'll take the Underworld. And no one will be the wiser because, dear sweet Ivy Taylor... I look just like you."

As she spoke her voice changed, sounding more and more like my own. As she smiled at me, the pit of my stomach went cold with fear. She looked like my twin. Some form of dark magic twisted the Demon Princess into my likeness. She even had the patches of scales where Lorren had healed mine. That was the only difference. A difference easily explained away. She rose, pressing the tip of her boot into my side, rolling me into the mirror.

CHAPTER TEN

Horror washed over me. Choking, I shot up out of Collin's lap. I couldn't let him touch me. The pain still coursed through my body making my muscles spasm uncontrollably. My hands clenched my hair and tugged as I screamed.

Collin was behind me. "What's wrong? Ivy?" When I didn't turn, he grabbed my shoulders and forced me to face him. Tears streamed down my face. The black lines filled with who-knows-what didn't heal. They marred my arms, and I could feel them on my face. He sucked in a shocked gasp as his eyes slid over me. "She took you. How? I was talking to you. Your mind was here. How did she pull you into the glass?" It became clear that as I rested in his arms, my body didn't portray any of the pain Locoicia cast upon me.

I trembled under his touch. It was too much. It inflamed every sensation of agony inside of me. Twisting my shoulders out of his grasp, I answered, "It doesn't matter. Collin—she trapped me. There's no way to survive what she's done. And I can't tell you!"

He nodded understanding, "Because the blood bargain prevents you from speaking of it. I know." He reached for me, but I pulled away. She was going to take my place! She'd planned it all along. That was why her hood was always up. That was why she studied me so closely. She knew me inside out. She watched me writhe in pain and cry out for mercy for hours upon hours. Sucking in a deep breath, I said to Collin, "I don't know how to stop her. I don't know what to do."

His eyes were wide. Helpless. When they narrowed, he offered, "I can kill her. Ivy, if you can conjure the mirror, I can kill her."

My bottom lip pressed tightly. When he went inside, he'd think the Demon Princess was me. He wouldn't know which of us was real. I couldn't do that to him. I shook my head, "You can't. There's... it won't work. Trust me." Collin nodded, not challenging my words. I sat down on the floor, trying to calm down. "Tell me everything you know about blood bargains."

Collin sat opposite me. He didn't try to reach for me again. As we sat and talked, Collin spoke the healing incantations one at a time, and I felt the open wounds begin to heal. He said, "That was extra fowl. She filled the wounds with..." He paused, and reconsidered his words, "with something that wouldn't heal with normal magic. These may scar. I'm not sure if they'll fade or not."

I nodded, not caring. The Demon Princess completely screwed me. And I fell for it. And now, I couldn't even tell Collin that she was waiting for me to do the dirty work, and then take over. Collin continued to speak, telling me about blood bargains.

"She wanted me to drink from the cup," I said. "I refused. She said it wouldn't have the same effect on me as your blood. Was she lying?" I glanced up at Collin, feeling the sting of the wounds healing on my face.

His eyes were troubled as he answered, "Yes. And no. No, she wouldn't have the same connection to you that I do, or Eric does for that matter. But, drinking from the chalice would have intensified the bargain—made it more powerful. It would have given her means to call you to her at any time. The one who holds the chalice holds the power. She would have used it to weaken you, no doubt. She keeps draining you when you need to rest. It's like she set you up to fail." He was quiet, thinking about it. And he had no idea how close he actually came to what she was trying to do—kill me and take my place.

"I spilled it, Collin. I dumped our blood onto the floor." I wanted to tell him about her desire to alter it, but found the words would not form. The bargain prevented me from saying it.

His eyes went wide, as he looked at me in shock. His lips pulled into a soft smile. "You spilled it? No wonder she did this to you. She can't call you back without it. As it was, she had to wait until you were weak to pull you through, but now—now she can't. You shifted the balance of power."

I nodded. "Yeah, that woulda pissed her off. Pinning her to the floor probably didn't help." Collin laughed. I glanced up at him.

"And you freed her?" he was more serious as I nodded. One question formed on his perfect lips. "Why? You knew she would go after you. You had to … and you freed her anyway. Ivy, why would you do such a thing?"

I looked away. I couldn't tell him. I couldn't say that I thought it was worth the risk. Or that she looked exactly like me. I couldn't tell him that she would be coming after him, as soon as she disposed of me. As soon as I killed the Demon King. I couldn't tell him that I risked it to save his life. So I said nothing.

Coldness raced through my heart. I wanted to press my eyes closed. This couldn't be happening. I couldn't be in her debt, and there was no way to get an angel into Hell to appease my end of the bargain. Lorren had his wings ripped off. I doubted he'd qualify, and there was no way I was asking him to do that. He'd be slaughtered. But, I had to figure out how to fulfill my end of the bargain. I had to give her an angel. Leaning forward, I pressed my face in my hands. It was hopeless.

CHAPTER ELEVEN

The door above slammed opened and closed. Eric bounded down the stairs. His cheeks were red, and white flecks clung to his hair. It was still snowing. Collin sat on the couch with his feet on the table, ignoring Eric. I stood and walked over to him, not expecting the look he gave me. Eric tossed a bag on the table. The brown paper bag was covered in snow. "Clothes. I thought you'd want to change."

I nodded, reaching for the bag. Eric's brow flinched as his gaze narrowed. His eyes darted from me to Collin, and back.

He blinked once, and said, "Why?"

Startled, I asked, "Why what?"

"Why him? Why now?" He stared at me with his jaw clenched tight. Collin ignored him, but my cheeks blazed red. He knew. He knew we were together. How? As if he could read my face, he added, "Fucking him is one thing, but you took his blood? Didn't you? I can smell it. You're different. You put yourself... That was just stupid, Ivy!" His fist flew into a canvas. The wood frame splintered as the fabric tore away. He reached for me. I let him wrap his fingers around the base of my neck, tangling his hands in my hair. His voice dropped to a whisper as he pulled me closer, "Do you want to be a slave for eternity? Do you want Kreturus to win?" His lips were in front of mine, forming each word with the precision that only comes with acute anger.

His words infuriated me. I'd been through hell that day, and I wasn't going to discuss the only thing that brought me joy. My jaw locked. I hissed, "My relationship with Collin isn't your concern."

His grip on my neck tightened. Eric spoke so softly that I could barely hear him. "It is if you fuck up my life too. Your blood bond with me is weak. It'll fade. You know what's happened. You saw it," he snapped, shaking me. "So don't act like that was a reasonable thing to do." He pointed to Collin.

Collin moved from his slouched position on the couch and was standing behind Eric. The tension in his shoulders said he was ready to pound Eric into the floor. I put my hand on Eric's face, knowing my words would enrage him, "Love isn't a reasonable thing to do." Eric tried to pull away, but I didn't let him. His golden eyes bore into mine. I wouldn't let go or look away. "I know you know. I know you know why I let you do what you do. It's not guilt. It's not pity." I shoved him away from me. Eric's hands fell to his sides, watching.

Eric stared at me for some time, without speaking. His eyes never drifted off my face. When he spoke again, the tension in his body eased. "Just because your feelings toward me are not one thing, it doesn't mean they're another." He turned, looking to Collin.

Collin's jaw clenched tight. I'd blindsided him without meaning to, and there was no way to tell him what I was thinking or why I said what I said. I'd have to tell him later and hope he trusted me. For some reason, I cared about Eric. It wasn't the same as my love for Collin. It was more of an affection based on a need I had—a need he fulfilled. I didn't know why. And when it came from him, it was different. Nothing like Locoicia's pain. My eyes darted to Eric's face. Was it so bad to convince him that I cared about him?

I answered, "Then why else would I let you beat me? Why else would I allow you that release? I've seen it the second after your mouth or your hand takes its toll. It's cruel. And it makes you cruel. And I know what it is. I know it's the curse." I was near ranting. I sounded insane. My reason didn't make sense without all the pieces. Collin didn't have all the pieces.

But Eric did. His brow pinched together as he spit out the words, "Fine. Deny it. Fuck whoever you want, Ivy, but you might was well remove your ward and kill me if you drink more blood."

"Eric," I paused. He made everything so vile. So hopeless. My mind drifted to the Demon Princess—to knocking the chalice on the floor. I refused. Even if her words were true, I couldn't take more blood. It would sever the bond with Eric.

And the lie. It was still there. He thought I held his ward. But I didn't, Lorren made it, and I didn't know when it would end. Or why it was there in the first place. Reaching forward, I took his hand. Pressing my thumb into his palm, he watched me. "I just want to make it better. I..." but I never finished speaking.

Panic straightened Eric's back, as he lunged for me. His hand flew over my lips, making me stop talking. My eyes were wide, as I looked at him. He removed his hand from my mouth. "Hate me, Ivy. It's the only thing that will save you."

***

Eric was pulling off snow-soaked boots in his corner of the basement while Collin and I sat on the couch. Collin leaned in close, "Why didn't you tell me you have feelings for him?" He didn't seem hurt, or defensive. It was just a question.

I wrapped my arms around myself not wanting to talk about it. "Because that's not really what it is. I would have said misplaced affection, if anything." I looked at Collin. He looked at his hands, not knowing what to say. "It was after he was Valefar. I..." I broke off trying to find the right words. This was something I didn't like. Something I was barely aware of myself.

But Eric knew.

"She doesn't care for me, Smith. She just likes to play with fire," Eric said as he sat down, barefooted on the floor in front of us. His gaze was vacant again. The mask he wore, solidly in place. "The pain made her feel alive, again. She has a dark side that seems to evaporate when you're around. But when she looks at me, I see it. It's self-serving. And I terrify her." His gaze was intense, watching me as he spoke. "She wants me because she's like me. I want to cause her pain, and she wants to feel it. Isn't that right?" He smiled, stretching his legs out in front of him.

While he spoke my jaw dropped lower and lower. I wanted to refute what he said, but as I opened my mouth to cut him off no words came out. I just wanted to feel something. And Eric made me feel something that I knew was my own. I wanted to fight off the numbness that was seeping deep into my soul. There was a need within me to try to control it. Until now, there had been no controlling it at all.

But I'd noticed something. Around Eric—especially when he was being cruel and doing things that would make a sane person run—I wasn't so numb. Maybe it was a false sense of security. Maybe I couldn't feel anything and it was all in my mind. At those moments, I didn't care because it felt *real*.

Allowing Eric to torment me became a desire. Dark thoughts flickered through my mind like tiny flames wanting to combust. What Eric did wasn't an act of violence in my eyes. It was a gift that brought me back to myself. As to the reasons why he acted that way, I wasn't entirely sure yet. I didn't need to know. And getting a straight answer out of the fallen angel was difficult.

But this… I never expected him to latch onto what I was doing, and voice it in front of Collin. I didn't know how to explain what this was or why I needed Eric. I never told Collin because it sounded more twisted than it was. I didn't know what to say.

Eric arched a brow at me, "What's the matter, Ivy? Are you too prim and proper to admit that's why you're drawn to me? That you have some carnal desire that you can't control."

Every muscle in my body tensed as I glared at Eric. He was so smug, saying things that appeared to be true on the surface, but we both knew they weren't. There was a reason why we were connected. A reason why I needed the pain he inflicted, and he needed me just as much. I worked the muscle in my jaw, trying to unlock my mouth. Without warning, I shot out of my seat and rushed at his face, pushing him back with my hands splayed on his chest. Eric's eyes went wide as he took in my fury. "Never make him think that I'd choose you over him." I shoved him hard, and backed away. Eric's eyes narrowed, but he remained silent.

Collin leaned forward, and abruptly ended the conversation. Tension lined his body. "Where's the stone, Eric?" he demanded.

Eric didn't remove his gaze from my face. "It's where I left it. In the hilt of a dagger. Wanna guess which dagger?" His lips snaked into a smile.

My face fell. He couldn't be serious. "You didn't…"

Eric beamed, "I did. The stone is in Shannon McClure's weapon."

All this time I didn't want to ask what happened to her. I had assumed Eric tormented her until she died. I didn't want to know what Eric was capable of, and I didn't want to see Shannon again. When he said her name it felt like stitches were ripped from my throat. I couldn't breathe.

Collin leaned forward, watching me. When I said nothing, he asked, "Why does a Martis have the stone?"

Eric shrugged. I watched him, unable to fathom who he was or what he did. "She has no idea she has it. I was the one in charge of her and the Celestial Silver. I placed the stone in the hilt. To her it looks like a polished stone, a decoration—obsidian maybe. But it's not. It's the inverted match of yours," he said pointing to my necklace. "We need to take her weapon."

I found my voice, "I thought you killed her. Where is she?"

Eric pulled his legs in and leaned forward, draping his arms over his knees. "Why would you think that? She was alive last time you saw her. She was fine. Why would I kill her?"

I scoffed, "She was far from fine. And you wanted to kill her because she killed you in the Lorren!" Was he crazy? Did he really let her walk away? There had to be another explanation.

He laughed, "You are so short-sighted. If you have eternity ahead of you, you can't kill every person who tries to fuck with you. There would be no one left to entertain you." He paused, watching for the disgust that filled my eyes. When he saw it, he continued, "I didn't kill her. I made her life hell. She's a Martis addicted to demon blood. It was amusing for a while. When I was done playing with her, I sent her back and watched her fumble. Julia would have killed her if she could manage it. I'm sure she suspects, but it's so ludicrous that most of them don't even realize what happened."

Collin's hand was over his mouth, as he tried to suppress a smile. He knew Shannon was a traitor, that she betrayed me when I needed her. "You turned her into a blood slave and sent her home? She must have..."

Eric smiled, recognizing that Collin understood the complexity of his revenge. "And she did. She still can't function. She kills people she's supposed to heal. A healer with no power is an abomination. Julia's banished her to the archives where she shuffles through piles of books trying to find a cure. I show up every few weeks and she begs for more blood. It's her punishment." His golden eyes stared vacantly, no doubt recalling the terror he thrust on Shannon on a daily basis. Not only did he remove her skill, but he screwed with her mind. If she couldn't heal, she couldn't think. Shannon had healed me once. If she hadn't, I wouldn't be able to see. It bothered me that he tormented her. I could accept her death easier than torture. Eric cut his gaze to me, "It's a much better punishment than killing her."

CHAPTER TWELEVE

"So you say," I said quietly. A million thoughts were on my tongue. One of them finally slipped out, "Where is she? Rome?"

He shook his head. "No one is in Rome. Rome burned. Have you not stuck your neck outside to see what things look like?" He glanced at Collin and then back to me. "Of course not. Fucking lovebirds and all. Go push open the door and look. The beast that attacked us at the Pool—the Dreanok - there are more of them. They fill the skies. Demons walk the earth tearing a path of destruction through the landscape as they take city after city. The Martis moved to the center of the battle, protecting the remaining humans. But there's no point. The Martis are overpowered and outnumbered." He grinned, as if it amused him, "And it seems that the Martis have forgotten how to use their powers. The corrupt bastards finally figured out how far they've fallen." He paused, and added an afterthought, "The angels are here. The world you knew is gone. It's a warzone for the third and final Angel Demon War. The war that you have to win."

I sat on the couch, shocked. As his words sunk in, I jumped up and raced up the stairs and threw open the door. Collin was on my heels. We moved through the remains of the school and over a pile of rubble that was once the wall. Standing outside, my heart sank into my feet. My throat tightened, as my hand slapped over my mouth to stifle a scream. The sky was filled with grackles—the hellish kind. They swarmed like a massive black cloud. The only thing that broke them apart was the beast that'd attacked us in the Underworld—the Dreanok. Craning my neck from side to side, I could see three of them circling above, as if they were patrolling the area looking for something.

Or someone. Shit! They were looking for me!

Collin realized it at the same time I did, and yanked us back into the cellar and shut the door. We stood at the top of the steps, and stared at each other. Collin wasn't alive during the last war. Did it ever look like that? Did the sky bleed last time? Did humans die? Did the creatures of Hell soar through the skies?

Eric's voice echoed below, "Ivy, stop it. Terror is wafting off of you. If you want me to leave you alone, you can't do that." He was serious. I knew what he meant—what it did to him, but I couldn't suppress it. Not with Collin standing next to me. I could feel things when he was near. It wasn't just a distant echo in the back of my mind. It was palpable fear.

And that was the kind of fear that Eric liked best.

I nodded for Collin to go ahead. He looked back at me, questions in his eyes. Questions that I couldn't answer. "Go ahead. I can't calm down if you're next to me." Collin turned and slowly walked down the steps. I heard him sink into the couch. I exhaled deeply and tried to relax with my back against the metal door.

Eric stood at the bottom of the staircase. "This is the only safe place I've found. If you allow yourself to feel that much, it'll make it impossible for me to..." I already felt it. His blood. Had he been repressing it? Why didn't it bother me until now?

I kept my back pressed to the door and closed my eyes. I could hear Eric walking up the stairs. His shoe hit the metal steps one at a time. My heart raced harder and harder. His scent grew stronger and stronger, until he stopped with only a step between us.

He mouthed, *Tell him not to follow.* It was all I could do to nod. The enclosed staircase was small. I stood on a tiny landing with Eric pressed close below me. The former angel called back to Collin, "I need to show her something."

I heard Collin rise, and Eric nodded at me to speak. That horrible sensation was there again. My muscles weren't my own. Eric used his blood to force me, and I did as he said, "It's okay. I'll be right back." Eric pressed his body into mine as he pushed me through the door, his hand on my shoulder leading me onto the dark stage. My knees went weak, but I felt them stumble forward one step at a time. I tried to fight the bloodlust. I had been able to many other times. I didn't understand how he was able to do it this time. Or why I couldn't fight him.

Our bodies pressed together, making me inhale sharply. Before the door closed behind us, I saw Collin standing at the bottom of the staircase with clenched fists. He would allow it. I'd asked him, but I didn't anticipate on Eric forcing me to do anything. For half a second, I hoped he'd follow and stop this. But I knew he wouldn't. I knew Collin would honor my request, even if he didn't like it.

Collin called up to Eric, half growling at him, "If you go too far, I'll kill you. She's already had you fuck with her mind enough." Collin didn't like this. He didn't trust Eric, and he didn't understand why I did—especially when he did things like this.

Eric turned and laughed over his shoulder, "Yeah, I fucked with her mind, but you got her body. That was the better part, if you ask me." Before Collin had a chance to respond, Eric slammed the metal door shut. The knob scraped closed with a loud clack. We stood on the other side, behind the mangled black curtains that separated the stage. Eric stopped, pushing his hair out of his eyes, and looking at me for a while. His golden gaze slid to my feet, as he took a deep breath. I watched him, unable to look away, unable to speak. The power of his blood held my tongue still. When Eric glanced up, he shook his head, as if he couldn't believe what I'd done; that I'd chosen Collin over him. His hands gripped my shoulders firmly, pressing into my skin before shoving me across the stage and into the lighting cage.

The metal box was exactly like a cage—a cage that contained electrical equipment used to control the lights during a show. There was barely enough room for one person. Eric pushed me into the tiny space, and turned and pulled the cage door shut behind us. It creaked closed, and it was all I could do to watch him. The tiny space had my heart racing. I hated feeling trapped, and that was exactly how I felt. Stuck in a tiny space, surrounded by metal slats, with Eric blocking the only way out. I swallowed hard. This side of the theater was still intact and far from the open hole in the roof. We were shrouded in darkness, but I could still see the hole in the roof. The winter sky was stained red, with gray clouds casting sleet from their folds.

A gust of winter wind blew through the opening, lifting my hair from my shoulders. I shivered. It was frigid and I had no coat. Eric watched as the cold tremble crept from my fingers, to my back, and throughout my body. The whole time I fought to suppress his blood lust, so I could ask what he was doing—but the best I could do was subdue it. I couldn't ignore the desire. I couldn't thrust it into the back of my head and make it disappear like I'd done so many times before. Eric's close proximity made it worse. Between that and the fact that he hadn't spoken, and shoved me in a tiny metal box, I felt like I couldn't breathe. My heart hammered in my ears.

Fascinated, he watched me and said nothing. His amber eyes rested on my face, transfixed on my mouth, watching me fight to control the fear that was coursing through me. The fear he was inducing. Minutes passed and Eric said nothing. He just watched. When my lips were blue, and I couldn't stop trembling from the cold, Eric leaned closer to me and traced them with his finger. His touch was warm, hot compared to the frigid air. It shot a bolt of heat though my stomach.

I managed to jerk away, and he laughed. "I wish we had more time, but we don't. Not since your crazed boyfriend will be here any moment. Listen. I needed to tell you something." My gaze snapped, focused completely on Eric. I couldn't fight him. It was as if someone turned my head and made me listen. "Good," Eric stated. "The bloodlust isn't totally gone. But, his blood complicates things. A lot… " he sighed deeply, as he leaned back onto the lighting control panel. It ran the length of the cage and was like a little table covered with switches and levers. None of it worked since there was no power. We sat in total darkness.

"I needed you to come with me," Eric explained. He shifted his weight, and leaned on his hands. The muscles in his arms curved taught as he leaned back. "But, I can't just waltz into the Martis camp and steal the dagger with you like this. You've been compromised. That's why Locoicia taught you to fight. That's why she taught you to bury your feelings. It makes you fearless. But, like this—you're no fucking good to me like this. You can't even fight me off. You're staring at me like a fucking zombie. Ivy, fight back." It was a command, but I couldn't. Eric didn't lessen his hold on me, but he demanded that I fight him off. Yet, I could only stand there staring at him, feeling like a trapped animal. My mind was screaming, willing me to move, but my body remained still.

Unmoving. Something changed. The power of his blood was too strong, too potent.

Eric sighed, pushing his hair out of his face. "You can't, can you?" I shook my head, unable to say more. Eric silenced me. My jaw was locked tight. It felt like a sandbag had fallen on my chest, crushing me flat. Eric was beyond irritated this time. He screamed in my face, "Why'd you have to do this! And now? Out of all the stupid-ass things you could have possibly done! This made you weak. The more demon blood you have in you, the less you become. The Ivy that fought back has been subdued. Tamed." He stepped away, leaving me standing in front of him with my heart racing in my chest. "Listen. She's not gone. The girl you were is still in there, but she's weak. And we can't afford weak. There are already so many things stacked against us." Us. The word rang in my mind, not connecting to any other thoughts, but I couldn't ignore the usage. Eric kept saying us.

He continued, "The second we have the stone, you'll have to use it. You can't hesitate. And, I know you saw my price. I know that you saw what it did to me and your price will be so much worse. It will be the third time the stone has been used." His amber eyes slid over my face, fixating on my lips. When he realized he wasn't blinking, he turned his face away, breathing deeply.

My mind fog started to clear. The lust induced haze that rendered me silent faded. All I could manage to say was, "Eric, I have to use it. There's no other way, is there?"

He shook his head somberly, serious for once. When his gaze lifted, I felt like I was staring into his soul. I could see and feel everything. Sensations choked me in a cloud of emotion. Eric stood in front of me, casually leaning back and literally bared his soul. I gasped, but he took my hand, explaining, "You can see me, because you touched my soul once before—when it wasn't in my body. Healing me at the Pool allows you to see things others don't." His lips parted as if he was going to say something, but he stopped.

I felt confused. Afraid. There was an otherworldliness that felt wrong. Like I shouldn't be able to see what I was seeing. That Eric couldn't be so... My mind had difficulty wrapping around the idea. It was like his body was a shell, containing something far more vast and powerful than I could comprehend. I averted my gaze, looking away. Swallowing hard, I asked, "That's what I see now? That's what I feel now?" It was strange. I could sense him in a way that didn't make sense. It was like I could feel him thinking. My consciousness was aware of the feelings that went into his thoughts, pulling on memories that made him what he was—the tormented fallen angel sitting in front of me.

He nodded, tilting my face up to meet his gaze, "The blood, plus the way you touched my soul—it makes it hard to hide anything from you. Add that to the power I stole from you, and it makes it worse. It takes so much effort to keep you from seeing me for what I am. What I was … "

"Then why?" I asked, shivering at his touch. Eric's hand dropped from my chin. I wanted to understand why he felt the need to hide things. If he trusted me, why bother?

He smiled answering softly, "Are you serious?" He ran his fingers through his hair and looked at me with a surprised expression on his face. "Would you allow me full access to everything you were, and everything you are, and all you want to be? Do you really want me to see every shattered hope? And feel every bit of pain? How could you even ask me that? You, out of all people, should understand." He was quiet for a minute, blinking, looking past me instead of at me. When Eric's gaze refocused on my face, he added, "Self-preservation. Same as you. It's the same reason you shut people out, and push them away." Eric watched me as I spoke, taking in my reaction. And he was right. I understood what he meant. But I also knew there was more. More he wouldn't say. More he couldn't say.

After a moment of silence, he asked, "You know how this ends, don't you?" I glanced up into his face. Eric looked down at me, with an expression I couldn't identify. Eric continued, cutting off my thoughts, "There is no other possibility. My curse is on a collision course with you. When you use the stone, if not sooner, my curse will destroy you. I can't stop it. I've tried, but it's too late. Ivy, my curse will intertwine with yours, and however this ends, it won't be good. Adding Collin into things, and his blood—you need to understand—you'll just suck him down too." He paused and I felt his blood take control of me again. My stray thoughts stopped, as Eric made me listen to him. "Ivy, Collin can't come with us. His blood will weaken you. If the pain price of using the stone is too great, you'll feel it even more with him standing there. It'll destroy him. And you."

Eric released me. I sucked in air, once again feeling like the cage was too small. It was as if someone was pumping the air out. The cold night suddenly felt hot. I couldn't breathe. I heard what Eric said, but my gut reaction said he was wrong. I searched my mind, looking for the exact reason, "He has to. Al said I needed both of you."

Eric nodded, "Yeah, Al said that was part of the prophecy. But there's one other prophecy that no one's ever seen. The last one. Ivy, no one knows how this'll end, but I'm telling you sincerely, warning you—do not take him with us. If you love him, keep him safe. Make him stay here until it's over." He took my hand and placed it on his chest. A swell of emotion flooded me. Pleading, Eric said, "I risked too much already, showing you this. But I had to say something … "

I nodded. I knew he wasn't lying. I could feel it—hell, I could see it. There was no motive behind his words other than compassion. And, there was nothing like seeing a soul without anything to hide it. The thought made my stomach clench. Eric was right. I did understand why he hid it from me. From everyone. I would do the same thing.

My gaze flicked up to his face. "Fear feeds your affliction, doesn't it? It makes it harder for you to control yourself." His gaze slid over my face, locking on my eyes. My stomach dropped. I couldn't comprehend the horror of what he lived through. Or what was to come. But his curse seemed to feed off of it, never giving him a moment of peace.

"You have no idea," was all he said.

I stared at him, openly studying his face, his eyes. The curse that the stone cast upon him twisted his life. It made him angry, and bitter. It twisted who he was, making him into the sadistic bastard he was now. Half the time I hated him. The other half, I was confused. His actions didn't always line up with evil Eric. He was more than that. Eric was beyond good or evil. I could see it. I didn't know what that meant. But I did know how it affected me. Pressing my lips together, I glanced at him, "Does it help? Does it ease at all—in those moments? When you're hurting someone?" It was a question that I didn't want to ask. I already knew the answer. I could see it in his eyes when he hurt me.

Eric's gaze didn't leave my face, "You know it does. I know that's why you were allowing it..." he sucked in a breath and looked away. His jaw stiffened, as he worked the muscle. "Listen, Ivy. We don't have time for this. I had..."

The blood lust wore thin. It was nearly gone, subdued by Eric and all but gone. He was in full control. But as I watched his lips, and he spoke, my mind drifted back to the Underworld where his words were wild and damning. Evil Eric thrusting me into a rock and saying things that made my blood run cold. The anger, the fury in his eyes when he first found me after I turned him Valefar. The emotions I felt at that moment, pressed through the memory and into the present. Terror raced through my veins. Terror that would feed Eric's affliction and calm it for a moment. I wanted to give it to him—one last second of solace before we faced the Demon King.

I did it on purpose, allowing him to take what he needed from me. And before I could blink, he could feel it. The veil that hid his soul slammed back down, shutting me out as his instincts warred within him. He was a good man being forced to do bad things. The only way for him to have a moments peace was when he was inflicting pain.

"What are you doing?" concern was in his voice. His brow wrinkled as he turned away from me, trying to fight his natural instincts. But he couldn't. His control on the bloodlust slipped. It slammed back into me full force. Eric tried to choke it back, but my heart was racing so hard. My body was tense. Ready to run, but trapped—which made it worse. I didn't try to calm myself down. I allowed my fear to feed him, but he fought it. Eric rejected the terror coursing through me, as if it was causing him pain.

I answered, "You know what I'm doing." My voice shook as I watched the muscles in Eric's arms coil tighter. I was drawing out the dark part of him, and he tried to resist. But that wasn't what I wanted. It wasn't what he needed. "Stop fighting it, Eric. Be what you are. Take what you need." Amber eyes flew open as I spoke, wide and wild. He looked crazed, fighting the instincts that were trying to overtake him. My heart raced faster and I found my voice again. "Take some of my power. Take what you need. Do it." My body tensed as he moved closer, like a wild animal ready to tear me apart. My heart pounded against my ribs like it was ready to explode.

"Ivy..." he breathed unable to say more.

Eric reached me, twisting me in his arms, and pinning me to the cage door. He moved me fast, and my head slammed into the metal mesh with a soft thud. The wind blew at my back, making me shiver against the chilled steel. Eric pressed his hands to the door on either side of my head, locking me in place. I'd seen him in here so many times, and never thought things would be like this. I remembered him kindly smiling at me after my lessons with Al. The boy pinning me to the door was the version constantly fighting for control. The one that went denied and underfed. It made Eric weaker than he was, denying himself like that. And he was right. We couldn't steal back the dagger and kill Kreturus weak.

My throat tightened as he leaned closer to me. I could feel the heat of his breath slide across my skin. This version of Eric scared the hell out of me. He was still fighting, trying to withhold the bloodlust, attempting to restrain himself. His gaze narrowed as he watched me try to respond. My mouth was dry. Every muscle in my body was flexed, stretching, leaning away from him and pressing my body harder into the metal mesh door at my back.

I whispered, "It's necessary. Do it." As his face loomed closer, I turned away. My breath caught in my throat as my pulse pounded, deafening all other sounds. The winter wind howling at my back no longer chilled me. I didn't even hear it as Eric leaned his warm body onto mine.

His face was so close. His lips were barely brushing against my skin as he spoke. Eric lifted his hand, and traced a vein in my neck, slowly feeling it pulsate under his finger. The thumping of my heart pounded harder. In a heavy breath, he asked, "And Smith?"

I didn't expect him to ask. I didn't think he would care. Eric seemed to take what he wanted and not make apologies for it. It was as if he were an animal and didn't know better. But this—this version of him frightened me the most. It was as if he knew what I was, and he twisted it, using it to mold me into what he wanted—what he needed. The bloodlust coursed through me. I inhaled softly, not wanting him to notice, but knowing he would. The heavy scent filled my head.

I pressed my eyes closed and answered him, "He knows." It pained me to say it, which made Eric smile wider. Collin knew I'd do this. He knew it was something I needed, that Eric required of me. It was unexplainable, but in the moments I saw Eric's soul—I knew. We were connected. Our fates were tied together. It was a tangled destiny that allowed him no freedom. No reprieve from me. It left him in a constant state of pain and longing. Loneliness and devastation followed him, weighing heavily on his heart—crushing it to bits. But this. This removed that burden. It freed him, making him into something else. A being I didn't understand. A being I feared. My voice shook as I added, "Collin's probably watching. I told him that you would. That you had to." Despite the cold, sweat rolled down my spine. Eric noticed the shiver. My hands clawed at the locked door behind me as Eric's finger remained on my throat, moving in a slow gentle movement down my neck.

He stopped when his finger rested on the hollow of my throat. The lashes on his eyes lowered as Eric watched the vulnerable place beneath his hand. The muscles in my neck strained, becoming taught as his finger pressed deeper and deeper into the soft flesh. I sucked in a ragged breath, pushing myself back against the cage wall. It didn't matter that I could comprehend that Eric wouldn't kill me. My body completely ignored the fact. Fear raced through my veins. I couldn't stop pushing into the steel cage door, trying to get away from him. And I knew what he was doing—how he was playing with me. He watched as his finger pressed harder, and my body tried to melt into the metal. If he pressed a little harder, a little deeper—I'd die. Eric's finger would crush my windpipe.

A bead of sweat rolled down the side of my face. My hands were gripping the metal mesh, bending it as I tightened my fingers between the slats. Pushing back into the door forced out my chest, and straightened my spine. My long curls fell over my shoulders. Forcing myself, I glanced at Eric. It hadn't dawned on me how hard he fought to control himself. How hard he tried to be something he was not. This side of him was deeply hidden, and deeply starved.

Eric was fascinated, watching me breathe and listening to the hammering of my heart. When he pressed down harder, I gasped. Pleading, I said in a panicked voice, "Eric, don't!" He paused, not applying more pressure. His gaze lowered, seeking to meet mine, but I couldn't look at him. I wheezed in another rough gasp, and Eric lightened his finger more. I could breathe. He watched my lips, and my chest rising as I sucked in air.

He glanced over my shoulder for a split second, and a smile twisted his lips. Was Collin so close? Was he watching? Is that why Eric seemed pleased? I didn't know. I couldn't feel anything but the fear that Eric pumped into my body. If Collin was near, I couldn't sense him. I couldn't smell his blood. And he remained out of sight, so that I couldn't see him. Pain coursed through me, thinking that he was watching. I knew he didn't understand. Hell, I didn't understand.

But that pain and fear wasn't enough for Eric. And he took things farther than I'd expected. And the bloodlust didn't let me stop him. The fallen angel pressed his body to mine. His lips brushed past my ear, breathing in deeply as he did so. His chest pressed against mine, sliding, feeling the swell of my body—the desperation of my breaths. I could feel his wild heart beating frantically beneath his chest. His desire was palpable. Lust overtook me, swelling within my middle until it reached every inch of my body. He held nothing back. Nothing was tempered. My body flushed, heated from head to toe. The only thing I could think about was Eric. Eric's hands. Eric's skin … Eric's taste on my tongue. He'd never done this before. He'd never released himself fully. Eric always tempered the lust, holding it back or contorting it into fear or rage. He controlled my mind and body. And I couldn't resist.

As he breathed heavily, I felt his firm chest move against mine. Eric's hand was suddenly at my waist, as he looked into my eyes. They were rimming violet. I couldn't resist him. I couldn't push him away. When his hand touched my skin, I sighed. But he didn't leave it there. Sliding his fingers under my shirt, Eric pressed his palm against my breast. My heart shot into my mouth. Startled, I yelped. Eric's gaze didn't waiver. He watched every reaction swim across my face, and then his fingers clamped down squeezing the sensitive skin hard. Pain registered, cutting through the haze clouding my mind. But Eric's blood held me in place. When I cried out, Eric slammed his lips down on mine. And I melted. His blood was still inside of me, calming me, letting him steal and take anything he wanted. The kiss continued and his hand lingered, pressing harder and harder. Pain continued to shoot through my body until I thought I'd scream. My head swam, feeling large and heavy on my shoulder. Eric's lips pressed into mine so hard, his tooth nicked my lip. The kiss softened for only a second, a second in which he slid his tongue along the wound—tasting my blood. My stomach twisted as I watched him. Felt him. I felt so lost. So far gone. Eric took my lip in his mouth and bit down gently. Then his lips pressed down on mine. I felt myself weakening, knowing that he was taking from me. I remained tangled in his arms, until Eric increased the pressure on my breast, and twisted hard. My back arched as a scream tore out of my throat. Eric suddenly ripped his lips away from mine, and his hand slid down to my waist.

He leaned in close, breathing raggedly in my ear. He squeezed the bare skin at my waist and withdrew his hand. "He's across the stage." A wicked smile spread across Eric's face. My heart was still racing. I felt the absence of power. I knew he took it. And Eric was beaming, ready to fight. He seemed happy, almost.

~ 137 ~

I sat there for a moment, catching my breath. Fury built inside of me. I didn't like him touching me. He hadn't done that before. My anger made my fists ball up. And before he could move, I swung. My fist connected to the side of his face. Eric staggered. I'd hit him hard. "You didn't have to do that. I gave you enough without it." I gave him enough pain, terror, and fear for a moments reprieve, but he took more. He melted me, and used me—feeling me beneath his palm. My breast ached from what he did.

Eric wrapped his fingers around my wrist and jerked me closer. I fell into his chest, and he held me there for a moment, saying, "It doesn't work that way, and you know it. Having an idea of what you're doing—of what I'll take—subdues your fear. It alters the pain. Next time, don't plan anything and I won't have to resort to such drastic measures." He threw me into the cage wall, pushed opened the metal door left me staring across the dark stage into Collin's flame red eyes.

CHAPTER THIRTEEN

Rage had engulfed Collin, making him shake as he was forced to allow Eric to manhandle me. I was certain Eric grabbed my breast, because he knew Collin and I were finally together. And that Collin was watching. The action would force a wedge between us, making it easier to push Collin away—making it easier to convince him that he had to stay behind. Apparently, Eric planned it that way. A fight would make him give me some distance, if not make him so pissed off that he left me entirely. From the looks of it, Eric and I were intimate. But we weren't. It was a plan to leave Collin behind. A plan that would keep him safe. I sighed. Eric was smart, but he had no heart. It was cruel. I supposed that was why he did it that way.

As I neared the side of the stage, I stopped in front of Collin, and looked up into blood red eyes. This was the very spot we first spoke. I sat in a chair where he now stood, as he exited the stage. I remember that day in vivid detail. I never expected to be standing with him in this same spot with half the ceiling missing, surrounded by splintered wood and shattered concrete. A breeze blew through the decimated room, lifting the ends of my hair.

Collin's hands were balled into fists, crossed over his chest. His words were eerily calm when he spoke, "Does he always do that to you?" He asked as if Eric and I did this a lot. Fucking Eric. I scowled, shaking my head. I could explain, but I didn't. Telling him that Eric only did it because he was standing there would make it worse. Collin looked into my face, studying my eyes. Then he asked softly, "Did you like it?"

My heart lurched. I never expected him to ask that question. My face grew hot as I blushed. I pushed my way past him, saying "I don't want to talk about it. I told you I had to do it. It's over now."

But he grabbed my arm, stopping me. I spun around and looked up at Collin. "It'll never be over with him. You two have some kind of connection. Am

I supposed to just let him do what he wants with you? Ivy..." he growled, shoving his hands through his hair. The muscles in his arms were corded tight, ready to snap something in half.

I pressed my lips together. Sorry for causing him pain. Sorry that my fate was tangled with Eric's. "The only way he'll need more power is if something goes wrong when we try to take the dagger." I paused looking up at him. This was the hard part. The part I knew he wouldn't consent to. "I need to go with him. Will you wait for me here?"

Anger flashed in his eyes, "I'm not going to stay behind and let him... Ivy, he screws with your mind as much as Locoicia. I can't let him..." I cut him off.

"You promised. You said you trusted me. Please Collin. I have a plan, and if it works, I'll need you here. I'll need you here even more if it goes wrong." I told him what we planned to do, and why I needed him to stay behind. Collin took my hands, wrapping his fingers around mine.

The fire in his eyes faded. His blue gaze tore into mine. "I can't let you go into battle with a sadistic lunatic as your only means of help. Ivy, you're asking me to sit back and watch..." Horror gripped his throat, cutting off his words. His hands reached for my face, and tilted my chin to meet his gaze. "Don't ask me to do this."

I pressed my hands to his, wanting to feel his skin against mine forever. But that wasn't possible. I had to convince him to stay behind. So I nodded. "I have to. Eric's the one who has Shannon under his control. He has to come." I wanted Collin to understand, but the pain in his eyes said he didn't. I took his hands in mine, "I have to go."

As I turned to leave, I swallowed hard. I didn't like leaving him behind, but Eric was right. He shouldn't come this time. It was risking his life for no reason. And if things went screwy, someone needed to be here to restrain Shannon.

It was necessary.

As my hand slipped from his, I said softly, "See you in a little bit."

With his jaw locked, Collin nodded in one smooth motion. There was nothing else to say. I was doing something he didn't like, with someone he hated. Collin watched me walk toward Eric.

Eric's arms wrapped around my waist, pulling me tightly against his body. "Go to Heckscher State park—the campgrounds by the field. I know you've been there." I had. I knew exactly where he meant. I wondered what it would look like now that demons walked the Earth.

A grin spread across Eric's face. If Eric said a single taunting word, I'd punch him. I could feel

Collin's gaze burning into the side of my face. It had to be this way. He was safer here. Swallowing hard, I closed my eyes and effonated Eric and me to the dagger.

CHAPTER FOURTEEN

Eric glanced over his shoulder. Snow covered the bloodstained ground, hiding a multitude of sins. Flurries flew by, not recognizing the horrors that surrounded them as they drifted from the heavens to the earth. The Martis encampment lay in front of us, across a barren field. I would have never seen it if Eric hadn't brought me here first. There were rows and rows of tents. They varied in size, and every single one of them blended perfectly into the background. Eric had to tell me what I was looking at when we arrived. There was a slight shimmer around the edge of each tent—a white line that was almost completely lost against the newly fallen snow.

Glancing at Eric out of the corner of my eye, I asked, "How'd you find this place? I can barely see it."

"Angels are creatures of habit," he whispered, gazing over the frozen land. He turned to me, explaining, "It's the same type of encampment they made last time. The tents are made from ethereal linen and blend in almost perfectly. But there are ways to tell." He grinned. "See the circle around the camp?" I nodded. "It's from their sentry. It's the guard's line, the perimeter that they are protecting. And the center of the camp is squashed flat. Basically it looks like a massive circle depressed on an area, leaving a rim of untouched ground around it." He shrugged. "It's easy to find when you know what you're looking for."

Tugging my hand, Eric and I moved closer to the Martis camp. If Shannon was still alive, she was in there doing something mundane—the equivalent of washing dishes because of what Eric did to her. We'd effonated to this point to avoid the Dreanoks. But other things screamed out in the night in this place. Things that made my blood run cold. I wasn't certain exactly where we were, but Eric said we were still in New York, close the epicenter. Close to home. Close to where the gates of Hell stood wide open.

I followed Eric until he stopped at the base of what had been a massive oak tree. All that remained was a splintered trunk that jutted out of the earth like a massive hand. He pressed me to the tree, protectively, looking past me to the camp. The bloodlust whispered at the back of my mind.

I fixated on Eric's lips as he spoke, "Shit. There are more here than there were this morning. And, is that?" His face fell. He looked down at me with wide eyes. He leaned his head into the tree, pressing me harder into the stump as he sighed. The broken tree base was the only thing between us and the camp.

"Eric," I breathed. He was suffocating me.

He looked down at me, still crushing the air out of my lungs, "Your heart's racing." A faint smile lined his lips.

"I'm about to die. Of course it's racing." Eric's brow pinched as he removed some of his weight from my body. "Don't give me that look. And that wasn't what I meant, but thanks."

He lowered his gaze toward the frozen ground, "You're talking about my curse, aren't you?"

"Yeah. I am." I looked up at him. Eric's amber eyes met mine. "You know as well as I do what's going to happen if I use the stone. There isn't anyone left, is there? Everyone you cared about is dead. I know. I saw. It's part of your curse." Eric looked away, not wanting to hear my words. "You never let yourself get close to anyone, but you screw up every once and in a while. You loved Lydia and it was the reason she died such a horrific death. You cared about Al, and the curse twisted that death so that it was by your own hand. Despite how hard you've tried to make me hate you, I don't. And I know you care about me, which means I'm next."

Eric's lashes concealed his eyes as he looked down. His heart beat slowly under his shirt. "You shouldn't say such things. It'll only..."

"No, it won't. You can deny stuff all you want, but the curse isn't going to ignore it because you do." Eric's face was still downcast. I tilted my head to catch his eyes, "Our futures are intertwined. The repercussion of me using the stone is the only variable." I paused, "Eric, I'm going to die no matter what. You've gotta know that by now. Even if I survive using the stone, and your curse doesn't lead to my death... there's still something else. Something I can't escape from. The death angel's gotta be following me around, waiting, because it's only a matter of time. I've accepted it. Now, you need to."

Eric's golden eyes watched me, but neither of us spoke. The wind whipped across the land, tangling my tendrils in its frigid breeze. Eric's hair lifted and blew into his eyes. He didn't reach to smooth it down.

Finally, he said, "The stone won't kill you." He glanced back across the field, speaking softly, "It has to take a price, but death won't be enough." He paused looking down at me. "I'll help you learn to bear it, Ivy. And survive whatever comes next." He pressed a kiss to my forehead, softly. Completely unlike anything that Eric's ever done.

Confusion wrinkled my brow, "What was that for?"

A soft smile spread across his lips, "Ancient traditions. That's all." His hands were pressed to the tree, holding me in place. Eric's mask slipped, and what I saw made my throat grow tight. Sincere affection, and admiration burst through, shining transparently on his face. I smiled. I couldn't help it. He leaned in, touching his forehead to mine, and said, "Stop doing that." I hadn't meant to, but I melted the veil away and got a glimpse of what he was feeling for a second. I grinned at him.

When he looked up, he released me, and his veil was back. It instantly blocked the softness that I'd seen. Glancing across the field, he took in a deep breath. His smile faded, and I could see the worry in his eyes.

Conniving, ruthless, Eric was worried. This wasn't good.

I twisted around to see what he was looking at, using the tree to shield me from being spotted. Eric's hand rested on my shoulder, and he pressed into my back, whispering in my ear. "The camp is set up as a place to heal the wounded. Shannon would have been healing if I hadn't..." he paused. His hand rose next to my ear, his finger extending to a tent the same brown and blood red color as the ground, topped with snow. "Earlier today, she was in there. But, the angels weren't here then. I don't know how to get past them. They'll sense us if we take another step toward the camp." He dropped his hand and turned. A burst of cold air took his place at my back. He stepped away from me, pressing his fingers to his temples.

"What's wrong? So there are a few angels? So what?"

Eric glanced at me. "No, you don't get it. Warrior angels are guarding the camp - Seraphim. You're basing what you know about angels on the ones you've met. Seraphim don't pat you on the head if you wander into places you shouldn't be and then send you on your way with a cookie. They kill you."

Watching Eric, I asked, "Is that what you were? Before you used the stone?" He glanced down at me, not meeting my gaze.

"It hardly matters now, but yeah. I was." Eric remembered his life. The things that had been forgotten were shoved back into his mind with acute clarity when I merged his soul with his body at the Pool.

I added, "That's why you know so much. That's why you were a warrior Martis—the best. That's why you're able to help me now and know so much stuff. It wasn't chance. It was fate." I glanced up at his face to see his reaction, but as always, Eric remained coolly composed.

"Yeah, fate sucks like that. You spend a couple hundred lifetimes learning stuff only to get martyred—twice." He looked at me for a moment. His lips parted. I waited for him to speak, feeling the intensity of what he wanted to say, but none of the words. Instead of speaking, Eric closed his mouth and looked back at the camp. At the problem that barred our entry.

I gazed at the camp. Figures moved inside of tents illuminated from within. An encampment filled with healers. I whispered, "Is there anyone else here? Only Seraphim and Dyconisis?"

He nodded. "And the injured."

"Okay, the guards—they smite first and ask questions later?" He nodded. My eyes moved across the tents. I lifted my hand, pointing, "And Shan is in that tent, there is only one guard, and he's protecting the entire perimeter?" The camp was huge. I didn't see how that was possible. So I asked, "How is he doing it? How is he guarding the entire camp?" I wasn't stupid enough to think that just because I couldn't see him, that he wasn't there. I blinked once, wildly. I would have never thought something like that a year ago. Now it was a cold, hard, deadly fact.

"Yes, it only takes one Seraphim to guard a healing camp. The circle around the camp is his path. You can't see him moving, but it allows him to circle the entire thing at once. It's like he is the circle. The only way to make the angel materialize is to cross the line. But we can't. They put up wards to keep us out. And we can't effonate inside. They'll know the second we cross the line into the camp, and the angel appears and kills us," he replied.

Eric's face was blank as he stared at the trampled ground around the camp. I didn't understand how an angel could do that. I knew angels were powerful, and I suspected they were more powerful than I was, but there was no way to know. And I certainly didn't want to kill one. When I made the pact with Locoicia, I hadn't thought of her killing the angel. My throat tightened. What did she want it for? Or did she just pick something I couldn't deliver?

I felt Eric's gaze on the side of my face and turned. "What's going to kill you if you survive this?" The moonlight slipped across his cheeks and illuminated his amber eyes like small suns. He finally asked, "The blood bargain? That's what it is, isn't it? Damn, Ivy. Why didn't you tell me?"

I raised an eyebrow at him. I couldn't tell him if I wanted to. "That's kind of a stupid question, Eric. It doesn't matter now, anyway. She fulfilled her part. I'm the one who'll default." His hand clamped over my mouth as someone stood, walking the perimeter of the camp.

A smile flicked across his lips. He asked, "How much do you trust me?"

I snorted, "Are you kidding?" Trust and Eric were like puppies and vultures—they didn't go together.

He looked down at me, "There's no time for your witticisms, Taylor. Do you trust me or not?" The pit of my stomach twisted and I nodded. Once. Fear tightened my muscles. Eric smiled, shaking his head, sensing it. He reached into his pocket, and pulled out his brimstone blade. Lifting it to his hand, he sliced open the skin on his thumb. Crimson welled up in thick red droplets. He thrust his hand toward me. My eyes saw nothing but his blood. My jaw locked, not understanding, and I looked up at him. He didn't want me to drink that. He wasn't serious … was he?

"Quickly," Eric said, "drink it. My blood's not as potent as before. The demon blood is working its way out of me, because of the curse. But, it should be enough to help you relax so you don't feed my... ah, affliction." Comprehension slammed into me. If I drank his blood, I wouldn't feed his fear. He could help control my emotions.

"Is that what's happening? Back in the cage you seemed to have no trouble controlling the bloodlust. It seemed stronger. I thought you were controlling me and making it worse."

He shook his head, quickly adding, "No, it's the curse. It's twisting things and making them different. Ivy, this is the only way I know to mute your terror, and we have to—or God knows what'll happen. Drink it!" he hissed. There was a command in his voice, but I could fight it.

Eric pressed his bloodied thumb to my lips. Fear shot through me. Here I was making the same stupid choice I had to make earlier, but this was different. Eric's future and mine were intertwined and I knew it. And so did he. Looking up into his eyes, I pressed my tongue to his wound and swallowed three times before the fear snaked out of me. The lightheaded feeling returned, and I smiled. Eric cursed as he tore his hand away. I giggled. "The initial buzz will wear off fast, and then it'll be like before. Or it should be. But right now, you'll have to do what I say. Let me speak when we are over there. Got it?" I nodded.

Without another word, he placed his hands around my waist, tugged me closer, and effonated us. I could feel him using my power and taking the pain of the effonation for both of us. I had no idea that was even possible. What the hell was he?

When we landed, Eric and I were directly on top of the circular path etched into the ground surrounding the camp. It was beyond bold. Slightly insane was more like it. But it had the effect he wanted. It made the guard materialize. When the angel turned around, Eric thrust me in front of him and pressed the black blade to my throat. I gasped, feeling it biting into my neck, but I didn't care. His blood swam through my mind making it difficult to think.

The angel stared at us. Under the dark clothing that appeared to be made out of the same ethereal linen as the tents, a pink tee shirt popped out. Blonde curls were pinned to her head under her hat. Jenna Marie still looked like the picture perfect personification of cuteness. Her eyes narrowed in on my face. Recognition hit both of us at about the same time.

"Ivy," she said. The shock washed away as she continued speaking, "Last time I saw you, you took off. And now you're standing here, with... him?" Jenna Marie didn't seem fazed. Her eyes moved over the pair of us, like she knew our little plan. How was she a Seraphim? After all the time I'd known her, Jenna Marie seemed like a valley girl, not a vengeful sword-swinging angel.

But Eric had other ideas, "I brought her for you. I heard you were looking for her." My eyes darted to the side as I tried to turn and see Eric's face, but the knife pressed into my throat. My brow pinched. I hadn't known she was looking for me. Why did Eric? But my mind couldn't think more than a step or two ahead. I couldn't put the pieces together. His blood was fogging my brain, making lust burn and twist inside of my stomach. His fingers touching the skin on the side of my neck were making me nuts. A strong sense of calmness crashed into me. That must have been Eric manipulating my emotions.

Jeanna Marie ignored me, and stared at Eric. Snow flurries drifted down, falling on her shoulders. Her perkiness turned to anger, "Do you think I'm stupid? I know why you're here."

"I don't think you do," Eric replied. Jenna Marie scoffed, about to say something else as Eric pressed the blade into my throat. Fear welled up in my stomach, but I felt Eric replace it with another emotion. I melted, not caring about the razor sharp blade pressing into my neck. Then, Eric's weapon nicked my skin. Something warm ran down the side of my neck. My hands lifted, trembling, and I touched my throat where I felt the warm tickle. My fingertips came away covered in blood. My eyes went wide. Fear raced inside of me, but Eric squashed it promptly. Completely. It was enough that

Jenna Marie saw the look of horror on my face, but not enough fear to awaken Eric's insatiable lust for pain.

He tilted his head, and said to Jenna Marie, "It's harder to get your information when she's dead."

Jenna Marie's eyes were wide. She watched the expression on my face as my hand withdrew covered in blood. Up until that point, she acted as if it were a game. Like Eric wouldn't really harm me. But now she thought otherwise. A gust of wind tore between us, tangling my hair and smearing it in the blood dripping down my neck. The wound wouldn't heal as long as Eric held the blade there. I felt the warm burn of the torn flesh, but it wasn't screaming pain, as it should have been. My heart raced, wondering what Eric was doing. He didn't anticipate the Seraphim, but he seemed to know Jenna Marie would be here. Either that or it was luck, of which I had none. The mind fog started to lift, and as if Eric could sense it, a wave of thick emotions splashed over me again—everything from anger to lust. Eric did it. The rush of emotions made me stop thinking, so I could suppress the feelings he pushed into me. I barely heard what they said.

Jenna Marie snapped, "What do you want for her? I'm assuming you want something." Her arms folded over her dark coat.

Eric breathed behind me, making me shudder. "Shannon McClure. A trade. One girl, for another..."

Jenna Marie's narrowed eyes slipped over me. Her jaw locked, as her gaze drifted between my face and Eric's. She didn't know if she was being played. That was exactly how I felt. When Jenna Marie spoke, her voice was low, "They'll kill her, you know. You won't get your little pet back." Little pet? What did she think I was to him? Could she tell I was doped up on demon blood?

"Why would I care?" Eric asked. The tension in his arms didn't ease. The black blade held the wound on my neck open. Blood was running down my throat and pooling between my breasts. Eric never took his eyes off the angel. He could sense that she wasn't going to take the bait. Me.

"Last chance," he urged, determination in his voice.

Jenna Marie glanced over her shoulder, back toward the camp. Angels were weird. They seemed to be like Martis in some ways, but not others. I had a feeling she wanted me for a different reason than the Martis, which worried me. Finally she turned back, and answered, "Fine. It's done. Give her to me." Something swam in Jenna Marie's eyes - something that made me wary of her. She had other intentions. Intentions Eric was aware of, but I was not.

Eric laughed, amused, "No, no, no. It doesn't work that way. You deliver Shannon right now. Bring her outside the camp, and we'll switch."

Jenna Marie's lips parted, as if she were going to say no. Her perfectly pink lips turned up at the corners to laugh at him, but her jaw fell open instead. When Eric saw the laughter on her face, the expression that challenged him, he pressed the blade deeper into my throat. My eyes shut tightly as the blade slid deeper into my skin. A small cry escaped from my mouth, as it opened in horror. I felt Eric's warm hand on my neck. He didn't subdue the pain that coursed through me. It filled my body in a rush. Eric breathed in deeply, ever so slowly, adding more pressure to the knife. His hand didn't shake. There was no remorse in his voice. And I could feel every ounce of pleasure shoot through him as he did it. Warmth slid down my neck, covering it in a red river, as blood flowed down, soaking my shirt. Eric pressed a kiss to my temple, slowly, as if he was caressing a lover.

Jenna Marie's eyes were wide. She hesitated for a moment, shocked, before she said, "Enough! We trade now." She said a word I didn't know and moved her hand. Shannon appeared next to her as if she were plucked from scrubbing the floor. She was still on her hands and knees with a soapy brush in her hand. Her long cinnamon colored hair was tied at the nape of her neck.

Shannon gasped as she looked up at us. She jumped to her feet and tried to move behind Jenna Marie, but the angel clutched her wrist and stopped her. "You'll be going with him." She shoved Shannon forward and Eric grabbed her arm.

Eric withdrew the blade from my neck, and a smile twisted across his lips. When he released me, he pushed me toward Jenna Marie. She clasped my wrist tightly. A single brow on her face arched, as she said, "A pleasure, Eric." He nodded and effonated out of sight with Shannon.

The look of terror on her face made my heart sink. I slumped back into her arms, blood still flowing from the wound. I tried to speak, but Jenna Marie shushed me. I blinked once. Then again. Then the world went black.

CHAPTER FIFTEEN

My head felt like it was in a vice. As I opened my eyes, I saw a soft white light glowing above me. It wasn't contained in a bulb. It was just there, illuminating white fabric that flowed in long stretches above me.

I heard her voice before I saw her face, "How long have you had to endure him?" I turned and looked at her face. Jenna Marie didn't mask her emotions, but I suspected she had a veil like Eric that masked other things. Pity was strewn across her face, plainly visible for anyone to see.

I swallowed, and reached for my throat. When I pressed my fingers to the flesh, I was surprised that it was smooth. My eyes darted to her face. She must have healed me. The wound was too deep to heal on its own. My brows pinched. I didn't know what to think of Eric. If he could use the stone, I'd be worried. Why the hell did he slash my throat? I hadn't a clue. Our original plan didn't look anything like what happened. And right now, if Eric wasn't depositing Shannon with Collin and coming back for me, I didn't know what I'd do. I was inside the angel camp. There was no way out. I couldn't effonate. Eric said their wards were powerful. They not only shielded their camp from the insane grackles and Dreanoks, but kept out Valefar and Demons as well. It was a safe house. Except, I wasn't safe.

Sitting up slowly, I rubbed my throat and whispered, answering her question, "Long enough."

"He forced you, didn't he? I could smell his blood in you, exactly like the girl he took." She studied me, the way Martis do, but her gaze was gentler and less damning. She wore a pale pink shirt and a pink plaid skirt. Little cute shoes adorned her feet. She changed her clothes since we saw her outside. Her long golden hair was perfect, without a hair out of place. I didn't know if she already knew what he did to Shannon, or if she was trying to get more information. Either way, I wasn't helping her.

Staring at her blankly, I asked, "What do you want with me?"

She sat down in a chair across from me. I was sitting on a pristine white table. There were four other tables—all exactly the same—forming a line across the tent. The other three tables were empty. No one else was there. The angel folded her tiny fingers in her lap, and looked sad, "You don't trust me..."

"I don't trust anyone."

"Mmm," she nodded, not believing me. "Did you volunteer to be his blood slave? Or did he force it on you? I've been tracking Eric for a while. Watching how the curse twists him. He's very deceptive. You don't have to feel badly if he tricked you..." she paused, and muttered, "He's fooled many of us."

I looked away, "I don't want to talk about it." I was hoping that it came across as shame, but I have no idea what Jenna Marie saw. Before last year, I thought she had Twinkies for brains. Turns out that she was quite an actress. An angel. Al didn't even know that. She thought Jenna Marie was her teacher—a Seeyer Martis—one of the last of her kind. This angel fooled the wise and the foolish.

"As you wish," she replied. "I don't want to cause you more pain." Jenna Marie was quiet, studying me openly. What she really meant was that she didn't want to cause me more pain than necessary. Warrior angels—angels that fought demons—killed humans, and whatever I was. She'd told Eric that they would kill me. I wondered if she meant the other angels or the Martis. And did they know I was here? Was Eric coming back? Collin couldn't find this place on his own. The lump in my throat swelled, but terror didn't grip me. My feelings were a dying ember at the back of my mind, nearly non-existent.

Jenna Marie's gaze moved over my face before she leaned forward in her chair. Her golden hair fell over her shoulders, as she wrung her hands. "I have a question for you. I've been looking for you, because I needed to ask it." Her eyes met mine. Based on the look on her face, this was a plea, not a question. "Will you take me to Lorren?"

She insisted that I take her to Lorren once before. I didn't tell her where he was or what happened to him. Only that he was alive. Suddenly, I realized something. Jenna Marie was there both times Satan's Stone was used. She said she was watching Eric. And she remembered Lorren, because she was there. My lips parted slightly as I gazed at her. She had information I needed. She could help me, if she didn't kill me first.

I snapped my jaw shut and asked, "Why do they want to kill me?"

Jenna Marie flinched, "Who? The Martis? They condemned you to death at the Tribunal. You were there for part of it, as I recall."

"And the angels?" I asked, making sure the angels had no vendetta against me as well. "Are they trying to destroy me as well?"

A soft smile spread across her lips, as she shook her head. "No, the angels have no issue with you. If you destroy Kreturus, as the prophecy says, then you're an ally. Some of them are just a little worried that you won't. But none of them will kill you. Not yet, anyway."

Confusion twisted my face. "The Martis are your creation. Why do they want me dead, if you want me for an ally? Why didn't you stop them?"

She laughed lightly, as if this were a merry moment. "You think we didn't? Our creation was damaged during the first Angel Demon War. The Martis were allowed to survive out of compassion. As long as they were trying, we left them alone. I suppose you already know that having angels around checking up on them was a flag?" I nodded. I'd heard that. If angels were snooping around, then things were very bad. I just had no idea at the time. "You continue to escape by the skin of your teeth. You think that's luck? Seriously, Ivy, I thought you were smarter than that." Her last words were scolding, as if I disappointed her.

I was numb again, so my snarky response died in my mouth. She didn't anger me with her carefree words. It made me wonder if they had been protecting me. I glared at her, "I thought angels didn't interfere. Saving me goes against that, doesn't it?"

She shrugged. "I've been watching the Martis fall for some time. I'd hoped you would revive them, but they were so bent on your being evil that they couldn't see the good you had to offer. I tried to give them time. Time to adjust on their own. Time to redeem themselves and do the good they were created to do. But their hearts hardened and they were fixated only on killing Valefar. Their purpose perverted to darkness masked in light. The war will end and with it—the Martis."

My jaw dropped opened, "What are you saying? The Martis that survive the war will be exterminated by angels as their reward?" That was disgusting. How could she even suggest it?

She laughed, a perky bubbly laugh, "You make it sound so simple. As if this decision costs us nothing. As if it didn't bring pain to all of us. Satan's Stone was used once, and then twice. The seed of destruction was planted, and the Martis grew into a twisted version of what they were meant to be." She saw the disgust on my face and asked, "Name one good Martis. I'll save every single one you can name, and I know you've met many. Tell me the names of the ones who guarded you. Tell me the names of the ones who sought mercy before judgment. Tell me, Ivy, and I'll set them aside from the angels' wrath."

My mouth flew open, but the only names I had were the names of the dead. Al. Eric. There was no one else. No one I'd met. Not here. Not in Rome. Not anywhere. My voice was soft, questioning, "There were two... And if I met two, there have to be more." Surely there were more Martis who were good. Good the way Al was. Good the way Eric had been, before I changed him.

"You have the heart of an angel, pleading to save a race of beings that don't deserve it." The corners of her mouth didn't lift. There was no upbeat pitch to her voice. She shook her head, making her blonde hair shift at her shoulders, "I'm sorry, but the decision has been made, and I alone cannot change it. If the Martis redeem themselves, they will survive. But if they do not, their days are numbered."

Silence filled the room. I stared into space, no longer afraid she would kill me. When I glanced up at her, I asked, "Are there more of you in this camp?"

She nodded. "Two more. We usually travel in pairs. As I told you before, I thought that my pairing—Lorren - was destroyed ages ago." She stared into space, remembering something that I didn't want to know. Pain seeped across her face, painting years of grief and loss. But I felt nothing for her. No compassion. No empathy. Normally I wouldn't have been able to watch her, but this time I could. When she looked up, she asked again, "Will you take me to him?"

The question flew out of my mouth before I had time to decide where it came from. "Will you hurt him? Lorren has had a horrifying life. I can't let..." I stuttered, "I can't bring you there if it'll cause him more pain."

Tears were in Jenna Marie's eyes. A hand covered her mouth as she swallowed a happy sob. Then she moved out of her chair, and walked to the table where I sat with my feet hanging over the side. They had dressed me in new clothes—pink clothes. She fell at my feet, wrapping her hands around mine, "I love him, Ivy. I thought he died. All this time, I thought that he was destroyed. Do you know how wonderful it is to find out that your true love survived?" Actually, I did. She pressed her lips together, eagerly asking, "Where is he?"

"Sit," I said. She did as I said, and slid onto the table next to me. I glanced at the door to the tent. "I'll take you to him. But I want to tell you what happened before you see him. You need to know … " Why was I being protective of Lorren? I didn't know. I had treated him harshly all this time, but I wasn't sure why anymore. All I knew was that if I was trapped down there, I would want someone to bring me Collin if he asked. But, Lorren thought he was deformed. I didn't want her crying over his wings, so I told her, "The stone took its price. It ripped his wings off his back, and trapped him in the Lorren. He's stuck inside the tomb he created in the Underworld."

Her hands covered her mouth, shaking. Her pink nails, pink clothes, and bubbly personality stood in stark contrast to Lorren, and his dark mood and black clothing. Everything about them was opposite. It was as if they were paired for that reason. I couldn't imagine a stranger couple.

Jenna Marie grasped my hand, excitement on her face. As she opened her mouth to speak a shriek echoed through the camp. Jenna Marie jumped off the table, panic in her eyes. "Oh my God. The wards have been broken," her voice was barely a whisper. "Leave. Ivy, leave now!"

I raced after her, following her to the edge of the tent. I started the effonation, and felt heat searing through me. I held it until I saw between the flaps of the fabric. Eight large Dreanoks walked through the camp, headed directly toward us. The one in the front tore open the tent like it was a tissue. The fabric ripped apart, as screams filled the night. The other Dreanoks used their razor sharp beaks to impale Martis. Jenna Marie's voice pounded against my ears, her screams piercing the night as the Dreanok slashed at her just as she opened the flap. Its lethal golden claws flashed as the beast's leg swatted her out of the way.

The effonation continued building within me as I ran for Jenna Marie, trying to dart around the creature. It shrieked as its demonic arms reached for me. I narrowly missed its grasp. I could feel the flames building in my belly, and spreading into my limbs. It was only a second, but I had to save her. I threw myself, hurling my body through the air. I would have saved her. I would have effonated away with the both of us. Instead, she lay on the frozen earth with her golden hair covering her face, and an expanding puddle of red soaking the ground beneath her. Before I could reach her, the Dreanok, plucked me from the air. He grabbed me right before the effonation took effect. The beast's touch was like ice, cooling the burn of the effonation. I should have effonated. I should have been free of the creature, but I felt his grip tighten on me. My power didn't work. I was trapped.

I screamed, kicking and biting the beast, but he acted like I wasn't there. Seven creatures cried out and flew off into the night.

And they took me with them.

CHAPTER SIXTEEN

The wind ripped through my hair as we soared across the night sky. Anger coursed inside of me. They were taking me to Kreturus. There was no other explanation. These things were from the Underworld, which meant the Demon King controlled them. I swallowed hard, and pressed my eyes closed. I tried to summon my magic but every time I tried, it felt like my power was sucked away. Something was draining me. I could feel my power slide away as soon as I summoned it. It had to be the beasts.

The Dreanoks were giant leeches sucking away my power. The added power made them grow larger, and fly faster. It took two attempts to effonate out of the beasts grip before I realized what happened. After that I knew that I couldn't use my power while it held me. But the beast didn't respond when I tried to make it drop me. I punched it, bit it, and ripped my nails into its fleshy arms, but it acted as if it was immune to pain—numb to everything. Like me.

I slumped in its arms as mountains jutted into the sky. Each cascade of rocks grew taller than the last with spires of stone that reached into the heavens. The beast wove between the formations, passing them all, and flew higher and higher. The air had grown frigid and thin. I shivered and looked below. The only thing I could see were my dangling feet suspended in air. There was no sign of land. As far as I could tell, there was nothing but the jagged stone spires surrounding us.

The Dreanok finally slowed, rearing back to slow his approach as we neared one of the stone spires. His wings flapped backward once, then twice before dropping me on a plateau the size of a small bedroom. The rock on top of this spire was smooth, and flat as if it were worn away by the elements. I fell forward onto my hands and knees, staining the pink jeans I was wearing. The rock stung beneath my hands as my palms scraped open when I tried to stop the momentum. Sucking in air, I glanced up to see the beast fly off, backing away as if they were afraid.

His voice cut across the space, "Pink hardly seems appropriate for the Demon Queen. Especially today." My neck twisted toward the voice. A thick shadow masked the edge of the cliff across from me. I focused on my power, ready to effonate, but his words stopped me, "This place is like my Dreanoks, it devoids one of power."

I searched within me to see if that was true. Pressing my eyes closed, I tried to call my power, just a little to test his statement. But nothing happened. Swallowing hard, I looked across the seemingly empty space, asking, "Then how are you here?" I looked for the ancient demon, but could not see him. The shadows were so thick that I thought the shadows themselves were his form, but I wasn't sure.

"Show yourself." If Kreturus touched this place, he'd be trapped too. I hoped. If he was a hovering shadow, I was screwed. As I glanced around, a gust of wind rumpled my hair. The spire I was standing on was high above the cloud line, below an inky sky with stars surrounding me.

A boy stepped toward me—a beautiful dark haired, blue eyed boy. His complexion was flawless. He body was toned, and taller than me. He was wearing his hair combed to the side, but it protested and fell in his eyes. A memory brushed my mind, and I realized that he reminded me of Collin. Sneaky demon. Beautiful boy.

His dark blue eyes swept over me as his polished black shoes touched the earth, stepping closer. My spine was straight as he approached. I'd risen and dusted myself off as best as I could. The boy stopped in front of me. His voice was like honey, deep and rich, caressing me as he spoke, "Does this form suit your tastes?" he asked. My stomach fluttered, and I had no idea why. I shouldn't have been able to feel anything, but I felt that. I felt the attraction to him. My throat tightened as he continued to speak, "The last vessel I had chosen was suddenly ripped away." He smiled at me, as if impressed. As he spoke he circled me, his eyes touching every inch of my body, making me flush. Why was I flushing? What the hell happened to my emotional deadness? Kreturus seemed to bring it back to life. "You're a clever girl, using her to help you. A woman scorned will do anything for vengeance." He stopped walking and stood directly in front of me.

"You surrendered all your power to stand here and chat?" I doubted it, but I had to know. Flickers of emotions shot through me, but it was as if they were disconnected—like random fireworks streaking into the sky that weren't part of the show. My arms had folded across my chest.

His eyes dipped to my breasts, lingering for too long. I dropped my arms, and his gaze returned to my face. I wasn't sure what he was doing. I had expected him to kill me, but not this.

"Of course not," he answered. "This place affects you, not me. I cast a powerful spell here after I found out what you were capable of." He smiled, revealing perfectly white teeth. My stomach slid into my feet. His eyes slid over my face, "I underestimated you. A mistake I won't make again. Especially not now." He folded his arms and tilted his head. The black tux he wore fit him very well. It was impossible not to notice. Kreturus smirked. He noticed my eyes moving across his body. "Good. This form does please you. Now to make you, ah..." he paused searching for the right word, "more presentable."

I was going to protest, but as I opened my mouth Kreturus' magic had already started. A stream of darkness—thin as night—shimmered out of the air, and scrolled off a bolt as if it were fabric. I shrank back from it, but it followed me to the edge. Kreturus' eyes were on me as the fabric began to wrap around my body, Jenna Marie's pink clothing disappearing. One moment it was there, the next it melted into nothing and left me exposed. Horrified, my hands moved to cover my body, but the bolt passed over my chest before the last of the pink faded away. I glared at Kreturus. This seemed to amuse him. The fabric continued to dance around me circling again and again, taking the shape of an elaborate gown. The silky fabric had the otherworldly feeling of the tents the Martis were using. It was light as air, though it draped mound after mound of fabric across me. As the bolt moved downward, I felt the panels wrapped around my chest and waist constrict. The gown conformed to my body, hugging closely to every curve. When the dress was complete, the bolt faded from sight.

I stood perfectly still, feeling the breeze upon my neck as my heart sank into my throat. Kreturus walked to me with his hands clasped behind his back. He circled once, admiring the dress. "It suits you. Darkness with flecks of light." He pointed to the fabric. It was darkness, the deepest, richest black I'd ever seen. It was as if the gown were made of shadows and lace. His finger rested on the neckline of the bodice that dipped down low. He touched a dark sparkling stone, and pressed it against my skin. His eyes locked with mine, waiting to see my reaction. But I did not move. I just stared at him. "Jewels cover your gown. Black diamonds. Black pearls. Black opals. This is a gown fit for a queen." He removed his finger and turned from me. His arms folded across his chest, revealing his narrow waist. "I have forgiven so much and yet you still act distant. Cold."

My eyes were resting on the view of the mountains and the night sky behind him. His words made me shift my gaze. "I don't want this. I don't want your presents," I yanked the gown, shaking the skirt. "I don't want you. The last time I saw you, I tried to kill you. What the hell makes you think that I'd be your queen? What twisted thing inside your mind thinks that I'd submit?" Anger reared inside of me. I tried to control it, but he made me feel out of whack. Why was I feeling anything?

As if he could read the question on my face, he answered, "Demon blood is powerful, Ivy. I don't have to feed you mine for it to have an effect." His arms unfolded as he turned from me, looking out into the night. The only reason he turned his back was because he didn't think I was a threat. And with my powers voided by standing on this stone, I wasn't.

I was trapped. There was no way out. My heart was racing in my chest, making it hard to stand still. The main question, screaming in my head, blurted out of my mouth, "Why haven't you killed me? You could just take my power, and not deal with me. It seems much simpler. And I won't have to look at you every day, and see what I've become." My chest filled with remorse—his remorse. A feeling he placed inside of me. I tried to push it away, but couldn't.

Kreturus was standing in front of me. His movement was so fast that I never saw him take a step. One blink he was out of arms reach and the next, he was nose to nose with me. I sucked in a shocked gasp, unable to step away. The edge of the cliff was too close. His beauty was breathtaking. A single slender finger tilted my face up to his, forcing our eyes to meet. I didn't flinch away. My emotions were stabilizing. He was doing it. He was making me complacent.

"I'd hoped you'd like looking at me every day. I chose a form that suits you, so similar to the one you yearn for. Possibly better, is it not?" He arched an eyebrow at me. I didn't answer. "A living vessel is preferred, though not required. You're correct. I could destroy you, but I prefer to have you for a companion, to rule by my side and share our power."

Lies, sweet lies dripped from his lips. My mind knew he wasn't telling me the real reason, but I couldn't look away from his face. I couldn't think. The depths of his eyes went on and on. I blinked once, trying to remember this was a boy who Kreturus turned into a puppet.

"If you refuse me again, though," his eyes instantly burned red, like coals stoked in a fire, "I will drain your power from you. You'll become a Valefar—one of the demon kissed. A mindless slave that does my bidding for all eternity. The fate I am offering you is much better."

"And then what?" I asked, taking a step back closer the edge. Heights made me dizzy. The drop off the side went straight down. "I accept, and you use my power—for what? You already destroyed the earth. You wouldn't be content with that though, would you? You're planning something. Something more." I glared at him, as my heel slid backwards. There was less than an inch between me and a sharp plummet into oblivion. I swallowed hard, trying to tear my gaze away from his face. My mind felt hazy. My fingers wanted to see how silky smooth his hair would feel in my hands. Warring within myself, I pushed those feelings back. Silencing them. I stared at him.

He arched a dark eyebrow. His feet were planted shoulders width apart, his arms folded, "I'm trying very hard to make this painless, Ivy, but you keep pushing away my attempts at kindness."

"Forcing yourself on someone who doesn't want you is not a kindness, Kreturus." He smiled when I said his name. Rage flowed through me in response. It spread within every inch of my body. The wind caught my hair, tugging it gently. I saw the tips turn to violet flames. Akeyleah started. I could feel power building in muscles, but it was snaked away by the ground. I stared at the demon, feeling my eyes turn violet. Intense heat filled me, but I had no idea where the power went.

He smiled at me, taking a step forward. "Such beauty. And anger. You are truly perfect. And so selflessly feeding me your power." His hand brushed against my cheek. Butterflies exploded in my stomach. My knees felt weak. Kreturus was doing it. And the sensations were becoming stronger.

I couldn't stand there another minute. I couldn't wait for him to take me away, and use me, or turn me Valefar. I'd rather die. A smile snaked my lips. My muscles tensed and I threw myself backwards before he had a chance to grab me. I fell off the cliff and disappeared into the night.

CHAPTER SEVENTEEN

The wind rushed past howling as I plummeted toward the ground. Pressing my eyes closed, I tried to focus and effonate, but my powers seemed fried. When I called them it was like trying to snap on a lighter that was out of fluid. There was only sparks. No surge of strength. Nothing.

Fear raced through me as I tried to focus, calling the power to me with increased desperation. But nothing came. My stomach was in my throat as I fell, head-first into the night. Rocks jutted out of the side of the mountain. They were too far away to try and grab hold. Wildly, I looked around, reaching for something to stop the plummet. But there was nothing. I'd die. I'd die and my power would crash into Collin. Kreturus wouldn't get a drop. The wind tore at my hair, pulling it behind me like a streamer on a kite. It left a glowing purple path in its wake as I fell. The moment the ground came into view I thought I'd puke. The gown billowed around me, feeling like it was going to be torn off, but it clung.

Closer. Nearer. Faster. The earth grew larger and larger. A scream erupted from my throat. My eyes pressed closed as I covered my face with my hands, anticipating the instantaneous impact that was less than a second away. My nails dug into my skin without meaning to. Everything was always without meaning to. I regretted that my life had so little intention. It was literally swayed by the breeze. And now it was too late to change anything. Peeling my eyes open, I screamed as my face was less than ten feet from the rocky earth. The second my nose touched the rocky terrain, gravity stopped thrusting me downward. My dress billowed around me as I jerked to an abrupt stop, floating like I was in a vacuum. Shocked, I twisted my neck trying to see what happened.

Kreturus stood next to me, his voice bringing tears of frustration to my eyes, "Did you think I would let you fall? After all I've done to secure you, did you really think I would let you smash yourself upon the rocks?" Irritated, he grabbed me by my neck and raised my face to his. Cold blue eyes narrowed behind dark lashes. Breathing hard, he demanded, "Stop this childish attempt at defiance. Chose. Now. Valefar or Queen?"

With a sudden rush, time unfroze and the momentum that my body had lost returned. The layers of my skirt flittered down, lying properly in place. His fingers loosened around my neck as he returned my feet to the ground. My mind was screaming, telling me to do anything I had to do to escape. I couldn't accept his offer—either of them. But, for once in my life I was going to choose. I'd choose. And if I chose wrong, I'd deal with it. But there was no way I was going to sit by and just allow things to happen to me. It was time. Life didn't usually give me a choice between something that was likeable and something that sucked. That ability to choose and accept the consequences was the difference between a cowardice and courage. Determination shot up my spine, as wave after wave of thoughts flew through my mind. I'd decided. And I'd live the consequences for the rest of my life.

Breathing hard, I stared at the ground, at his shiny black shoes and whispered, "I surrender..." Raising my eyes to his, I added, "Conditionally." It was insane adding that part, but I had to try.

Kreturus' eyebrow pulled up as he placed his hands in his pockets. Cocking his head, he asked, "And may I inquire as to what this condition is?" There was laughter in his voice—amusement. It was as if the peasant were commanding the king.

My fingers were twisting in the folds of the fabric on my dress. A nervous tick. When his eyes drifted to the motion, I realized what I was doing and stopped. Swallowing hard, I placed my arms at my sides. They hung there rigid as tension crawled across my shoulders, and down my spine. Looking him in the eye, I said, "I surrender. Fully. Eternally. I'll be your queen. You can use my power. I won't protest," he didn't blink once while I spoke. "But... you cannot destroy those of my choosing." I worded it vaguely on purpose. I didn't want to get caught on a technicality by calling Collin, Eric, Lorren and Jenna Marie people.

The corners of his mouth curved. "Then you would have me destroy no one, which will interfere with my plans. Plans I will reveal to you shortly. And Ivy, I will keep my word. It will be our pact. If I make a promise, I will abide by it, but I cannot offer more than one life. I will spare one being of your choosing. No more. No less." His dark eyes studied my face. His arms were folded, with a single hand touching his chin. It was as if he was excited and trying to contain it.

I'm sure my thoughts were scribbled across my face at that moment. I'd wanted to save anyone I deemed worthy—which would be everyone. I didn't even seek vengeance on Shannon, or any of the Martis who tried to kill me. I couldn't.

Swallowing hard, I stared into his gaze without blinking as I thought. Only one. I could only save one person. Instantly, I thought of Collin. But... I didn't want harm to come to Eric either. Or Jenna Marie. Her kindness made me question everything I knew. She had the traits that I admired in Al. Pressing my eyes closed, I turned away. My fingers pressed into my temples. One person. I could only save one person. That was unacceptable, and yet, it was the best I could do. Turning back to him, I straightened. My bare shoulders squared off, and my gown swished around my ankles as I took two steps toward him.

It was my fate. My choice.

I looked into Kreturus' face. He stood confident, relaxed—as if this wasn't a pivotal moment at all. His lazy gaze slid over my face, dipping to my waist and back up to my eyes. I thrust out my hand, and said, "I accept."

Kreturus grabbed my hand, and yanked me toward him. His eyes glowed with greed. Satisfaction dripped from every perfectly formed muscle on his body as his hand slid around my waist. "Done." The weight of his words was palpable. My body steeled at his touch, forcing back any emotion he was trying to instill within me. His hand brushed the curls from my shoulder. His gaze drifted to my neck. Heart racing, I stood perfectly still, not knowing what he was doing.

When he spoke his voice was deeper, full of desire, "Darkness calls to darkness. I feel it inside of you, yearning to be of use. And it will be. Soon." He brushed a kiss against my neck. The vein in my neck throbbed as his lips pressed the soft skin above it. I wanted to be steel in that moment. Feel nothing. I wanted the control, but it was beyond my control. It was as he said. Something about him called to me. It scared me and thrilled me at the same time. As his lips brushed my neck, a gush of air rushed out of my body. My knees buckled and were powerless to hold me. My mind swam, as his soft lips touched my throat, making my heart pound harder. I hated him. I hated what he was and that he trapped me.

Kreturus' eyes returned to my face. A smile twisted on his lips, utterly confident. Utterly certain. "A ritual is required to make you Queen. It will join us together, for eternity. We need a chalice. Come," he took my hand. Heat surged through us, but the effonation didn't hurt. Kreturus pulled me tightly against his chest, and released me shortly after. We were in a dark home. Torn drapes hung haphazardly in the windows, as if they would fall at any second. The sky bled deep red, with gray snow clouds stretched across the heavens. Plumes of gray smoke filled the air. The house smelled of ash and charred wood.

Glancing around I asked, "Why didn't it hurt? Where did the pain price go?" Where are we? His broad shoulders were already turned away from me, but he stopped, turning back to answer.

"We are near the place of your birth." Startled, I looked up at him, wondering if the question was on my face or if he plucked it out of my mind. Terror coursed through me, but I pressed it back. I was enabling the demon to destroy everything. That is what I was doing. That was the only thing I could think... because if he heard the things in my heart—he'd know. He may know what I planned already. He continued, "Others pay the pain price for us. We feel only pleasure." He watched me, taking in my sickened reaction.

My jaw dropped while he spoke. My hands lifted, as if I could fix it. I wanted to fix it. "I don't want anyone paying my price."

He smirked, "That's very noble of you, but your request is denied. And soon you will see why. When creatures like us—beings with our vast power—try to use it, the price is too great for one person to bear alone. I bet Locoicia taught you to endure more pain than any demon thought possible," his smirk faded as he spoke of her with his eyes narrowing into slits. "And perhaps you did, but when we fight you will not have time to rest. There will be no reprieve. Others must shoulder our pain. It is their burden, as it is our right." He walked into the darkened house, turning his back to me. Dreanoks and grackles shot into the sky like someone had thrown a stone.

I stared through the window. Reaching for my power, I tried to effonate again, but only felt the power dulled. It was drained away like it was before. It felt like water dousing a spark. I turned my shoulders toward him, hearing Kreturus tutting, "Still trying to leave? Don't bother. We are connected. You cannot use your power without my permission." Rage flamed inside of me, but I tried to remain docile. The thought of asking his permission for anything was deplorable.

Turning toward me, Kreturus held a black glass in his hand. It was the size of a wine glass with an ornately carved stem. It was a woman, standing half naked, draped in cloth triumphantly holding up the cup above her head. Long curly tendrils of soft hair fell down her back. Lifeless black eyes stared at me, making my breath catch in my throat.

Kreturus held out the goblet for me to take, "You recognize her?" I nodded slowly, stunned. Trying to swallow. Trying to figure out what this was. "Hmm, there is a great likeness, but you are more beautiful than the prophet predicted. Ivy, this is the thirteenth prophecy. It shows what will happen—what your kind fears most. Take it. Examine it. See that you are the means by which we win, and take pride in who you are. Your beauty. Your power. The darkness that lies within you. There is a reason you were the Prophecy One." His voice deepened as he spoke.

My fingers wrapped around the goblet in fascinated horror. I rolled the stem to examine the upper portion of the chalice, which was even more ornate. It depicted scenes of demons brandishing weapons, and slaying angels. The skies were filled with fighting, as was the earth. The demons crawled upward from the stem in a vast army that was far greater than the scattered angels spread in the heavens. The demon's deformed bodies were twisted and hunched. Their hands were tearing off the wings of prone angels that had fallen in battle.

I stood there holding the glass, horrified. My jaw wouldn't move. It just hung there. Open. I couldn't think.

Kreturus reached for the cup and spoke as he turned from me. His lean form walked toward the remains of a wooden liquor cabinet. He stood with his back to me like he was mixing a bar drink. "You shouldn't mourn them. All this time you've seen that good and evil are merely labels that people assign to make themselves feel better. The Martis are good. The Valefar are evil." His voice was mocking. He turned, glancing over his shoulder, "And yet, you saw that was untrue. You surround yourself with demonic beings and call them friends, do you not? The Martis shunned you, and called for your death. They assassinated their own. Anyone who spoke against them. That is not goodness and light." He walked back toward me. The chalice was full. Its dark contents were at the rim.

I remained silent standing in front of the window. The red glow of the sky lit the room with faint light, lining my figure in the window frame. I clutched my hands together in front of me. Demons lied. But Kreturus wasn't lying now. I agreed with his words, which frightened me. Stopping in front of me, he said, "We are more alike than you would care to admit." His gaze bore into mine, but I didn't flinch or look away. "Why would you favor them over us, when mere titles no longer convey meaning?"

That was a good question, a question that I hadn't yet pondered and no longer had time to consider. But his challenge made something flare to life inside of me. And I knew why. "You are right. There is more than good and evil. Most of life, and most people, fall into the gray—that spot between the two. A good man might do something horrid. A bad woman might do a good deed. It means that no one is intrinsically evil. Or absolutely good. It means they have a choice. By siding with you, I remove the choice. I'm saying decimation is preferred, above free will."

"There would be no need for decimation if they would submit," his eyes shone as he forcefully spoke, sounding more like a king than a demon. "A ruler cannot allow his people to ignore him. He commands them and they must listen." His dark brows were pulled together, irritated. "Your examples are naive. They ignore the obvious."

I smirked, "Yeah? And what is that?"

He pressed closer to me, careful not to spill the contents of the chalice. His hand brushed against my bodice as he held the glass flush with his chest. He was so close that I could feel the warmth of his breath as he spoke. "Beings have an innate desire to be ruled. They want to submit. Very few fight against it. And that is what a leader does, meets the needs of the masses." My lips twisted into an incredulous smile, but he snapped, cutting me off, "Wipe that look off your face. Just as the world will submit to you, you will submit to me. Respect is mandatory."

The smile on my face faded as I considered him. He didn't sound insane. Why did I think demons were evil? Was it possible I was wrong?

As soon as the thought surfaced, Kreturus placed his hand on my bare shoulder, jerking the thought away. He glanced at the glass in his hand, and back up at my face. "A blood bargain, willingly entered cannot be broken. This right will make you Queen. You will command the Underworld after this day. It will be your domain. I will command the heavens and the earth, after the last angel falls."

I stared at him, and at the cup—the lost prophecy that showed the angels losing. I was about to make another blood bargain. My eyes flicked up to his. There was a question pressing on my mind—one that I wasn't certain if I should make known or not—my blood bargain with Locoicia. I didn't know what would happen if I joined Kreturus and didn't kill him. I didn't think it would cause me to default since our pact was for the knowledge, not murder. But the murder was implied.

Pressing my lips together, I asked, "How will this bargain affect previous bargains?"

His eyes narrowed. "Explain." An eerie red light bathed the side of his face. It accentuated each dark chunk of hair that was tousled on his head, and the curved muscles in his strong arms.

A shiver raced down my spine, as his hand slid away. His eyes were cold, frozen, inhuman. I suddenly had a pang of sympathy for the boy he was using. I slid my hand across his cheek wishing I could free him from Kreturus. But dislodging the demon from this body wouldn't be possible. It was luck that it happened last time. No doubt, this boy's soul was lost long ago. Kreturus seemed surprised by the touch, obviously unaware of the thoughts drifting through my mind.

"I have a bargain with another. It's still in effect. I cannot speak of it. How will... ?" but I didn't get to ask.

Kreturus roared, grasping my wrist so tightly that it started to break. It sounded like a dried out twig being snapped slowly as his fist tightened. Pain shot up my arm. "Locoicia trapped you!" He released my wrist, making an obvious effort not to toss me across the room. Placing the goblet on a table he turned and smashed his fist through a window. It shattered, breaking apart into a shower of glass. The tiny fragments gleamed like ice on the dark carpet. Kreturus stopped, hunching over a chair, thinking. After a moment of silence his neck snapped up to meet my stoic gaze. "We have to kill her before we can do this." His gaze slid sideways to the goblet.

I stared at the stem—at the depiction of me. Was she really me? I didn't think so. I'd never stand so confidently, with my body half covered. Yet, it was a prophecy. She and I were the same. What happened to me? How will I become her? What makes me that way?

Kreturus' eyes followed my gaze, before flicking back to my face. "You are the perfection of femininity, despite your doubt." My throat tightened as the words poured out of his mouth. I wanted his words to roll off, and not matter. But they didn't. Instead they pierced that soft spot inside of me. The place that doubts my abilities and makes me uncertain. "That rendering does not do you justice, either. Have you no clue how others see you? Is your perception of yourself so twisted that you cannot see it? Your strength, power, courage, determination—it's in every inch of you. In every curve of your flesh. In the lines of your lips, and the curls of your hair. You refuse to accept what you are, and you're the only one who doesn't see it."

I glared at him with flushed cheeks, arms folded over my chest, "I'm not what you think I am. I'm not going to slay people and angels without remorse. If I do so, it's because you forced me to."

Tiny lines crinkled the corners of his eyes as he laughed, "You lie!" A smile spanned ear to ear as he walked in front of me, examining my folded arms, which were gripped so tightly that my fingers had turned white. "The great Ivy Taylor has deceived herself! Your lies run so deeply within your mind that you twisted the truth to suit yourself. You would not needlessly slaughter without remorse. Ha!" he mocked. My blood turned cold as he spoke. Each word cracking the wall of protection I built around my mind. Truth rang through his words, crumbling it, forcing it to break apart and shatter. "The day you slaughtered my

Valefar... I saw you cut down one after another. I heard their cries for mercy, and saw their screams fall on your deaf ears. You didn't even have the compassion to terminate their lives. You left them damaged beyond repair, to suffer until they died, crying out for help.

"You are no savior. You are already the monster that you have tried to deny. That is the darkness that lies within you. Until you accept who you are, you'll live your life with duality—and that will be your downfall. It has nothing to do with your inner darkness, and you know it."

As he spoke, I felt more and more exposed. His words crashed into me, wearing away any defense that I could possibly retort. I was the one who did that. And killing the Valefar wasn't the only time I'd swung my blade and not cared who was on the other end. Choking, I felt his hand on my shoulder. Looking up into his face, he said, "Accept who you are before it destroys you."

CHAPTER EIGHTEEN

Kreturus' words rang out in my mind, even after he'd stopped speaking. My throat tightened so that I could barely breathe. My hands ripped at the bodice of my gown. I wanted a tee shirt and jeans. I'm not what he said! I couldn't be! But no tears streaked my face. Only anger burned through me. My fists clenched tightly, waiting for the demon king to say something. But he only sat muttering spell after spell, which appeared to do nothing.

Finally, I turned away from him to look out the window. Snow covered the ground in a pristine white blanket. It covered the horrors that lay beneath—crumpled bodies of people I'd known. People I couldn't save. Across the street were fallen trees, their branches forming a web of shadows that stretched across the snow. Dreanoks circled above us in the sky. And at the very end of the street, perched on top of the last home on my block, was the dragon. His lacy wings were spread like giant pieces of jagged lace. The creature reared up on its hind legs, stretching, showing its mass to the other monsters nearby. The grackles and Dreanoks gave it a wide birth. The dragon's glittery red eyes fixated on me, watching me from the other side of the broken glass. A breeze gusted through the open pane, and I shivered. Wrapping my arms around myself, I turned away from the window.

I didn't want to know what the dragon was doing, and didn't want to ask. A couch sat across the room on the other side of the door. Turning, I moved toward it to sit down. Weariness was pulling at me. I wanted to hide my exhaustion from Kreturus. I didn't know if he could remove the poison, and I didn't want him to have any clue that Collin had part of my soul. As I padded across the room and neared the door, I felt a rush of wind at my back. Before I knew it, Kreturus thrust me into the wall.

His eyes were wild, "Oh, how you test my
patience..." His finger pressed on my temple and slid
down the side of my face. My body tensed as he pushed
into me, making it impossible to move. "I should just
drain you now, and end this. Your lifeless, powerless
body will belong to her, and I'll have your power to use
how I see fit. Why keep you?" I wasn't certain he was
speaking to me anymore.

My brows pinched together as I asked, "Why keep
me at all, Kreturus?" When I said his name, he snapped
out of his gaze. His arm pressed into my chest just
below my throat, pinning me in place. "By the way... I
wasn't leaving. I was going to the couch to sit down."
My eyes darted to the side, were the ugly blue check
couch sat on the other side of the door.

The demon didn't blink. Instead he reached for my
face, gripping it firmly in one hand. "I would kill you.
Slowly. Watching you scream and beg for mercy. Look
into my eyes, Ivy. See the truth, and make no mistake
about it. Sharing power isn't something I want to do.
It's a necessity. A requirement to gain the things I
want." He released me. My body slumped forward as he
backed away, watching me suck in air. "Your power is
still growing, still forming. Taking it now would be like
plucking a rose before it's budded. Your abilities will
grow and manifest slowly. I will try to keep you around
until then, but if you try my patience—if you push me

too far..." His finger crushed into the center of my chest, pressing hard on the bare skin above my low neckline, "I will not wait."

Kreturus' eyes darted to the side, looking out the window at the enormous form of the dragon perched on the roof top. His jaw went slack as he stepped away from me. "It's the Omen." His voice was barely audible. Anxiety twisted his features as he stood there staring at it.

A plan was forming in my mind. A backup plan. Plan X. The plan that I'd do when every other plan failed. It had something to do with irritating the King until he killed me. If I kept Collin alive, it would shift the balance of power. All my powers would go to him. But that was a last resort. And I wanted to know what he meant. Why he was standing there dumbstruck.

"The Omen?" I asked, stepping behind him. "It's just a dragon. Aren't there hundreds of them in the Underworld? I'm surprised I haven't seen more."

Whirling around, he cocked his head and asked, "You've seen a dragon before? That dragon?" He pointed behind him.

I couldn't tell what was wrong. I missed something somewhere. Why was he freaked? I nodded once. "I saw it in the Underworld." I left out the part about the dragon finding me. Something was wrong. For once I felt like my senses weren't betraying me. The sight of the massive beast had him spooked.

His eyes washed over me, and glanced back at the dragon briefly. "Of course. Of course you saw it before. That makes sense..." he ran his hands through his hair, staring at the creature. Stepping away from the panes, he said, "That's an Omen, not a dragon. And there's only one. Seeing it is an oddity. Especially now." His arms folded over his chest as one hand stroked his chin. Thinking. His eyes were blank, revealing nothing. The apprehension I saw moments ago was masked, and disappeared from sight. "Did the Omen touch you? Did it seek you out?"

Oh shit. Yes, it did both. More than once... "No," I shook my head hoping the lie reached my eyes. There was no way he'd believe me. "I saw it sitting high on a cliff in the Underworld. I thought it was yours. It snatched Collin away from me the first time I was down there. You were there... Surely you saw it?"

"Yes," he snapped. "I saw it. That damned thing almost ruined my plan, running off with the boy like that." Something was in his eyes and on his face. Kreturus didn't like the Omen. But I didn't know why. "In the end, it didn't matter. It left. Come. We can't stay here. It's not safe..." he grabbed me, wrapping his fingers around my hand, but I jerked away from him.

"I'll stop being such a pain in the ass if you tell me what's going on. You can't expect me to follow you around for eternity and be clueless. Tell me Kreturus. Why is the Omen bad?"

He didn't reach for me again. Instead he laughed hollowly, "Why is any omen bad? Since when is that a good word? The word itself has a feeling of foreboding, like something lurking, seeking to do damage. And that's what that thing is. It's the manifestation of darkness, interfering and meddling with us. The person who sees it can expect their path to darken. And if it touches you..." he released a harsh laugh, but didn't finish.

Turning my head, I gazed through the pane. "What? What happens?"

But he wouldn't answer me. Instead he grabbed the chalice and me and effonated elsewhere, leaving the Omen behind.

CHAPTER NINETEEN

When the effonation was complete, my jaw dropped. I recognized the place before glancing around. My heart felt like someone was standing on it. Turning to Kreturus, I said, "Take me somewhere else. I can't stand to look at this place." My fingers wrapped around his arms, as I pleaded, looking into his face. My pulse raced as the lub-dub of my heart hammered rapidly in my ears. We were standing in the school auditorium. Collin, Eric, and Shannon were less than ten feet away, hidden by a steel door that could swing open at any second.

Kreturus looked down at me, expressionless. "This is the only other building standing. And we need to be protected from the elements to bring her here." He pulled out of my grip, walking to the back corner of the auditorium. Bending at the waist, he gripped a chair and tore it from the floor. He threw it across the room. He did it again. And again. He tossed the chairs like they were couch cushions. The noise was so loud that I was certain they heard him. I just hoped Collin and Eric had the sense to remain hidden.

I didn't miss Kreturus' meaning. He was going to call Locoicia. "You're calling the Demon Princess? Here? That's insane! That's what she wants!"

"I know," he retorted as he threw another wooden chair. It splintered when it crashed into the pile of rubble slowly growing across the room. "We'll call her here, and kill her. More specifically, you'll kill her. It will break your bargain, and whatever debt you had will be gone." Another chair hit the cinderblock wall and splintered.

I stood there, watching him as he worked. The two of us looked like a deranged prom couple ripping apart the school –him in his tux, and me in a ball gown. And we were about to summon a demon. I pressed my hands to my face. I wished the bond worked. I wished I hadn't fried it. Collin would know he was in danger. Bringing Locoicia here would only make things worse.

And I had the sinking feeling in my stomach that the Omen's touch was something too horrible to say. And it touched me. And Collin. Was it possible that there was a creature that was worse than Kreturus? From the times it'd followed me, I didn't think it was dangerous. Well, no more dangerous than anything from the Underworld. What could it do that would make the ancient demon nervous? I looked through the hole in the roof, half hoping to see the beast swooping across the opening. But the dragon was gone.

When Kreturus cleared a space large enough, he commanded, "Call the mirror. Locoicia is powerful and used magic to hide from me. I cannot call it, but I suspect that you can." And I could. This was the end then. I'd kill the Demon Princess and go from being in her debt to being in his. Biting my lip, I did as I was told, thinking fast. With any luck the two of them would kill each other, but I knew I wouldn't be so lucky. I focused on the black glass. The mirror materialized in front of us. The pane set within the dark mirror was cracked. Kreturus stood next to me, with his arms folded over his chest, and an eyebrow arched, "How long have you been able to do that?"

My stare was blank. The thought of seeing Locoicia made something change inside of me. Numbness flooded every inch of me in order to drown out my fear. Staring blankly at the glass, I said "Too long." Kreturus took my answer and didn't press for more. This mirror had been appearing since I was hauled into the Martis compound.

Kreturus stepped up to the mirror, touching it with his fingers to test the stability of the sheet of glass. When he was done, he turned and said, "Call her to the pane. I will pull her through and subdue her. It will be easy for you, Ivy. Combine your weapon and your spells to kill the Demon Princess." His words were urgent, rushed. Seeing the Omen spooked him. A sound startled me and I looked to the hole in the roof. Dreanoks screeched in the sky as they circled the building. They must follow Kreturus wherever he goes.

I nodded, ready to do as he said, hoping to God that no one chose now to come out of the basement. But as I pressed my eyes closed to summon the Princess to the glass, I heard his voice. My heart dropped into my toes, and my mouth snapped shut.

"Hey boss," Collin's voice was light. Mocking. When I turned I saw there was laughter in his eyes. His hands were in his pockets like he was strolling through a field of daisies, and not facing the demon that damned him and stole his life. "Didn't expect to see you again."

Kreturus tensed. His eyes narrowed as he spit words at Collin, "You ignorant fool. Have you come to plead for your soul back? Or someone else's? Someone near and dear to Ivy that you were responsible for destroying?" The smile faded from Collin's lips as Kreturus spoke. When Collin didn't respond, Kreturus placed his palms together excitedly. A grin stretched across his face, dark eyes sparkling, "You didn't tell her… She doesn't know." Kreturus looked at me with glee in his eyes.

But I wasn't fazed. Nothing he could say would shock me. Absolutely nothing. I've heard everything. There were no more surprises between me and Collin. I gazed at Kreturus as if I was bored and didn't care what he had to say, but I caught a glimpse of Collin out of the corner of my eye. He was tense, his muscles strung tighter than before. The confident swagger was gone.

Kreturus laughed, and continued, "Such lies! And you think I'm the deceiver." He walked behind me, placing his hands on my shoulders, thrusting me toward Collin. My throat tightened as my feet stumbled to a stop in front of him. There was something in his eyes—that expression—I recognized it. I couldn't breathe. Not more lies. No! I tried to tear out of Kreturus' grip, but he held tight. Placing his face next to mine he spoke in my ear, loud enough for Collin to hear, "Your precious sister died because of his mistake. You see, he was hunting the Prophecy One; he mistook Apryl for you."

Shaking my head, I tried to pull away, saying, "No. Nicole said... The Valefar said that it was Eric. That he was responsible." I remembered their words. The sting when Eric had confessed it was his fault. That meant what? That Collin stood by the whole time and didn't tell me? It couldn't be true. "You're lying," I snapped.

Still grinning he said, "Not this time, Ivy." His fingers dug into my bare shoulders as I tried to twist away. But Kreturus' grip only tightened, as he held me firmly facing Collin, forced to watch his face as he spoke, "Eric may have led the Valefar to her, but who do you think was the one leading the Valefar? Eric didn't watch her die from a room only a few feet away. He wasn't the one who demanded her death. He wasn't the one who allowed the Valefar to rape her. The one responsible is standing in front of you. Collin Smith watched the entire thing. They killed at his command." His fingers loosened, releasing me, and he stepped away.

My eyes shone with unshed tears as I stared at Collin. His lips were in a straight line, smooth. Tense. His gaze was on the demon over my shoulder, not me. My throat tightened. It felt like someone was strangling me. All this time. He could have told me. I knew he'd done things, things that were deplorable. We didn't speak of his past, though. Watching him, I knew it was true. His sapphire blue eyes slowly drifted back to mine.

"Why didn't you tell me?" My voice was a whisper, barely audible.

Collin reached for me, but I stepped back, a step closer to Kreturus. "I was a Valefar. I did what I had to do to survive. It wasn't an option." His response was cold, unfeeling. He didn't apologize. He didn't sound remorseful.

What was wrong with him? How could he do this to me? How could he hide it for so long!

Disgusted, I stared at him stunned. I couldn't believe that I trusted him, and what he'd done. Something bubbled up inside of me. Rage. Anger. It coursed through my veins, until I slammed both fists into Collin's chest. A gasp of air was pushed out of his lungs as the force of the hit launched him backwards through two rows of chairs. Collin jumped off the floor, dusting himself off. My eyes were warm. Rimming. He slept with me. We were together and he never told me that he... I couldn't even think it. Processing what he did was too horrible.

Collin rose, grinning, like he was glad. My muscles twitched. With every ounce of my being I wanted to wipe that smile off his face. Swiftly moving across the room, I lunged at him. My hands connected with his chest, thrusting him back again. Kreturus stood there, watching us—watching me unleash my power on Collin. The distance between me and the Demon King grew until I'd cracked Collin's back through every row of chairs and he was pressed against the stage. The stupid grin on his face finally faded. He hadn't fought back very much, and I hadn't noticed. Until right then.

Collin's hand shot out, grabbing my wrist, as he yanked me toward him, and tried to whisper in my ear, but I didn't want to hear him. Power built in my hands as spells lined the roof of my mouth. I wanted to hear him cry out for mercy. Ruthlessness consumed me, blinding me to what was happening around me. As I tried to land the power blow on Collin's chest, he twisted, grabbing my hair, and moved out of the way. With a swift tug on my hair, my neck snapped to the side and up.

"Look!" he hissed in my ear. And I saw it. Eric was standing in the darkened wing on the stage, holding Shannon's dagger. He arched an eyebrow at me with a look that said I was stupid. Shannon stood behind him, masked in shadows. Her gaze was lowered to the floor. She didn't move.

At the same time Collin yanked my head back, Kreturus realized something was wrong. My shoulders slumped as I stopped throwing my power at Collin. Between the time it took Kreturus to effonate to my side, Collin threw his arms around my waist and hauled me back and up onto the stage. Placing himself between me and Kreturus, he stood poised to fight. My mouth was dry. I didn't know what to believe. They must have decided to lure me to the stage. But why? I glanced around, seeing only Shannon standing submissively in the wing. Her wide green eyes gazed at me with an expression I hadn't seen in a long time—regret.

Tearing my gaze away from my ex-friend, I turned my attention back to the demon now battling Eric. When Eric effonated he landed right where I stood. That led to Kreturus grabbing him, expecting my body to still be in that spot. Collin had moved me so quickly that Kreturus didn't have time to react. But Eric had the upper hand, if only momentarily. They'd planned it that way. That explained Collin's infuriating smirk. And now—now Kreturus was trying to force his way through Eric to get to me. Eric used the remnants of my power, which made him stronger than Collin.

Urgently, Collin said, "Effonate to the Martis camp. Now!" My jaw dropped as he shoved me to the side of the stage. I tripped on the hem of the gown. I didn't have time to tell him that I couldn't leave. As long as Kreturus was standing there, I couldn't wield my own power.

Shannon's hands reached for me, and she pulled me to my feet. "Nice dress," she joked, but I just glared at her. "If you don't leave they both die. Leave. Now." Her voice was deep. She didn't sound like herself, but she didn't sound like the lust-induced blood addict I'd last seen either.

Her hands shoved into me, turning me around to push me through a side door. But, it felt like we hit a wall. Kreturus' power extended, pulling me back to him, making it impossible to walk away. Even with the boys fighting and someone helping me, I was still trapped. Shannon felt the jarred impact as well, and her eyes went wide. "Their plan falls apart if you don't leave."

"Time for a new plan then, because I'm stuck here." Kreturus was powerful. The ancient demon had done something to me that made it difficult to use my powers. But it seemed to only affect me. Collin and Eric didn't pause, but I knew they couldn't win either. They were no match for the Demon King. I yanked my comb out of my hair and extended the tines. Three against one should help. I didn't think we'd kill him, but I thought we might wear him down enough that we could escape.

Eric and Collin had flanked him, both fighting Kreturus at the same time. Eric's lips moved as he slashed his blade at the demon. There was a thin red line were Kreturus had bled. They must have gotten close enough to hurt him. And that was all they needed. Hope swelled in my chest. This could be over. This could end right now.

I ran and jumped off the stage to the empty space below. My gown filled with air as my body rushed toward the floor. Grabbing the skirt in one hand, I ran toward Kreturus. I hurled my comb at his chest. As the weapon left my fingers, I spoke an incantation. Swallowing hard, I watched the silvery tines sheen and turn red as they sped toward his body. The power of my spell would drive the blade to him, and through him. As if he sensed me, Kreturus turned—taking hits on both sides and snatched my deadly blades out of the air. Anger flashed in his eyes, as his hand tightened on the tines and crushed them. The scent of seared flesh filled the air as Kreturus held up his fist, bending the Celestial Silver into a ball of metal.

Rage filled him, his eyes turning to red coals. "Enough!" he shouted, thrashing with the full force of his power at Collin and Eric simultaneously. Their bodies flew through the air in different directions, hitting the floor with a sickening thump. Swallowing hard, I clutched my skirt with one hand, and watched the demon move toward me. His tux was torn. Blood lined his cheek. A smile twisted across his face, "You cannot defeat me! Accept your fate!" He moved toward me, reaching for me. Hatred flared in his eyes.

Dreanoks screeched wildly above us, halting his step. With his hand outstretched, Kreturus looked up. We were standing under the hole in the ceiling. The sky was chaos. Dreanoks scattered like they were under attack. Screeching grackles darted like arrows flying past them. My foot slid back as my jaw dropped. Something was plummeting toward me, about to land on the spot where I was standing. Jumping back, a dead Dreanok fell with a thump at my feet. Its body was slashed by talons. There was no other sign of injury.

Then, without a sound, the Omen narrowed its body and flew into the open roof. Kreturus stood there, stunned, staring at it. It landed between us, crushing the dead Dreanok with his massive claws. I didn't care what Kreturus thought this thing was. It liked me, and leaving with him was better than staying here. As I climbed onto his back, I glanced around quickly. Eric and Collin were watching. Their wide eyes were focused on me. I only hoped this beast could take me where I needed to go and that they had the sense to meet me there.

The beast flapped his wings once, then twice, before we lifted off. It was then that Kreturus decided to move. His hand still held the ball of Celestial Silver. He spoke an incantation into it just as the Omen started to beat his wings. The silver ball glowed bright blue and was dripping with something. I could actually see it drip down onto the ground as it flew through the air at me. It would hit. I couldn't stop it. My stomach clenched. At the same time the silvery ball left Kreturus' grip, something moved. I couldn't twist my head to see. The ball was coming too fast. It would knock me from the dragon's back. At least, that's what I thought it would do.

I was wrong.

The dripping blue ball flew closer and closer. We were barely off the ground. Attempting to use my powers to stop it, I tried and failed. Kreturus made certain that I couldn't defend myself. On instinct I covered my face as the ball was about to collide with my body. But before my face was covered, a flash of cinnamon hair flew past. Shannon. Her body sprung from the ground, using Martis power to gain enough height, and was suddenly in front of me. The ball collided with her chest as her body flew in front of mine.

On contact, her skin hissed. Black veins spidered out, covering her body as she screamed. Shannon's body stopped its arc through the air and fell. It was like she was hit by a truck filled with poison. Her body cracked as it hung suspended. Agony creased her face, closing her brilliant green eyes. One minute Shannon was close enough to reach out and touch. The next, she was laying on the ground convulsing. Her hair spread around her head like a halo. Her limbs twisted in unnatural directions. The ball forced her to the ground, crushing her bones. She no longer moved. Breath did not fill her lungs. Wide green eyes stared blankly, no longer seeing. The brimstone dust and sapphire serum Kreturus put into the ball worked its way further into her dead body. My jaw hung open, watching her, waiting for her to jump up—but she didn't. The black lines continued to grow, covering her body in a black web of poison until there was no fair skin remaining. The fourth flap of the Omen's wings put us out of the hole in the ceiling and into the night sky. As we lifted away, I felt the jarring sensation of Kreturus' spell trying to hold me in place. The dragon turned his head and violet flames shot from his snout. The sensation stopped, and the spell broke. Clutching his back, I leaned down, pressing my body to the dragon so that Kreturus couldn't try to hit me again.

As we flew, my eyes stung. Wind whipped my hair wildly around my face. Every living creature that normally inhabited the skies gave us a wide birth, wanting nothing to do with us. I was on the back of the only thing that frightened Kreturus. And he saw that it touched me. That was when the Demon King hurled the death ball at me. He realized the beast not only sought me out, but was familiar with me. I didn't scream as it landed. I jumped on his back like we were buddies.

Pressing my eyes closed, I rested my face against the beast's cold scales. Shannon. Why did she do it?

Did Eric compel her to do that? Or did she do it on her own? I didn't know what to think. I couldn't think. It was too horrible.

And I had the feeling that revealing my relationship to this beast just changed the game. Kreturus would no longer be hunting me with the intention of sharing my maturing power. Next time he saw me, I'd die.

CHAPTER TWENTY

The Martis scurried like ants when he hovered over their camp. It was luck that we found it. I had been thinking of the location of their camp, wishing I could effonate there when the dragon arched his wings wider and banked into a rapid turn. It was long after that, that I spotted the glimmering tents. They'd moved. Either that or this was a different camp. I didn't know what to do. We circled high above, away from the sentry, waiting. Thinking.

I spoke to the dragon as if he understood me, although I didn't think that was entirely true, "We can't land. I don't know why they told me to come here. Or if this is even the right camp..." my voice trailed off. Wind tugged at my hair and stung my face. It was so cold. And this gown did nothing to keep me warm.

On the third pass over the camp, the wind abruptly stopped, and I sat on the dragon's back suspended in air. Turning my head, I looked for the cause. An angel was nearby, causing this—freezing time. Her voice floated across the empty space, "Are you ever going to land?" It was Jenna Marie.

Turning toward the source of the sound, I saw her. She was in the air, high above the camp below, standing next to me. At least she appeared to be standing. A rush of relief shone on my face, "You're alive! I though the Dreanok killed you."

She hovered next to me. I looked behind her, wishing I could see her wings. She replied, grinning, "Nope. Long story. Are you coming or going? I can't hold time like this forever and the beast you're riding is strongly protesting what I'm doing. He's going to flame me if I don't release him this instant. Land. Come inside. See you in a moment." Then she was gone, and the wind burst against my cheeks again, tangling my hair. The dragon snarled as if he was aware of the entire conversation and pissed off that something held him still like that.

"Shhh," I patted his back trying to sooth him. "She meant well. Don't kill her, okay?" I was half joking, but part of me was seriously asking. I didn't know how the beast would react. In response the creature roared, making the most bone chilling sound I've ever heard.

He descended, gliding in slow circles toward the ground. As the camp became closer, I could see Jenna Marie's familiar face. Standing next to her was Eric with a smirk on his lips. I smiled crookedly at him. My eyes darted between Martis, searching for Collin, wondering where he was. I half hoped that Kreturus' words were lies, but something inside of me said that they weren't. Apryl died. Valefar killed her. Eric led them there. I already knew this. Somewhere in the back of my mind, I knew Collin was also responsible. I just didn't want to admit it. But until now, I didn't know he was there. Somehow, thinking of him actually sitting there, and watching the Valefar destroy her—it damned him more. Searching the camp for his beautiful face as we sank lower and lower, circle by circle, I wondered what I'd say to him. Did Collin think this was in the past? Would I let it be? Could I do such a thing? Forgive someone that much? I didn't think so.

My heart sank lower with each descending pass. The dragon was cautious, hesitant to land. I wasn't sure why. Then it dawned on me. If this thing was the Omen, crossing his path had dire consequences. I cupped my hands and yelled down, "Clear the area, except for Eric." I would have said Collin, but there was no trace of him. The Martis scattered. Jenna Marie, paused, but did as I asked. As soon as they left, Eric stood in the clearing alone. The dragon dropped out of the sky, landing lightly on his feet. Twisting my body, I slid off his back and into Eric's arms. Stumbling, I landed my feet. Eric pulled me closer to him, to steady me. The dragon snorted a huff of hot air, warming my frigid skin and then took off. He disappeared into the night.

Eric's hands were on my face, tilting my head up as he examined me. It was as if he expected me to be broken. I swatted at him and he stopped. Smiling, he said, "I wasn't sure how you'd get here. Your pet followed you from the Underworld, huh?" He released me and stepped back.

I glanced over my shoulder, looking at the spot where the dragon had been. Ignoring his comment, I asked, "Eric, have you ever heard of the Omen?" His expression changed. His eyes darted into the sky, looking for the creature that was just standing before him.

Snapping his gaze back to me, he asked, "You think that was the Omen?" His voice rose, a tad higher than normal. Shit. Eric knew what it was. It seemed that he didn't think it was possible until I suggested it.

Jenna Marie walked up behind me. "I'm guessing it was. It's why he didn't want to land. He didn't want to cross paths with more people than he already had. That's why you were able to stay, Eric. It wasn't because you and Ivy are friends. That had nothing to do with it." Eric bristled at her words. I was uncertain what had offended him. Jenna Marie stood before me. Golden blonde hair fell in her face. She made no attempt to push it back. Studying her, I noticed her downcast gaze. She didn't look up.

Suspicious, I stepped toward her. Limp blonde hair dangled from beneath her flowered cap. The wind blew mine, but hers didn't move. It clung to her face like it was weighed down, so it would stay in place... to conceal something. Reaching out, I moved my hand toward her face. Jenna Marie didn't move at first. She just watched my hand move slowly toward her. When my fingers touched her hair, ready to move it away, her fingers wrapped around my wrist in a death grip and yanked them away. "Not today," was all she said, and turned walking back into a tent.

A gust of chilling wind blew hard, kicking up the fallen snow as it rushed past. The wind was bad enough, but when it pelted me with snow I couldn't stop shivering. Glancing at Eric, I asked, "She didn't die? What happened to her?"

He nodded, his eyes darting toward Jenna Marie's tent. The question was on my face, about to be asked when he replied, "The Dreanok scarred her. It didn't heal. I don't know why."

Shivering, I wrapped my arms around myself. I stared at Eric for a moment. It was odd that he was the one here to welcome me back. It was strange that his were the arms to catch me and hold me. His amber gaze locked on mine as we stood there, in the frozen air, gazing at each other. I didn't know what to say. And I was afraid to ask what I wanted to know. Did he sacrifice Shannon so we could get away? I broke the gaze and glanced away, rubbing my arms.

"We better go in," I said, turning to follow Jenna Marie.

Eric's hand shot out and grabbed me, spinning me around and into his arms. He was warm and I was so cold. I didn't look up into his face until he spoke, "I didn't make her do that. Shannon moved of her own accord. If Kreturus was trying to kill me, it is possible bloodlust would have made her move. But nothing but her own desire saved you." His fingers tangled in my hair as I looked up at him. The words he spoke made me feel crazy. I didn't know whether to be happy or sad. Shannon had already been dead to me. She betrayed me. But I couldn't accept it. And when I finally did, she sacrificed herself for me. Eric spoke, breaking my thoughts, "You realized that Collin was there the night Apryl died. You realized it before now, didn't you?"

I pulled away, my jaw hanging open. I wanted to say yes, but my expression clearly said no. Eric's gaze rested lazily on my face, watching. Waiting. When I spoke, I didn't answer him. Instead I asked, "Where is he?"

"He didn't think you'd want to see him. Plus his origin is questionable, so they wouldn't let him into the camp." Eric saw my face light up with fury. What did he mean questionable? Collin was like me. None of us were Valefar. As I started to growl a retort, Eric reached out and grabbed my lower lip so I couldn't speak. Irritated, I tried to pull away, but he held it, jerking me closer to his face. "You think I care what he is? Or what you are for that matter?" he released my lip. I didn't move. I just stared at him.

"What do you mean?" Warm breath slid out of his mouth. He was so close to me. The anger that was trademark Eric was gone. Or I was looking past it. I wasn't sure.

"At one point it mattered, and now it doesn't." His tone suggested a finality, ending the conversation, but I didn't understand. He turned to walk inside.

Tugging his arm, I yanked him back around, "Wait." Eric stopped, looking down at me with an expression that was unreadable. "I don't understand. What do you mean?"

Eric's gaze lingered on my lips while I spoke. Then he replied, "Ah, but I think you do." Leaning closer, he pressed his lips next to my ear. He opened his mouth, like he was going to say something, but thought better of it and snapped it shut. As my mouth opened to ask him what he was going to say, he pressed his lips gently to mine, and pulled away quickly, grinning slyly. "You ask too many questions."

Eric walked away from me and into the tent. The flap closed behind him, leaving me alone in the night. This was the first time I was alone, truly by myself, in a long time. Not caring about the cold, I sank to the ground and closed my eyes. The wind caressed my face as it screamed, racing by. My gown absorbed the snow, slowly making the fabric damp before it froze, clinging to my body in sheet of ice. No one came out to look for me. I don't know how much time passed, but when I rose, every inch of me was soaked. A thin layer of ice had formed on my skin. I had too many decisions to make, and no time left.

As I sat there, feeling the whip of the wind tugging at my hair, and blistering across my cheek, I decided something. It would dictate how I lived the rest of my life, whether that would be a matter of hours or centuries. I felt content when I rose—content with who

I was and what I would do. I would not sit idly by. Not anymore. The remaining decisions to be made were mine. And no one was taking that away from me.

Jenna Marie fussed at me for staying outside so long, but it was with less perk than usual. As I watched her move, it was like she was deflated or something. I didn't understand how she could be so vane. How could she allow a scar to alter her so drastically? For a moment I thought I was a hypocrite, but the Dreanok's scar and my mark weren't the same thing. My mangled Martis mark threw me onto a crash course of suckage and marred my skin. She just had a complexion issue. As I tugged on a pair of her sneakers, and was bent over tying the laces, I glanced up at her. Her hair hung down both cheeks, completely flat against her skull. She did her best to hide the scar, but I saw it as I finished tying my shoe and looked up. The gash started on her cheek and went back into her hairline where it thickened, and disappeared. My stomach twisted, as I sat up. The damage was more than that, although I didn't know what. I hid my reaction, not wanting to bring attention to it. She seemed like she was doing okay, now that she had found us again.

Jenna Marie sat next to me. Eric was across from me, and Collin was glaringly absent. I didn't fight with them about letting him into the camp. I just hoped I could find him again. I had no idea where he might have gone. Eric continued arguing with Jenna Marie.

He was back to his jack-ass self, snapping "If the dragon was the Omen," he mocked in her voice, "Are you insane? If? The Omen was something angels told demons to scare the shit out of them. It's not real. It never was."

She snorted, "Yes, and we all know that you only believe in the things that are right in front of your face." Eric sneered at her. "It makes sense. If Kreturus paused as you said, when the Omen appeared, it makes perfect sense."

Eric leaned forward, his fingers resembling claws as he shook his hands at her, half wanting to strangle her, "It's a fucking dragon, not the Omen! It has scales, breathes fire, flies like a deranged cow with wings. If it was the Omen—the one you and I heard of when we were kids—then there's no way Ivy and I would still be alive." He leaned back, arching one eyebrow at her, as if to say, there, I told you so.

"You only think with your head, Eric...," Jenna Marie retorted, but was cut off before she could finish. Titling her head to the side, she took a deep breath through her nose, listening to Eric berate her intelligence before she continued, "Think with your heart. You know it's the Omen. You know it makes sense. It's the only explanation. It followed her in the Underworld. It protected her from the Demon King. The Omen is messing with Kreturus. For some reason, the Omen has marked him."

Eric shook his head, "No, if we go with your fucked up reasoning, then the Omen has selected Ivy—not Kreturus." He continued to rant, but I cut him off.

"If one of you doesn't fill me in on the Omen and what it is, I'm going to bitch-slap the both of you." I glanced at Jenna Marie. Her brow wrinkled in distaste as Eric laughed. "Let's assume the Omen is real for a moment," Eric started to speak, but I cut him off, "Yes, I know you think it's moronic. I got that. But I need to know what it is, because it doesn't matter if it's real or not. Do you understand? Kreturus thinks the Omen is real, so we need to act like it is." I stared at Eric, daring him to challenge me, but he remained silent. I turned to Jenna Marie as she spoke.

"The Omen is an ancient creature—like angels or demons—but it kept to itself for so long, belief in its existence slipped. The only place that I've ever heard it mentioned was in ancient fables angels used to tell their kids." She smiled at Eric, but he didn't seem to appreciate it.

"Angels have kids?" I couldn't help it. I didn't realize that was even possible.

Jenna Marie arched an eyebrow at me, as Eric exhaled loudly and rubbed his hands into his hair. "Focus, Ivy," she snapped. I think I liked her better when she was perky. "The Omen was reduced to a myth, which is what Eric so clearly thinks. The fables claim that if the Omen crossed your path, destruction would soon overshadow your life."

"And if the Omen touched you? What then?" I asked, eager and nervous to hear the answer.

Her pink lips smiled softly, "Ah, he mentioned that, did he? Kreturus didn't want you if the Omen had touched you. He believes the touch of the Omen is tantamount to certain death and devastation. Since the beast touched you, he thought it was better to kill you and take what power you have now. Did he talk about it? Did Kreturus say anything about the Omen before it flew in and rescued you?"

I glanced at Eric. Although he didn't act like it, he was listening, "Yes. I saw it down the street. Kreturus took me to a house where he showed me the Thirteenth Prophecy. Kreturus has it. It was a cup—a carved chalice. He was going to make a blood bargain with me, when I saw the dragon looming on a roof top down the street. I felt like it was watching me." I no longer glanced at either of them. They didn't understand my connection to the creature. Neither did I. "Anyway, Kreturus saw it. He said it was a bad sign."

I continued to retell the rest of the story. When I finished, I twisted my fingers together in my lap, staring at my hands.

Eric's palm gripped my entwined fingers and squeezed, making me look up into his face, "He has the prophecy?" I nodded. He sat next to me. "What did it show?" His voice was soft. Softer than I've heard it since before I drank his soul. It sounded something like hope—hope that was false—hope that would shatter as soon as I told him.

Jenna Marie's eyes burned into the side of my face, but she didn't speak. I pressed my lips together. "The prophecy rests in my hands. There is, fighting, demons slaying angels, ripping off their wings." Jenna Marie flinched, but Eric just continued to stare at me as I continued, "The Underworld, Earth, and the heavens were all colliding. It was as if whatever lines separated their creatures were erased."

Eric shifted slightly. "And what did you look like, Ivy? What were you doing in the prophecy?" Eric asked eagerly. But his question made me blush. I felt the heat sear my cheeks, as I looked away. But he twisted my shoulders back toward him.

I tried to shake him off. I couldn't tell what I was doing in the prophecy. Kreturus thought it was one thing—that I was commanding the destruction—but that didn't feel right. So what was I doing?

"Get off!" I tried to twist away, but he wouldn't let go.

"Tell me," his voice was low, commanding. Something rippled inside of me. Suddenly I wanted to press my body against his. Feel his skin, his lips pressed to my body and taste him.

My eyelids lowered slowly, forcing the seduction of the blood lust away. When he exhaled, I could feel his breath slide across my skin. It was everything I could do to stifle a moan. My fist flew, attempting to collide with his cheek, but he caught my wrist and held it tight. Eric commanded, "Tell me. Say it." More seduction. More compulsion to spill what I'd seen, but I couldn't.

I didn't know who that woman was. She wasn't me. I wouldn't stand there half naked and command a demon army to kill everything and everyone. Eric held me tight. The muscles in my arms started to tremble because they were so tense. I tried to pull away from him. "Say it," his voice dripped with desire, trying to coax it from me. Jenna Marie watched wide-eyed, doing nothing to stop him. "Tell me, whisper it to me." My stomach filled with flutters as I started to melt in his arms. Part of me stopped fighting, wondering what would be so bad about telling him. But the other half of my mind wouldn't permit it. I had to squelch the desire so I could pull away. I leaned in to kiss him, to press my lips to his, but he made sure our lips didn't meet. Instead he dangled himself in front of me.

Pressing my eyes closed, I gave in to him. I was too weak. "I was half-naked." The desire evaporated as my words shocked Eric and he didn't hold the bloodlust in place. I sneered at him, and connected my fist with his stomach. Eric gasped with an *oof*. "Next time you do that to me, I'm going to beat the shit out of you."

He smirked, "You said next time... " I growled at him, ready to fight more when Jenna Marie cleared her throat.

"That was... interesting." Her voice was higher than usual. Her eyebrows were suspended in an odd expression too high on her face. When they finally fell to their normal place, she re-crossed her legs and put her hands in her lap. "Naked?" she questioned.

I shot out of my seat. "Yes. Okay? It was a battle and I was walking around like fucking Aphrodite, waiting to be... whatever." I turned my back from them, annoyed. Embarrassed. And tugged my hair out of my face. Sniggers broke out behind me, followed by a loud laugh from Jenna Marie. Turning sharply, I said, "What! What's so funny?"

But she and Eric just looked at each other and couldn't stop laughing. I stood there feeling even more stupid while they calmed down. Eric wiped a tear from his eye as he looked up at me. Disgusted, I folded my arms across my chest and turned away. He jumped up, grabbing my shoulder, and trying to be serious said, "Don't be like that. You just have such a way with words," his face broke into a smile as he laughed softly, like I was the funniest person he'd ever met. "Then she was laughing, and that made it worse. I'm sorry. That must have been embarrassing. Or something." And he started laughing again. With a huff, I twisted out of his grip and stepped outside the tent into the early morning snow.

Breathing deeply, I tried to calm down. So maybe it was funny. I just didn't feel it. I walked through the center of camp. It was nearly abandoned after the Dreanok attack. It was so close to the old camp, the camp that we took Shannon from. I gazed at the sky as I walked, folding my arms over my chest. The sky was blood red. Gray snow clouds covered it in thin streaks. A hand landed on my shoulder, making me jump.

When I turned around, I was staring at Collin's blue eyes. "How'd you get in here?" was the first thing out of my mouth. His eyes revealed nothing.

His mouth was in a thin line. Collin wore his black leather jacket, jeans, and biker boots. Snow clung to his damp hair. He'd been outside for a while. "I have ways." I wasn't sure what those ways were, not unless Jenna Marie was the only angel here and let him walk in. After a moment, he looked over his shoulder. A

Martis was moving in a nearby tent. Collin tilted his head, indicating I should follow. We wound through the camp, to the back. After passing three tents, he opened a flap and gestured me inside. He followed me in. Dusting snow from his hair, he asked, "Have they told you?"

Confused, I looked at him, "Told me what?" I wondered how he'd react to what I'd said. Would Collin have laughed too?

He pulled his jacket off, shaking it out. The supple leather was wet. He finally sat down, and kicked his boots up before answering. "What happened after you left? And the stuff about the stone?" I shook my head slowly. "Then what were they...?" he trailed off. He didn't understand what they could be talking about that was more important. I suppose finding the last prophecy was a bit of a distraction.

Pushing his fingers through his hair, Collin avoided my gaze and said, "Kreturus seemed to think the dragon was the Omen. He was pissed that Shannon took the spell that was meant for you. I don't know how she got there in time. Eric saw Kreturus throw it, but he couldn't intercept its path. And I was too far away. By the time I effonated, it would have been too late. We failed you, but she didn't." He was quiet for a moment. "Eric didn't force her to do it. I saw him. His lips didn't move. I know that you were probably wondering what to believe..." he gazed at the floor. I still stood in front of him, wearing jeans and a tee shirt Eric gave me. Thank God I wasn't wearing pink. Collin kicked out a chair with his foot—the only other chair in the small space. "Sit."

Glancing at him, I moved toward the chair, my arms still wrapped tightly around my middle. "I was wondering what to believe." For the first time since he'd started talking, he looked at me.

His eyes were flighty, as if they couldn't stand to meet mine. Collin glanced to the side, "About that." He meant, about Apryl—about my sister. "I thought you knew." He worked his jaw, as if he was trying to dislodge something bitter. "There were so many things I did, and I'm not gonna hide behind Kreturus and say he made me do it. I said those things back there to draw you to the stage, so you could tell that we were trying to help you. I do take responsibility for every life I took," his blue gaze met mine, "for every ounce of pain I've caused. I was damned before you met me, and now I've stolen everything that mattered to you. Everything I've touched was destroyed, utterly decimated. Your entire family died at my hand. I know you realize that. And I don't expect you to," he swallowed, choking on his words, "to do anything. To act any different than you would with anyone else." His fingers clenched and smoothed on his lap. Shame covered him thickly, slumping his shoulders, and pulling his gaze downward.

I stared at him. I'd already decided what I would do before I saw him. Allowing him to speak was a formality. He didn't cower or grovel. Collin expected me to choose vengeance. At least that was what it seemed. My arms tightened as he spoke, a lump forming in my throat. As he said the last word, I couldn't take it anymore. I didn't want to hear it. I knew! I already knew and there was nothing to be done about it. There was no changing the past. There was no bringing back the dead. I swallowed hard. Jumping to my feet, I grabbed his shirt in my hands, pressed his forehead to mine, and tilted him back in his chair.

Surprised, Collin clutched the seat of the chair as I dipped it back. "Look at me," I demanded. His gaze flicked to mine. Emotions washed over him, emotions that I could no longer feel. Eric's blood subdued his, making it like a weak whisper in the back of my mind. "I knew who you were before you did. I knew what you were capable of—what you did. I had the pieces to connect my sister to you, and I didn't. I didn't because we've already been over this and it doesn't change a damn thing. There is no point in discussing the past. It's over. It's gone. If we're lucky, you and I have today, and maybe tomorrow. Beyond that is too much to hope for, and there is no way in Hell I'm spending those days without you. I accept you. I know who you are. What you were..."

I released him, and stepped back. Collin's chair thudded down on all four legs. His hand smoothed his shirt as he looked up at me, surprised. Breathing hard, I asked, "The question is, do you accept what I have been and what I will become? Will you still love me after whatever happens, happens? Will you still love me when I murder without thought—as I already have." Swallowing hard, I looked down, shaking my head. When I looked back up at Collin's face, his eyes met mine, "I saw the thirteenth prophecy, Collin. Kreturus has it. I hold demons and angels in my palms. I stood watching a battle, without so much as a breastplate to protect me...without anything to cover me. I don't know how I get there. I don't know when or how that will become me. The question is, will you accept me then?"

My eyes stung. I'd just admitted a plethora of things that I wanted to denounce. I couldn't offer the prophecy, and my interpretation of it, to Jenna Marie and Eric, but to Collin—it slid off my tongue. I couldn't keep it a secret. He was my other half, my soul mate. Worry wrinkled the space between my eyes. My teeth sank into my lower lip, as I fought to keep my gaze cool and even. It killed me to say it. I didn't want to admit all that yet, but I had to. I had to say it, because... I was no better than him. All the things Collin did, I would do, if not more. It didn't matter what the reason was, the hand that killed was mine. Kreturus' words stung. I was so close to being the ruthless Queen everyone expected me to be. There was only one thing anchoring me, keeping me from becoming her—from wanting to be her. And it was this boy, the perfect boy standing in front of me.

Collin hadn't moved. As I spoke, his eyes drifted away from my face and down toward the floor. He pressed them closed a few times, and remained that way when I stopped speaking. His jaw tightened as he looked up at me. His eyes shone like twin pools, "I accept who you are now, and what you will become." As he spoke my heart soared. I tried to wipe the stupid smile off my face, but I couldn't. He stood slowly and walked toward me as he spoke. There was an intensity in his gaze and determination in his step. One of his hands slid around my waist, and the other tilted up my chin. His eyes lingered on my lips, as my heart fluttered in my chest. He pressed a soft kiss to my mouth, pulling back long enough to say, "I love you, Ivy Taylor. I always have. I always will. No matter what..."

CHAPTER TWENTY-ONE

Collin kept his arms wrapped around me tightly, my head tucked under his chin. I wasn't certain how long we remained like that until the tent flapped opened. My heart jumped into my throat. Collin wasn't supposed to be here. We pulled apart like we were caught doing something horrible.

"You two make me sick. You act like two fucking lovebirds who think that love will save the day," Eric chided. His arms were folded over his chest. A white tee shirt clung to his body like a second skin. His dark jeans and shirt were both wet, plastered to his body from the snow. He shook off the precipitation like a dog, ruffling his fingers through his hair, splattering us.

"Eric," I gasped, ignoring everything he just said. I loved Collin. I wasn't stupid. I didn't think it would change anything. And it had the potential to make things suck even more. But it was a risk I was willing to take. Collin's fingers intertwined with mine. I was worried about him. He shouldn't be here. Pushing my hair out of my face, I asked urgently, "Where's the dagger? Do you have it? We need to get out of here. All three of us..."

Before Eric could speak, I heard her voice echo from the other side of the flap. "No, I do." Jenna Marie, pushed her way through. A gust of wind tangled her hair. She held the hair down, against her cheek, hiding her hideous scar. When she stepped inside, she held Shannon's dagger between her fingers. A grin spread across her face. "Were you seriously going to leave without me? Ivy?" She glowered at me, scolding me.

But I wasn't apologizing. "Why wouldn't you let Collin in? I need to know. Now. Before anything else happens." I moved in front of him protectively.

All eyes in the room shifted to Jenna Marie. She sighed, tilting her head to the side. "I obviously let him in, Ivy. And kept the other angels away from him. We just wanted to keep him safe. There are Martis here that would kill you if I wasn't sitting with you every moment. There are even more that remember Collin and what he's done. It was an unnecessary risk. Collin agreed. It wasn't like I banished him."

Collin's hand rested on my shoulder, "It's all right, Ivy. Jenna Marie had your best interests at heart... and mine."

Eric turned to the angel, "So you lifted the knife off of me?" His arms folded over his chest. I'm not sure if he was annoyed or impressed.

She nodded, still holding it. "You have a serious problem. The stone is lodged in the hilt of this dagger. It won't come out. If it did, they would have given it to you to use already, Ivy. But it's stuck. Eric can't figure out why or how to dislodge it." She paused, licking her perfect pink lips. Her gaze met mine. Vulnerability was strewn across her face, "I say we take it to the other angel who used it."

I laughed, "Of course you'd say that." I reached out for the dagger, gripping part of the hilt and expecting Jenna Marie to release it, but her grip remained on the weapon.

Her eyes met mine, uncertain as to whether or not she should release it. The only thing she was asking for was to return to her love. I considered her request, not releasing the blade. Eric spoke next to me, "It's not a bad idea. And it's not stuck. There's something holding it in place, and unless we can get it out—you can't use it. Plus, the place is a tomb. Kreturus can't find us down there." He paused for a moment, and repeated himself, "It's not a bad idea."

Why was I resisting? Why didn't I want to go to the Lorren? If Eric could tolerate returning to that horrible place, I should be able to as well. But I couldn't. Something inside of me crept up my throat and choked me when Jenna Marie suggested it. I didn't want to go into the Underworld. Every time I went down there, I risked never coming out. And as for Collin and Jenna Marie, they'd never been in the Lorren. It may tempt them, or kill them before I find Lorren. Even then, I didn't know if he could turn it off. I didn't think the Lorren worked that way.

Speaking to Jenna Marie, I asked, "You know what the Lorren does to people who wander in there, don't you? Are you really willing to risk that?" She nodded.

As I turned to ask Collin, he spoke, "There's no need to ask me." He smiled at me. The joy that swam through me filled every part of my body. That's what Jenna Marie was asking for. The chance to be reunited with her long lost love. I couldn't deny her of that.

Voices carried on the wind outside of the tent. More people were coming. Possibly angels. Possibly Martis. I didn't want to wait any longer. If it was a risk they were willing to take...

"Let's go," I said. I wrapped my arms around Collin, as Eric pulled Jenna Marie closer. "Closer is better Jenna Marie, otherwise it hurts more for both of you. Eric, do you have enough power to do this?"

He nodded, "For now." Grinning at Jenna Marie, he added, "It burns like Hell. Get ready little angel. You're about to enter the forbidden zone. Crossing borders has devastating effects."

Her voice warbled, "I don't care. I'll endure whatever pain, pay any price. If I incinerate, if I don't make it, tell him," she paused and reconsidered who should take her final words to Lorren. She looked over at me, "Tell him I love him."

Something twisted my gut. "Tell him yourself," I smiled at her. My eyes cut to Eric. He wouldn't let her burn up. I trusted him fully. "Let's go."

CHAPTER TWENTY-TWO

Collin and I gasped as we crashed onto the golden floor. He'd never been in here before, so I held onto his hand and wouldn't let him wander away. He was admiring the golden flowers and jewels beneath our feet when Eric and Jenna Marie crashed into the ground next to us.

With a gasp, Eric yelled, "Something's wrong! She's not moving!" There was panic in his voice. Eric cradled her head between his hands, and lowered his ear to her chest. "She's barely breathing." We were in the place where Lorren usually sat. The table he'd healed me on was behind us, and empty. Lorren wasn't here. Where was he? It's not like he could leave.

Kneeling next to Eric, I glanced at Jenna Marie. Her perfectly pink lips were turning blue. The rose blush that was usually on her cheeks was gone. She had a sickly pallor that seemed to worsen as I looked at her. "Quickly," I said to Eric, "move her to the table." Eric did as I asked, abandoning his usual snide retort. When he laid her down on the golden slab, her hair fell away from her face. As Eric slid his arm out from under her neck, a dark trail appeared on his skin. I stared at it. His eyes met mine. We both realized what happened at the same time.

Jenna Marie had a wound that was inflicted by the Dreanok. Their talons were poisonous. I'd assumed she removed all of their venom, but the stain on Eric's arm indicated otherwise. The effonation put too much stress on her body. It caused the wound to worsen. She was being poisoned, the same way I was. Eric tore off her knitted cap by its flower and threw it aside. I took a hair band from my wrist and moved her hair away from her cheek and neck. Rolling Jenna Marie onto her side, I nearly wretched when I saw the extent of the Dreanok's damage. The long line of sliced flesh reached from her cheek back to her ear, and continued around to the back of her head. The Dreanok's talon sliced off the lower half of her ear, leaving a stump that had putrefied.

I blurted out, "Why didn't she heal this?"

"She can't," Eric replied. "There are certain things that can't be healed. The scars will remain, no matter what we do, but we have to draw out the poison before she dies."

His sarcastic voice pelted into my back like a brick. Lorren said, "Then let her die." The bitterness in his voice made me turn slowly. How would he react? I brought him his lost love, and now she was marred and half dead. Lorren's black hair hung in his face. His shoulders had that downward slant they always had. The muscles in his arms were tense as he swung his head around the room, asking, "What are you doing, Ivy? You never do what I tell you to! You never…"

Lorren was preparing for a full out berating, but before he could get going, I moved away from the golden slab, revealing a mass of blonde hair and smooth porcelain skin. He stopped speaking. Lorren's jaw hung open as his voice died in his throat. Lorren rushed at the table, not believing what he saw. His hands gripped her face, turning her lifeless body toward him. The expression in his dark eyes rapidly shifted as he recognized her.

A voice as soft as a caress slid from his lips, "Jenna. My God." His fingers traced the line along her cheek and back around to her ear. He stared at her and shivered, shaking his head. "I can't heal this. I can't..." he voice drifted off as panic choked him.

Grabbing his shoulders, I turned Lorren away from her. When he met my gaze he snapped back to himself and shook free of my grip. "Why can't you heal her?" I asked. "You drew poison out of me—why is this different?"

He stared over my shoulder, and then back down at me. Lorren's thin body was so much taller than my own. "It's Dreanok venom. She's an angel. I can't separate the poison from her body. Once they blend, they don't part." Lorren's face turned white, like someone flipped a switch as he spoke. He pushed past me and cradled her hand in his. "I thought I'd never see you again," he fell on his knees, placing his elbows on the golden slab and burying his face in the hand that held hers. The despair was so thick that I couldn't breathe. No one moved. No one spoke. My gaze remained on her ever paling face as her breath slowed and became shallow.

I couldn't watch anymore. I pressed my eyes closed and as my lids lowered, the world went black. I could see Locoicia's handwriting sprawled in golden letters in my mind. The spell would take all of my power. Possibly more than I could give. The pain price would drain me completely. My eyes flicked opened. I stared at her prone body wondering if it would work. My gaze shifted to Lorren. The question was, would he let me?

Collin saw my eyes narrow as I thought. He could tell I was thinking of doing something, and that I needed him to help me. Eric stared at Jenna Marie, no doubt infatuated by her pain. He was so fucked up. Thinking of the spell, I knew that I needed a golden spike. Turning, I twisted one of the flowers off the wall. The stem snapped in my hand. Collin was the only one watching me. I moved toward Jenna Marie like I was going to lay the flower on her chest. With a jerk of my head toward Lorren, Collin moved to stand behind him.

I flicked my eyebrows three times counting, starting the spell. Three words. One rose. I uttered the first word, smoothing the shirt across her chest, making sure there was nothing in my way. Lorren seemed to notice I was there and lifted his head. Tears stained his cheeks. His wet lashes clung together in clumps. He was going to kill me. I hoped to God that Collin understood what I wanted him to do. I uttered the second word. Recognition flashed in his eyes. Lorren heard the spell. The banishing word.

His eyes widened, and he asked, "What are you...?" but he never finished his question. I uttered the third word, and raised the rose over my head. Slamming the stem down quickly, it shook her body as the golden rose became rigid and cut through bone, plunging into her heart. Jenna Marie's body jerked as the rose pierced her chest. A raw scream erupted from her lips. At the same time, Lorren launched himself at me with his arms outstretched, ready to snap my neck. The pain in his eyes was too great to fathom. I jerked back just as Collin's arms wrapped around Lorren from behind, holding him back.

The first pain price ripped through me. Gritting my teeth, I snapped at Eric, "Help him! Don't let Lorren remove the rose. It has to stay there until the spell is done!" I screamed as the second pain price slammed into me. Collin's eyes were wide, as he maintained his iron grip around the tall and lanky Lorren. But every moment Collin held him back, Lorren became more enraged. Lorren no longer looked at his love. Instead, he glared at me with death in his eyes. Eric watched, utterly unable to move. The pain surrounding him—my pain price and Jenna Marie's dying body—trapped him. Eric pressed his hands to his head, trying to ignore it. Trying to do as I asked.

As the third pain price slammed into me, Jenna Marie's body arched on the table. She let out a wail of agony and when she was done, her body stopped moving. Her chest was covered in red as the blood from the rose buried in her heart soaked through her shirt. Jenna Marie was deathly still.

Lorren's hands reached for me as I fell to the floor, unable to support my own weight. I tried to numb myself, but I couldn't. The pain price tore through me, ripping, breaking, bleeding. It felt like acid was on fire in a streak across my chest. Pressing my fingers to my breast I looked down and saw the line—the sapphire serum—spider across my chest in tiny veins of deep blue. My body slowly curled into a ball as the pain price tried to take more than I had to offer.

As I lay on my side with my cheek pressed to the cold golden floor, Eric's foot appeared next to my face. He lifted me in his arms and pressed a kiss to my lips. A blast of relief filled me, starting at my lips, and rushed through the rest of my body. Eric held me, looking down at me as I heard Lorren screaming, still restrained by Collin.

Eric spoke softly so only I could hear, "It's not time. Come back to me, Ivy." My eyes flickered open as the last of the pain ebbed and ceased. I sucked in a gasp of air, my body shaking, unable to speak. Eric cradled me in his arms. His amber eyes were wide. A crooked grin lined his lips. It felt too intimate, but he didn't release me, and I was too weak to move. "You noble bastard. That spell would have killed you if I didn't help you."

I laughed once, weakly. It made me flinch. Every rib felt as if it'd cracked. "But you did..." My eyes drooped, as I fought to keep them open.

Eric watched my face, and said, "Sleep, Ivy. Me and loverboy will make sure Lorren thanks you instead of killing you." I couldn't protest. It wasn't a choice. My lids slammed closed like they were made of lead, and the world went black.

CHAPTER TWENTY-THREE

My neck was at an odd angle. It turned out that was because I was resting in someone's lap. Fingers stroked across my forehead, brushing the curls out of my face. My eyes were too heavy. I couldn't open them yet, but I could hear them talking.

"That shouldn't have worked," Eric stated. His voice was far away, across the room maybe. "Ivy wove together some nasty spells that usually kill people. Apparently her twisted mind works well under pressure." He laughed

Collin, the voice above me—the arms holding me—chided, "I knew the same spells. They wouldn't have worked if I said them. Not like that." He didn't bother scolding Eric for his mocking tone. There was no point. His hand brushed across my cheek, warm and strong.

"That's what I mean," said Eric. "That's why she is what she is. She can do things that no one else can." There was something in his voice—admiration? It sounded foreign coming from him. Then he added, "But she keeps using her powers for good and nearly killing herself."

Silence filled the space. For a long time, no one said anything. I wondered what happened to Jenna Marie? Did it turn out the way I'd hoped? Where was Lorren? He was quiet. Collin spoke again, "I heard you. Before. When you kissed her," his voice was strained. He'd let Eric do what he needed to take and give power, but he didn't like it. Eric was silent, not offering an explanation. "Tell me." Collin's fingers brushed across my brow. I breathed in deeply, trying again to force my eyes open.

With a flutter, they opened to meet Collin's gaze. "Hey," he said sweetly, smiling at me. "You're awake." His voice was relieved. I swung my legs off the ledge we were sitting on and tried to sit up. Collin kept his arm around my back to steady me. "Whoa, easy, Ivy. Slow. Move slow."

A quick glance around the room revealed an emotionally muted Eric who sat on the floor with his hands behind his head, like he was at a picnic. Jenna Marie still remained on the table. Someone had draped a blanket over her. The rose that pierced her heart was gone, absorbed by her body. Lorren rested his face on the slab, watching her chest rise and fall.

Gazing across the room, I asked, "Did it work? Is she all right?" Lorren glanced at me, and nodded once before turning his face back to Jenna Marie. His fingers gently stroked her cheek as he stared at her in awe. Her golden hair fell in piles around her head and shoulders, but I could still see the scar from here. It left a wide white path across her face. My stomach sank. "Her ear?"

"Still gone," Collin said softly. I frowned. "You saved her. It was more than any of us could do. She woke up before, asking for you. She's healing fast, and once this is over, she won't have to worry about it anymore. But, you..." Collin paused. His hand touched the side of my face, turning my gaze toward him. "You seem to have cracked open the venom in your chest. It's back."

"It was never gone, Collin. Just hidden. Locoicia said she could remove it. She said Lorren could have healed it, but... wouldn't.'"

Lorren's gaze didn't turn to meet mine. His voice boomed across the room, echoing with irritation, "I can still heal it if you had your soul." Horror made me try and jump up. As if that would be enough to silence Lorren and stop his flow of words.

"What do you mean?" Collin asked. He gripped my arm to steady me. "She has her soul."

Lorren's neck snapped toward us, "So do you."

I buried my face in my hands, and sat down hard. Lorren spoke softly, "I'm sorry Ivy, but I'm not lying for you. Not when it could save you. She needs her soul—all of it. The piece you have, she needs it back. If she has it, I can heal her. Now. Here. But she won't do it. She wouldn't tell you. She's known for a while, and from the look on your face, I'm guessing that it never came up."

Collin's hands slid over mine. "Of course I'd give it back to you. Ivy, why didn't you ..."

But I cut him off, "No! It's not an option. Lorren!" I growled at him. Fury made me want to say a million things to him, but I bit my tongue. Jenna Marie's eyes were closed. She was sleeping, healing from my spell. I pulled my hair, and huffed out of the space. Moving quickly I turned twice, then two more times, loosing myself in the Lorren. I needed to be alone. I had to think. Collin didn't follow me. He couldn't. Walking into the Lorren was death for anyone who hadn't survived it previously. I had. After walking forever, I slid down a flowered wall, landing hard on my butt. A rush of air was forced out of my lungs. I pulled my knees to my chest and lowered my head. I don't know how long I sat like that or when Eric appeared. I sensed him sitting next to me at one point. I could smell his blood and knew it was him.

"Go away," I snapped. But Eric ignored me, sitting less than an inch away—close enough to comfort, but not touch.

"You're a diva, you know that?" Eric's voice was scolding. I didn't take the bait. I didn't look up. I pressed my face harder against my knees and remained silent. "You're the only one who can help people. You're the only one who can risk her life to save someone she cares about, or someone who annoys her. I can't believe you risked your life for her. You knew the cost before you started, and tried to pay the pain price anyway—when you were weak. You're a fool, Ivy. A self-absorbed fool."

I lifted my head, and stared at him, not bothering to wipe away the tears on my wet face. "Fuck you, Eric!" I jumped to my feet, intending to walk further into the maze, but Eric clamped his hand around me, and thrust me into the wall. Golden flowers bent under my weight, poking into my back. His hands pressed my wrists next to my head as he leaned closer.

Eric hissed, "Very tempting, but not today. Thank you."

"I wasn't offering, Eric!" I twisted, trying to pull away from him. But the best way to deal with Eric—usually—isn't to fight back. I forced the tension out of my body and leaned back into the flowers. Usually, this was the right way to deal with him, but not this time.

He released my wrists. But he didn't lower his hands. Instead, his arm wound back with his palm open and it flew across my cheek. My face turned to the side, as he struck me. The sting blossomed, growing stronger. "Wake up, Ivy!" I turned, looking up at him. "You die! You die without him! You die without me! Collin's doing what he came here for. And it wasn't to hold your hand and pat you on the back. This is what he was meant for. This is why he's here—to give you back your soul. It protected you before, and it saved him. And now it's time to take whatever gifts anyone offers you, and say thank you."

I screamed in his face, "Fuck you." I didn't want to hear what he was saying. The things he suggested meant we were all martyrs—all three of us. I couldn't accept that.

"Yes, you said that already," he tilted his head, folding his arms across his chest. Eric's eyes were gold, deep gold. The same color as the walls.

"I wasn't done! You don't know what you're asking me to do! You don't know what will happen to him. I can't lose him, Eric. I can't risk it. It's utterly selfish, and I won't do it."

Eric growled. Reaching out he grabbed my face in his hand and jerked my gaze to meet his. "No! This is selfish—running off like a petulant child who didn't get her way. You don't get your way this time!" I ripped my face out of his grasp, trying to push him back. He was starting to piss me off. But my powers were still weak. Eric could strong-arm me now, and he'd win. When I tore my face away, he grabbed onto my shoulders and pushed me back into the wall, pinning me with his body. His hands moved down my sides as I tried to kick him in the groin, but I couldn't get a good shot.

When I felt his hands on my waist, sliding higher, I screamed, "Eric! Stop!"

He pulled away from me with lust in his eyes. I didn't try to control my emotions. I was afraid. Afraid of losing Collin. Afraid Eric would overpower me. Afraid. His hands lingered on the hem of my shirt. With a swift movement, the shirt was ripped over my head. I stood there in front of him in nothing but jeans and a bra. The look in Eric's eyes was carnal. His finger pressed against the deep blue lines on my chest. They spanned an arch from my shoulder to under my bra.

He traced the spidering veins of blue poison as he spoke, "This is a time bomb. You know it will kill you and you know you're already on borrowed time. Satan's Stone won't heal this, Ivy. You'd be a fool if you used the stone for anything but to defeat Kreturus." His voice softened as he stared at my breast, gently touching the soft marred skin with his thumb.

My hand caught his wrist, stopping him before he felt me up again. "I'll use it for both."

"You can't," he strained against my hand, leaning into me, feeling my body against his. But he didn't overpower me. It gave me a sense of control that I thought I lost. "One wish per user, with one horrifying payment." His lips were close to mine when he whispered, "It'll be worse than mine. Let Collin heal you." His body rested against mine, pressing me into the wall. His hands stroked my hair. My heart pounded in my chest. Angry. Embarrassed. Afraid. He breathed deeply, "If you don't get your fear under control, I won't be able to walk away."

I hadn't realized that Eric was fighting his instincts at all. But he was. Every muscle in his neck was corded tightly like rope. There was strain in his gaze, when he looked back down at me. It was a carnal caress. Gazing at his cheek, I asked, "What is it you want to do to me?

Every time you feel this—rage—or whatever it is, what does it make you want?"

Surprise washed across his face, "You. In pain. In ecstasy. And everything in between." He pushed away from me. I stood there for a moment, watching his back as he sucked in steadying breaths. When he finally turned around, he said, "We have to go back. And Ivy, this may be the hardest thing you've ever done, but you have to let him give you that kiss."

CHAPTER TWENTY-FOUR

I followed Eric back to the Lorren in silence. His words unnerved me. All of them. I couldn't speak. I couldn't breathe. When we walked into the golden room, I saw Collin sitting across from an upright Jenna Marie and Lorren. There was a grin on Lorren's face like nothing I'd ever seen before. He had just pressed a kiss to her cheek, when he saw me.

I couldn't help but smile awkwardly.

Lorren said, "I sent Eric after you. Collin wanted to go, but I wouldn't let him. This is the only place that is safe within the Lorren for him and you," he glanced at Jenna Marie. "I wish I could offer you more."

"You're all I could want. You're all I need," she pressed her lips to Lorren's and kissed him deeply. I blushed, looking away. Eric muttered something rude, and sat down on the floor.

Collin walked toward me, cupping my face in his hands. "Why didn't you tell me? You know I'd do anything for you—anything. I could have saved you a great deal of pain. Ivy, why'd you keep this from me?"

"It'll change you," I pleaded. "You'll be soulless. I don't know what will happen, or if you'll even survive. I couldn't turn you Valefar again—or worse... It's not like I can just give you back your soul. Our souls are fused together. They had to be or you wouldn't have survived that night Eric nearly killed you. I felt the magic as it left me and went into you. My soul isn't mine anymore. It's tangled with yours. Collin, taking that away from you. I just can't risk it." His fingers tangled in my hair as I spoke. His blue gaze focused on my mine. There was an expression in his eyes that was so powerful, I wanted to look away, but he wouldn't let me.

"You're worth the risk," he whispered. His hands slid from my shoulders to my cheeks, slowly. His eyes darted between my eyes and my lips as I spoke.

"I can't let you," I replied softly, unable to look away.

He released me, gazing at the jeweled floor and said, "Tell her." I wasn't sure who he was talking to, but it seemed that they had already discussed it.

Lorren spoke first, "When I used the stone, it nearly killed me. Ivy, it'll take every ounce of strength you have to command its powers and live."

I snapped at him, turning to the spot where he sat, laying back against the wall with Jenna Marie in his arms. "Would you be able to do it? Would you risk losing her?" But he had risked losing her, and did. I swallowed hard. Thinking. Not liking my options, but not seeing another way out.

Eric spoke from his prone position on the floor. His fingers were laced behind his head as he stared at the ceiling. "You know he did," he replied to the question directed at Lorren. "You're a smart girl, despite my criticisms." He paused, staring blankly. His jaw tensed, revealing his anxiety despite his cavalier pose. "When I used the stone, it destroyed me—and remade me. It ripped me apart, seam by seam. And I told them Ivy."

My heart lurched. He didn't! That was a secret between us. I wasn't even sure if it was true—if his curse would affect me. Anger and fear were mixing together, pooling restlessly in the pit of my stomach. "Stop it," he chided and sprang up. Walking toward me with a fierceness in his step, he looked down, saying,

"My curse—the price I paid to use the stone—will affect you. To date it has destroyed everyone I've cared about." His eyes were like golden flames, "Every. Single. One. No one escaped its reach. Everyone died. You know this! We already talked about it, and yet you sit here and act like this won't be a big deal." His index finger pressed into my chest where the poison was visible again just above my neckline, "This promises your death as well. The Omen, that dragon—if it's really the Omen—promises destruction. Your life is over. It's possible you'll try to use the stone, and just die before it even does anything." He removed his hand, and turned his back to me. Tension knotted his broad shoulders.

Eric's words made me shiver. They presented a finality that I hadn't heard until that point. They made me face the hopelessness that was presented to me. I had to use an incredibly powerful source of magic, and hope I was strong enough for its magic to course through me, like a piece of wire, without dying on contact. Collin remained leaning against the wall, his hands behind him with his feet kicked out in front. He watched me carefully as they spoke plainly, failing to sugar-coat anything. They said what would happen; they said what was real.

I nodded slowly, then turned to Collin, "And the price I pay for using the stone will be higher... " A hysterical laugh bubbled to my lips. "Collin, I can't do this! I can't. It's impossible. My body's supposed to be a conduit for some massive sort of dark power that will kill Kreturus—it sounds so impossible. He could snatch the stone out of my hands before I even have a chance to use it, and use it himself."

Collin shoved off the wall and stood in front of me. He could hear my resolve shattering, as I spoke. Reaching for me, he took my hands in his, "That's why Eric and I are going. That's why we have to be there. We can't use the stone down here, it has to be above ground, and in front of Kreturus. "

A puzzled look crossed my face, "Why can't we use it in secret? Why does it have to be in the open? In front of him? He'll make a grab for the stone, and if he gets it, everything will be so much worse."

His hands rubbed smoothly over mine. Assuredly, he said, "He doesn't get the stone."

"But how do you know?" I asked.

"Because of the thirteenth prophecy. Because the depiction of power on the stem of the cup was of you—not him. Kreturus knows he's fighting a losing battle without you. That's why he wanted you. That's why he waited..."

I studied Collin's hands, the strong fingers that tapered as gently as a sculpture. "He said he waited because my powers aren't fully formed. He made it sound like they were only in infancy."

Collin brushed a curl away from my eyes, "He doesn't realize you have the stone. The only thing he knows is that your powers change, and you become strong enough to destroy him as if he were nothing. He assumed your powers weren't fully formed, but they are. It's the stone that's changing things. It's the stone that gives you the power to destroy him, and make you the goddess you saw on the stem of the chalice." He leaned close, keeping his hand on my face, rubbing his thumb slowly across my cheek. "Let me give you this. Your sacrifice saved me. I'll always be yours. It won't change me—I promise."

"But how can you be sure?" Tears were pricking my eyes. I knew I had to accept his offer. I knew I had to drink his soul to reclaim my own. It was the only way we could win. There were no other options.

His voice was a whisper that only I could hear, "Because we were soul mates before we shared a soul, and we'll be soul mates after." He leaned closer, his dark lashes lowering as his full lips pressed into mine. His hands slid down my sides, pulling me closer as the kiss deepened. That was when I felt it—our conjoined soul was deep within him—mashed together like a ball of Playdough that had once been separate colors. They were now woven so tightly together that there was no way to pull the two souls apart. It was the gift that restored his life. And now I was taking it back. No, he was giving it. I kissed him deeper, wrapping my arms around his neck.

Our souls were floating freely, tantalizing my senses, and awakening the darkness that craved souls within me. At first the sensation frightened me, causing me to tense. I almost pulled away, but Collin slid his hand around to the back of my head, as his other hand lowered to the small of my back, pulling me even closer. Every inch of my body was pressed against his. When I stopped fighting what I was, his grip on me loosened, gently moving up my back, and cupping my face.

As Collin's soul was called to me, like a butterfly on a breeze, I thought I could hear him. His voice brushed my mind gently, but there were no words for what he felt. It was a mixture so intense that tears formed in the corners of my eyes. He thought I was brave and beautiful like a Greek goddess, like the version of me on the goblet. Confident and certain of what to do and when to do it. Admiration and adoration thickly coated his thoughts. The thing that startled me most was that there was no hint of fear, no underlying thoughts of losing me. He was certain we'd always be together. He was confident that nothing would tear us apart.

As his soul floated past his lips, I felt him sigh in relief. The mental connection I'd had vanished, and the only thing I could feel were his arms around me, his lips against mine. I kissed him deeper, as his soul melted into my body like it belonged there. It felt like wrapping your body in a warm blanket after being frozen. I felt stronger as the piece of lost soul fit back into the place I'd torn it from. Afraid to break the kiss, afraid to pull away, my lips lingered pressing gently to his.

Collin was breathing hard. He held our faces close, gazing at me. His chest swelled as his ragged breathing slowed. Finally he spoke, "I'm still here—and I still love you."

Eric's voice pierced my ears, clanging annoyingly like someone beating the bottom of a pot, "Lorren, heal her before I hurl."

CHAPTER TWENTY-FIVE

Having the remaining sapphire serum removed was somewhat humiliating. The only person who wasn't watching was Jenna Marie. Collin held my hand, as I squeezed mercilessly. As Lorren spun the rose, it made the venom move through my body. The pain was the only thing that distracted me from having three guys staring at my exposed chest. My back arched off the table as I grit my teeth.

"Almost done," Lorren said, swirling the rose so quickly that it was a silvery blue blur.

I gripped down on Collin's hand, trying hard not to scream.

Eric said, "Why is it hurting her like this? It seems to be draining her." But Lorren remained silent, working quickly to remove the rest of the poison. When no one answered him, his irritation became audible, "Lorren," he snapped, "is the venom spreading? What the hell's happening?"

"Don't know," Lorren replied. It sounded as if he couldn't speak as he concentrated on what he was doing. "It's close to her heart. She's weak. The poison may be spreading."

Another gasp of air and a silent scream ripped from my mouth, as I crushed Collin's hand. I could feel the venom ripping through my chest. It was like a wave of ice burning through my veins as the sapphire serum moved. The voices around me started to sound distorted, like we were under water.

"Her grip's weakening," Collin said quietly. His fingers remained wrapped with mine. I could feel his gaze on the side of my face.

"Awh, fuck," Eric growled. He hesitated, hovering over me as if he could do something but wasn't certain if he should. In a second, I understood why. Eric leaned down, and before I knew what happened I felt his lips on mine. It wasn't a kiss—it was a transfer of power. Eric infused me with some of his. As he did so, a cold rush of air filled my lungs. The trickle of power continued, and the pain that was shooting through me dulled.

Collin said to Lorren, "He's drawing her pain into himself. Finish this Lorren. Hurry, or you'll kill both of them!" Panic snuck into Collin's normally controlled voice. His fingers pressed against mine.

As I lay on the golden slab with my eyes closed, I felt peaceful. The pain coursing through me seemed distant, like a memory. But it wasn't the numbness that Locoicia taught me. It was better. Something else. Later I learned it was Eric, thwarting his curse, feeding me power and taking my pain for me. When his lips pulled away, I sucked in a gasp of air and sat up breathing hard. My hand flew to my racing heart, pressing it, willing it to slow beneath my palm. As my breathing slackened, my eyes focused again and I realized that I was sitting up half naked. And I didn't really care.

Breathe, Ivy, breathe, I told myself. My gaze was turned down, not seeing much, but I did see him—Eric—sitting on the floor ripping his hands through his hair. He felt my eyes on his face and turned his head toward me, his eyes still downcast.

"Thank you," I said softly, though I didn't think he heard. Someone wrapped a blanket around my shoulders, and lowered me down on the table. My eyelids were drooping, heavy with sleep, as I felt

Lorren's hands pressing into the soft tissue on my chest. Collin's familiar touch traced the path that the Guardian's tooth left across my torso.

"Will it stay like that?" he asked. But I didn't hear more. I blacked out into a blissful sleep.

CHAPTER TWENTY-SIX

There were no dreams, only silence and security in my sleep. I felt his arms around me, never letting go. I was aware of Collin holding me and speaking nonsense, stroking my long hair. When I stirred, I breathed in deeply and peeled open my eyes. I was lying against Collin's chest, and he was singing softly. I pressed my eyes closed to listen to his song, but he'd already seen I was awake.

"Hey," he said quietly. "Feel better?" He was smiling at me.

As I glanced up into Collin's face, my eyes widened in horror. His mark! I darted up in his arms, and twisted toward him, "Its red! You're a Valefar again!"

But Collin calmly took my hands and said, "yes, but I'm your Valefar. You made me this time... not Kreturus. It's okay, Ivy."

Licking my lips, I tried to stop staring, but couldn't. Eric's breath in my ear made me jump when he spoke, "Ivy's second Valefar is much tamer than her first. He seems the same." Eric sounded disappointed. I glanced at him, and he shrugged. "What? I had to make sure the guy wasn't still commanded by Kreturus. Couldn't have him fucking with you when you go to kill the bastard." Did they fight while I was asleep?

I bristled, but Collin turned my face toward his and away from Eric, "It's better this way. You have your soul back. I'm still me. And he's still..." he jabbed his thumb at Eric, "him. Only one thing is different. Your scar from the tooth—it has healed but drawing out the venom seems to have changed it. Look." Collin unwrapped the blanket that covered my shoulders. I looked down at my skin and saw the arch of pale blue vines tattooed on my distorted flesh. They spanned from my shoulder to the center of my chest, following the line of the scar across my torso. My jaw hung opened as I stared.

"I'm sorry," Lorren started to say, but I tugged the blanket around my body, suddenly aware of the gender of the eyes on me. "The magic I used to heal you left a mark and the scar from the tooth will always be there. I tried to remove it, but … "

I hushed him, "Don't apologize. It doesn't matter. And it's better than demon scales and snake hair. Thank you, Lorren." I smiled at him, hesitant to meet his gaze and was surprised to see him smile back. What's another scar? Another marking on my body? In a few moments it wouldn't matter much anyway. I'd fight Kreturus and kill or be killed. Living was the only thing that mattered right then. Living and having this strange collection of friends I'd gained since the night Jake attacked me. We were such an unlikely match that I knew it had to be fate that brought us together.

All eyes were on me, waiting for whatever was next. I cleared my throat, "So, somebody give me a shirt 'cause I don't care what the artist of the Thirteenth Prophecy thought—I'm not killing Kreturus half-naked."

CHAPTER TWENTY-SEVEN

Shannon's dagger was clutched tightly in my fist. We walked the frozen earth with the wind howling, looking for the demon. After much debate, we decided that Eric and Lorren couldn't free the stone in the hilt because they'd already used it. Collin couldn't remove it because he wasn't me. And that was true. When I touched the polished black stone on the bottom of the dagger's base, it slid out in my hand. Satan's Stone was identical to the pendant around my neck, except the center flowers burned like they were on fire. I'd pressed my finger against the glowing rock, surprised that it didn't burn. The tips of the intertwined peonies flamed white hot, with the centers burning deep reds and oranges. This part of the stone was alive. The flames moved within it, pulsating, and waiting to be used, waiting to unveil a surge of power so vast that it all but destroys the one who uses it.

Before going topside, I inserted the stone back into the dagger. It ensured Kreturus couldn't use it if something went horribly wrong. My feet were frozen as we trudged through ankle deep snow. The ground was covered with flecks of dirty sleet, the sky was bright and still stained red. Snow clouds drifted lazily above, unaware of the turmoil below.

Collin and I walked shoulder to shoulder. Eric trailed behind. I asked, "Do we need to worry about the dragon? Omen or not, I thought it was Kreturus'."

Eric spoke, "The Omen doesn't belong to anyone, if that's what it is. He may appear and interfere. But we won't know what that interference will look like until he does." Eric smacked the front of his pants, breaking ice off his thighs as he walked.

Collin lifted my hand to his lips, and pressed a kiss onto the back of my hand. Turning toward him, I could see him smiling. The boys seemed more stoked for this than I was. Killing stuff didn't make me giddy. I did it because I had to. I smiled back, enjoying his company until we heard a grackle screech in the distance. I stopped and turned. My jaw dropped in slow motion as my eyes widened. The horizon that had been blood red seconds ago was turning black. The bodies of grackles poured over the edge like hot tar. They shrieked through the air, intense and angry—and headed directly toward us.

My heart pounded in my chest, ready to run, when Collin grabbed my wrist and shook his head. "You don't need to run anymore. This is nothing for you. Blast them out of the sky."

Uncertain, I glanced at Eric and could see that he wasn't running either. He stood there with his arms folded, nodding in agreement with Collin. I was overruled. I huffed, "You both suck."

Collin smiled at me, "With any luck, you'll draw Kreturus out." A grin twisted across his face. But the only thing I could watch was the sky filling with grackles, pouring closer and closer in an endless stream. They covered the red sky like spilled ink. My throat tightened and my heart pounded in my ears. We were going to let them come. It would draw out Kreturus. It would end this battle once and for all. Knowing that, however, didn't erase the visions of these birds destroying Collin, plucking him apart piece by piece with their pointy beaks.

Eric turned away from us, watching the screeching birds flying closer and closer with fascination. He finally spoke, without turning around to meet my gaze, "These creatures terrify you, Ivy. I can feel your fear... Mute it. Now," he growled.

I had no doubt Eric was devising a way to torment me with the hideous birds, using them to rip my flesh open as he kissed me or some other deranged fantasy. I searched for the numb place within me. Locoicia taught me to be numb, to allow it to flood me so I could pay the pain price associated with my spells. Over time, the bloodlust weakened and no longer interfered. It dulled like it was supposed to. This time, I was able to pull up the apathy to spare Eric and to think more clearly. I knew I detested the birds, but I didn't realize how much they terrified me until Eric said something. When I finished, I looked up and saw an odd expression on Eric's face.

He grinned, and said, "You're far more twisted than I am." I blushed. It was as if he heard my thoughts—my fears. I wondered if he could. I didn't think that was possible, and yet—the expression on his face said he saw something within me. I pushed the thought away. Eric glanced up at the birds and then back at Collin and said, "Good luck with her."

I wanted to take the bait and fight with him, but I didn't. The birds were too close, swooping lower and lower. Their beady black and gold eyes were crazed, and they shot like arrows toward us. Eric and Collin flanked me. I held up my hands and moved my lips, saying a simple spell. My power flowed through me and formed a wall around us. The barrier wasn't visible. It didn't stop the wind, but it would prevent anything living from crossing its boundaries. It was perfect.

The first few birds, the strongest that flew ahead of the flock—smashed into the invisible barrier, cracking their necks and falling to the snow at our feet. Closing my eyes, I chose the spell. The spell that would decimate the entire flock of evil, flesh-loving creatures—and catch Kreturus' attention. The word rolled in my mouth and off my tongue in a whisper. Energy coursed through me, stronger than before. Starting with the grackle closest to us, the black glossy feathers slowly glowed red like embers, before they combusted into bright red flames. The bird's shrill screeches intensified, as one by one, the entire flock of birds fell from the heavens in a ball of flames. The black wave that covered the sky, burned brightly for several moments, screeching the loudest wail that I'd ever heard, before the last grackle fell dead in the snow. The charred bodies turned to ash, melting into the frozen ice at our feet.

Collin slid his hand around my waist, staring at the empty sky, "He definitely saw that."

"Or heard it," Eric added, staring at the horizon. "Get ready..."

As if I could be ready. As if there was a way to mentally prepare myself for what would happen. Instead of saying those things, I nodded and threaded my fingers through Collin's, squeezing tightly. The ring he gave me for my birthday bit into my skin as I squeezed.

Our plan was simple, but it hinged on Kreturus acting as he had every other time we met. He was insistent on gaining my allegiance. This time I would draw it out. Things would go differently this time. As soon as he was close enough, I would use the stone. Proximity mattered. It was everything. If Kreterus didn't come close enough, I knew I had to lure him closer. Collin and Eric would help me draw him closer if the old demon didn't comply. It was simple. It should have worked. All I had to do was surrender and say yes. One single word would change everything. This would end.

I smiled at Collin before returning my gaze to the horizon. That's when I saw him. The boy dressed in black was illuminated by crimson light from the moon. Kreturus. His dark hair whipped around with the wind. There was no coat on his body to seal out the frigid air. He stood there, still wearing his tattered tux as if he'd been waiting. He was too far away. He stopped out of reach. I had to draw him closer.

Without a word the ancient demon threw a spell at us. I increased the power on my shield to repel his incantation. The pain price hit me hard. I gritted my teeth and felt it roll off my back, feeling like it took my skin with the power it took from me.

My fingers twitched, wanting to use the stone, but Eric shook his head, "Not yet."

They'd explained that using dark magic was kind of like making a deal with a demon. It would twist things to suit its needs. My wish had to be concise, and those it affected needed to be present. I seriously doubted there was another innocuous Kreturus somewhere the Stone could kill, and say *tah-dah, I did it*, but I wasn't going to chance that.

Kreturus' shoulders were tense as he moved closer, blue eyes piercing me from a distance. He scowled at me from below his brow, "You are too weak to defeat me. I sense it. I know..." His fists balled at his sides as he stopped less than twenty paces from me. Hatred flared in his eyes.

I didn't respond with words. Instead I threw a spell at him. It plucked him from the place he stood and dragged him forward. Closer. He had to be closer. Kreturus laughed like a madman, as he lurched toward us and stopped a few paces away.

Before he stopped, his gaze darted between Collin and Eric. "No more time for delicacy." His hand flew forward as I drew my dagger, untwisting the stone from its hidden place. My fingers moved quickly. In a matter of seconds I'd snap the stone together and make my wish. In a matter of seconds the vilest being I'd ever encountered would be dead. Kreturus' spell hurled at us, but I wasn't worried. I assumed my shield was strong enough. Nothing should have been able to penetrate it, but that wasn't what he did.

CHAPTER TWENTY-EIGHT

Kreturus used a spell that seeped through the protective barrier.

Before I knew what happened, Collin gasped and fell to his knees with his hands at his throat. Every muscle in his body tensed. There were invisible hands putting pressure on Collin's throat, choking him to death. It all happened so fast. I would play this moment over and over again in my mind, wondering if I hesitated—or what I did wrong. But time and time again, I would realize there was no time. There was nothing I could do.

The spell crushing Collin's throat tightened suddenly. The motion went beyond strangulation. Before I could blink, a sickening crack shattered the silence. Collin's hands fell away from his throat. He seemed suspended in air for a moment, like something was holding his lifeless body upright. When Collin's eyes rolled back in his head, I felt my dagger ripped out of my grip. Within a breath, the Celestial Silver lodged deeply in Collin's chest. My weapon was moved by an unseen hand. Blood bubbled from the wound, turning to black tar as Collin's body was released from the spell. He fell softly onto the white snow.

Horror stole my voice as Collin died in front of me. His wounds bled black before he was reclaimed by the earth. It was as if the ground opened, swallowing him whole below the layers of snow and ice.

Eric's eyes were wide, as the ground opened. Thinking fast, he grabbed onto the dagger and tugged it out of Collin's chest before he disappeared. Eric stepped swiftly away from Collin's decaying body. He placed the dagger in my hands. Its cold metal felt surreal in my grip. I twisted it, not thinking. Shock washed over me, crippling me. Making it impossible to think. Impossible to respond. After all this time, after everything we'd been through, I lost him. Collin died standing right next to me and I was powerless to save him. My throat tightened. Breathing seemed unimportant. Raising my gaze, I looked at the demon.

A wicked smile spread across his lips. His dark clothing hugged his form. Kreturus' voice boomed, "Previous bargain still stands. Your false sense of security is enchanting, but I'm done playing nice, Ivy. Come with me now, or I'll kill your other friend, and anything that resides in this fucking place that isn't demonic." He wanted me. He still wanted me. I could surrender. A shiver raked my spine as I stood there, abashed and defeated.

Eric spoke wildly in my ear, "Ivy, don't. Don't listen to him!" But I pulled away, dropping my shield—the shield that did nothing. The shield that failed to protect. Numbness flooded me, as I stepped toward him. Eric swore at my back, unable to stop me.

The wind ripped through my hair, throwing it wildly around my face. The ends of my curly hair weren't violet. I was utterly calm. I hated Kreturus, but I couldn't feel it. In that second, I was everything Locoiea taught me to be. I knew Collin was gone, but I couldn't feel the pain from his loss. There was nothing I could do to bring him back.

And the plan - it was shot to hell. I didn't even have the stone. The dagger was in Eric's hand, and the other half of the stone was … I didn't even know.

Kreturus was correct. His powers were stronger than mine.

Sliding my hand into my pocket, I stopped in front of the demon. Clarity filled my mind, making it easy to see a path. And I chose it. Nothing was by chance. Not ever again. This was my fate. It was time to accept it. I knew what to do.

My eyes were dry, and narrowed into slits. I asked, "Our previous bargain still stands? In its entirety?" Kreturus looked over my shoulder at Eric and nodded. I stared blankly ahead, and locked my jaw. The muscles in my arms were corded tightly, ready to burst. But I didn't wring my hands nervously. I glared at the demon, and nodded once. "Then I submit. I surrender."

Kreturus stepped forward, clutching my chin in his smooth hand. I didn't jerk out of his grip. He gazed into my docile face, taking in the vacant expression and asked, "I assume this is your exemption?" he asked, gesturing to Eric. Swallowing hard, I nodded. A new plan was forming, and twisting in my mind. There was no going backwards. Nothing would change what'd just happened. Nothing.

The demon reached into his pocket and withdrew a knife. Its blackened blade was made of brimstone. Smiling he said, "A good faith payment, then. Something to prove you won't break your promise this time." He drew the blade across his palm, tearing open the skin as it passed. A trail of bright red blood filled his palm. He held it out to me. Cupped within his palm was more demon blood than I'd ever seen. It slowly dripped between his fingers forming scarlet drops on the snow.

This was it. This was the moment that I'd fought so hard to prevent. This was the moment when I lost and became the ruthless girl in the prophecy. It was his blood that would hold me. Blood is power. And I could no longer refuse. There was no stone in my hand, no magic within my reach. The best I could do was save Eric.

Taking his hand, I raised it to my lips, ready to drink the blood that was seeping between Kreturus' fingers. Before opening my mouth, I stared at the bright red blood. Blood is power. As I went to part my lips, Eric's scream shattered my thoughts.

"NO!" Before I drank, he lunged for me. Eric grabbed onto my arm and jerked me away from Kreturus. The blood in the demon's palm splattered on the snow, melting it as it sank. Eric's hand slapped my face, stinging the skin. "Wake the fuck up! Collin died for you! You can't let things end this way. You can't! Finish this! Finish this now!"

Wake up? Was I asleep? Is that what he thought? I remained docile as Eric shook me, not blinking, and not meeting his gaze. With a flick of my wrist, I used a spell that threw him back into the snow, surprised that Kreturus didn't quench my powers. I glanced at the demon. He gave me a cursory nod, as if to say that more power was mine—if I drank. If I did the thing that Eric was begging me to not do.

Turning back to Eric I laughed hollowly. I was speaking truths, and twisting them into lies. It was necessary. "What will it take for you to see what I truly am, Eric? Will you not see it until it is so blatantly obvious, until there is no shadow of a doubt that I am beyond redemption?" Turning to Kreturus, I asked, "Do you have the cup? The Prophecy?" He knew what I meant. I didn't have to explain. The cup by itself had no power. It was a memento—proof that he won. Kreturus handed it to me with a sick smile on his face. As I spoke, he moved closer to me, claiming me. Thrusting the cup at Eric, I shoved it into his hands, screaming, "Look! See? That woman is me! What she did—it's what I am!" My jaw locked tight as he looked at it, turning it over on his fingers.

His voice was deep, as if he were desperately trying to control himself, "No," he said hurling the cup to the ground. "That is not you. It will never be you." He growled.

An exasperated scream, tore out of my throat. Kreturus watched in fascination, with power crackling at his fingertips. I took Shannon's dagger and sliced it through my clothes, tearing away my shirt so it draped across my body like the carving on the chalice. I threw away the dagger, and it sank into the snow somewhere behind me. I didn't look to see where it fell. My hands reached behind me and removed my bra. I cast it aside. I was the Prophecy One. She was me.

I glared at Eric. This was over. There was no more fighting, no more wars. This would end it. It would end everything. The black goblet lay on its side next to the silver dagger. Bending over, I retrieved the chalice, sliding my fingers across the snow. My fingers slid along the silver blade, but I didn't pick up the weapon.

Covering the top of the cup with my hand, I said to Eric, "Never doubt me again." My voice was low, commanding as my eyes met his. The wind whipped my hair to the side and blew through my torn shirt. The garment draped off my body, not covering me. I looked like the girl on the goblet - exactly.

Breathing through my mouth, eyes hooded, I turned back toward Kreturus. Numbness flooded me. I did not shiver as the winter wind wrapped itself around my flesh, chilling it. The demon's eyes lingered on my exposed skin, the curve of my breast. I breathed deeply and he smiled in appreciation. His hand lifted—touching me. All the while his eyes were on me, wanting me, hungry for every inch of me, and desiring every speck of power that coursed through my veins.

So, I offered him exactly what he wanted.

"Again," I commanded, indicating the Demon King should slice open his hand. "I'll give you more than my word this time. And I will bind you to your word as well. You will not kill Eric. He has your pardon. Are we still agreed?"

Eric lunged at me, but Kreturus brushed him away like a gnat. Eric screamed as he fell to the side, forced to the ground where he was held in place with a spell. "Agreed."

The demon had a satisfied smile across his face. He drew the blade across his palm. My heart was beating so fast. I couldn't slow it. Eric screamed behind me, but couldn't move. Kreturus held him down, pinning him to the frozen earth—forcing him to watch me destroy myself. Eric should have been frozen in silent fascination, but he wasn't. Rage coursed through him as he screamed, trying to make me stop. But I didn't. I'd never stop. Not now. There was no going back. This was all I could offer. It was everything and yet, it was not enough.

Kreturus' bloody palm dripped with blood when he made a fist. I took it in my hand, sliding the slick warmth along my face and across my lips. Smiling at him, I licked his blood, tasting him in my mouth. He breathed deeply, as I drew his hand to the goblet, allowing his blood to fill it. His warm blood slid through my stomach, and forced a smile to form on my lips. Watching greedily, I saw him fill the chalice with his blood. When the cup was full, Kreturus, pulled me to him connecting our hips with the rough tug. I held the goblet by the stem, careful not to spill the contents. He moved his hand to my breast, squeezing me hard. Blood covered my pale skin—his blood—demon blood that would bind me to him and control me for the rest of my life.

Kreturus' beautiful face had a hint of the expression that Eric's held before he did something that caused me pain. "Drink it. Show me your repentance…" his words were seducing. His voice made me tremble with pleasure and I'd only tasted the tiniest bit of his blood. His grip on my breast tightened, as he stroked me with his thumb. My knees went weak as my mind reeled. His warm breath slid over my body.

The cup trembled in my hand, and I nearly dropped it. Kreturus wrapped his hand around mine, and helped me hold it up. He tilted it back and the warm contents slid down my throat. I pressed my eyes closed, feeling the power of his blood surge through me. The desire he inflamed in me tore through my body, making me press my body harder into him. My mind was covered thickly in haze and lust. Eric's screams died with the wind. I could no longer hear him. He no longer mattered to me. It was only me and

Kreturus—and his blood. The warmth slid down my throat, burning as it went, warming my naked body.

Kreturus purred, "Drink my Queen, drink..." I could not disobey his command. I did not want to. I'd forgotten what I was doing, and how I'd gotten here. Collin's death didn't flash behind my eyes as I closed them, feeling the slick warmth slide down my throat. Kreturus held the cup to my lips, watching me submit to him, and abandon myself.

As the cup emptied, I felt something bump into my lips. It was smooth and round. It remained pressed to my lips as Kreturus watched me drink, unaware. Through lowered lashes, I watched him. Moaning, I spoke as I drank, "Hmmmm," I moaned happily, "I wish," my tongue slid over my lips, but Kreturus didn't lower the goblet. He wanted to make sure I was completely under his control. He wouldn't stop until I swallowed the last drop.

He watched me, eyes wide and dark, transfixed on my mouth, "What do you wish, my Queen?" He tilted the glass back, and I drank more. The ancient demon's face was close to mine. He was mesmerized, watching me with blazing eyes.

"Hhhhm, I wish the demon who fills my mouth with his power, with his blood, and washes it over my lips," he tilted the glass up, and I gulped the last of its contents. I swallowed an entire cup filled with his blood. Blood that was powerful, and binding. With a satisfied smile, Kreturus lowered the cup. Running his thumb along my face, he stopped, feeling the bump in my cheek. The expression on his face shifted, but I spoke, completing the curse, making my wish, " … were no more." I pursed my lips and smiled, revealing the glowing Satan's Stone between my front teeth.

Kreturus' eyes went wide before the magic took effect. He threw me back, intending to kill me. My back scraped against the ice as I fell next to Eric. Eric watched me, wildly trying to free himself, when a loud crack echoed through the sky. The earth shook under us, threatening to break open and swallow us whole. Kreturus' voice rang out, caught in a silent scream as the power of the stone manifested within his body. It filled every ounce of his being, every bit of his spirit, and every cell of his blood. I watched as my wish was granted—my horribly terrifying wish. Eric pushed himself to his elbows next to me, and threw himself over my body, pressing me to the ground. I could no longer see the demon's gruesome destruction.

Eric worked his jaw before he spoke, "You're insane. Completely, fucking, insane…" He kissed me, fully on the lips, releasing the last surge of power that was contained within him. Every last drop surged into me in a flash. As he pulled away, he held my cheek in his hand, "I'll find you again. I promise…" he pressed a kiss to my forehead and I was ripped out of his arms, as the price of using the stone was paid.

CHAPTER TWENTY-NINE

Energy was drained from my body as the stone was ripped in half. Half of the stone remained in my palm, the other half was hidden again, awaiting its next victim. My body was twisted, deformed, and I was barely aware of my form when I was sucked into darkness thicker than tar. Wind rushed by my ears in a deafening scream. I was sucked lower and lower through the earth, finally emerging numb and naked on a marble floor. Lifting my head, my hair trailed over my shoulders. An empty dais sat in front of me. Demons surrounded me, filling the room with treacherous eyes.

Rising, I felt my chest constrict, but I did not panic as one of the demons approached me. This was the place from my nightmare.

The demon bowed down low and said in a gurgled voice, "My Queen." Hundreds of demons then dipped, bowing to the floor in a black wave.

When they rose again, I tried to cover my nakedness with my hands. My long hair covered my breasts, but as I gazed at my arm, my eyes widened. Suddenly not caring that I was unclothed, I lifted my arm to my eyes. My flesh was almost translucent, shimmering blue in the dim light. Swallowing hard, I touched my arm, wondering if I was real. My fingers pressed into cold flesh. When I grabbed my hair it felt like frozen silk. Every inch of me was cold beyond comprehension. Wildly looking around for answers I saw him standing in the back of the room. Eric.

Tears formed in my eyes, as my jaw trembled. He walked toward me, his gaze drifting over me from head to toe. "You're alive..." was all he said. No snarky remarks. Nothing else to belittle me. He reached for my hands, but they slipped through his touch like air.

"You cannot touch my Queen," the demon hissed at Eric. "She is no longer with body."

My voice came out half strangled, "What does that mean?"

The demon lowered its head, bowing deeply, "Am honored to answer for Her Majesty." He remained bent, facing down as he answered. I stared at the back of his deformed scaly black head, "You were damned, and your warm flesh was taken—but you retained your spirit. None can touch you for the rest of your days. You are amongst the dead, and Queen of the Damned, as you defeated our master."

Eric's voice sounded hollow, "No one can touch her? She has to live eternity without..." he didn't finish. My jaw hung opened. I was alone. Even though he survived, there would be no comfort from this friend. There was no warmth left in my life. Even my body was frozen, chilled through and through like a corpse. His eyes became glossy and he looked down, at my bare feet. Clearing his throat, his gaze turned up. His golden eyes remained on my face, "I have no idea how to console you, Ivy." He remained in front of me, his arms at his sides, uncertain.

Looking away, I replied, "There is no comfort for my loss." Collin. My throat tightened. I was to be deprived of touch, naked, and alone. Closing my eyes, I turned away. Numbness flooded me. Eric's voice rang out behind me, "Ivy, wait..."

But I didn't turn back, "There's nothing to be done." Stopping, I turned to make certain no one would harm him. "This boy has my protection. Anyone who seeks to harm him will suffer the consequences." I lifted my hand, surprised. Power, light and pleasant, flowed through my fingers. I gazed at Eric. His wide eyes were stunned as my power made my protection clear. A mark appeared above Eric's brow—a sprig of Ivy that glimmered pale gold. My mark. It was the mark of my chosen people. I smiled and walked away, knowing he would be safe.

CHAPTER THIRTY

Demons trailed after me, constantly asking if I needed anything. But I didn't. And they couldn't give me what I wanted—a sweatshirt and jeans. I'd always be cold. Always be alone and untouched. Eric remained in the Underworld. He wouldn't leave. Numbness flooded my soul, smoothing the ache of Collin's loss. I sat on my dais, my hair draped over my shoulders like a goddess, with my legs crossed. Eric sat next to me, trying not to look at me.

"The curse twisted, you know," he said one day. I stared blankly at the empty throne room. I didn't respond. "My curse tried to kill you, as your cursed tried to damn you... Combined, they did this. And you'll forever be a vision of beauty that no one can touch."

Glancing out of the corner of my eyes, I looked at him. He slouched back in his padded velvet seat to the right of my throne. His eyes were anywhere but on me. He always averted his eyes, not wanting to look at my body. I finally spoke. After weeks of silence, I finally said, "It's cruel. And humiliating. I'm on display like... like a... spectacle. Even the demons stare at me. They tried to clothe me, offering different materials, all made of magic, but when I put them on, they melt away. It's like this is a punishment for hiding every secret that I ever had. Now, I'm forever exposed."

He nodded, "I didn't think of it like that. You liked your privacy," turning his head to meet my gaze, he added, "your secrets."

"I did," I answered. His gaze started to drift lower, but he stopped himself and looked away. I'd watched him trying hard to ignore my body, and constantly looking anywhere and everywhere else. It was as if this curse pained him too. "This … ," I sighed, rubbing my face in my hands. "This pains you, doesn't it? You can't help me. You can't touch me. You can't even look at me." When he didn't answer I pressed my eyes closed and took a deep breath. Rising on my bare legs, I moved and stepped in front of him. "Look. Look at me, Eric," I threw my hair over my shoulders, exposing myself entirely. "Once you see, there will be nothing left to look at it." That was what I'd hoped. That was what I told myself. And Eric, well, he was constantly avoiding my gaze, looking over my shoulder as we spoke. It made me feel insane. It was bad enough that no one could touch me, but being denied his gaze, too. It was too much. I couldn't stand it anymore. Something inside of me snapped. "Look at me, Eric! This is who I am. This is what I've become! Accept it!"

His head turned, and he met my eyes. A sad smile spread across his lips as he stood. "It's not so easy. And it's not what you think." He reached for my hands, forgetting that I was untouchable. His grip slipped through mine. I was air to him, and nothing more. Turning his gaze away from me, he pressed his lips together and shoved his hands back into his pockets. "Your beauty is brilliant. Looking at you is like staring at the sun. I know I'm not supposed to, but I look again and again. Once is not enough."

I moved, catching his gaze with my eyes. "You loved me. Didn't you?" All this time, I suspected his feelings for me were more than platonic, but there was so much anger laced with his affection that I wasn't sure it was real. Now, seeing him looking at me like that... It was as if he was granted a wish only to have it shatter in his grasp. The longing in his eyes made my throat tighten.

"How could I not? But your heart was never mine..." his voice trailed off as his gaze slid over my form—looking at me with softness that was uncharacteristically Eric. He tore his eyes away when they reached the sloping curve of my hip. I would have blushed, if I was able.

I looked away and turned, walking toward the massive window, pulling my hair back over my shoulders to hide myself the best I could. I could feel Eric's eyes on my back. I didn't answer him. I would never stop loving Collin. This was my punishment. This was my price; to live eternity this way, without him. Emotionally, I was in such a state of despair that I couldn't take it much longer. If I were made of warm flesh and soft skin, I would have found comfort in Eric's arms. The way he blended pleasure and pain in such a carnal way would help me forget what had happened. What I'd lost. But there was no forgetting.

And I noticed the new twist on Eric's curse. He was in love with me. But all this time, he couldn't do a thing about it. Even admitting it risked his curse killing me. And I suppose it did, in a way. Eric could no longer touch me. Any hope he might have had that one day I may want him was gone. But the expression on his face said he already knew. For weeks following Kreturus' death, Eric was by my side. He never left me. He never faltered. His nasty remarks were a thing of the past. They'd been a way to push me away—a means to make me hate him. But it didn't work. I'd seen through him, even before he dropped his veil and allowed me to look into his soul. And now, that was all he could see of me.

Swallowing hard, I spoke over my shoulder, "I still owe a debt. I need to take care of it before the Demon Princess tries to claim her price."

CHAPTER THIRTY-ONE

Eric agreed to accompany me. He glanced at the golden walls after we effonated. I'd given him more power—power that wouldn't decrease with use. "Why are we in the Lorren?" Eric asked.

I didn't want to see Jenna Marie or Lorren, not like this. But I had no choice. I couldn't conjure the mirror in the palace. I wasn't certain why. And I couldn't go topside. The curse bound me to the caverns of Hell. This was the only place remaining. The only place I could go that I hadn't tried. And it was time to pay the debt. We moved through the golden maze, emerging in the small golden room. Jenna Marie had her arms wrapped around Lorren. They were laughing, teasing. A smile that I'd never seen before lined Lorren's lips. He was truly happy.

I cleared my throat to get their attention, but I didn't have to. Shocked faces with opened mouths stared at me. Eric stepped in front of me, hiding me from them, until they had the sense to look away. "Thank you," I whispered. Eric nodded. My heart fluttered in my chest. This was the last thing I had to do. Pressing my lips together, I said, "Kreturus is dead. I am Queen of the Underworld now."

Jenna Marie knew better than to be happy. Her eyes were wide, her brow knitted in concern, "Where is Collin? We don't hear anything in here. Neither of us can leave. Lorren's trapped here, and I can't move about the Underworld without something trying to kill me. We've been worried about you. What happened, Ivy?" I told her. My voice came out of me in a monotone, speaking factually. Her eyes grew wider and wider. Lorren's grip on her hand tightened when they'd learned of Collin's death.

Lorren's eyes slid to my face, "And this was your price? You've lost your form, your body, and can't conceal yourself?" I nodded once. Complete transparency. Complete hell.

"The demons said she's dead, a lost soul without a body. She can't leave the Underworld. She can't cover her form..." Eric's voice was softer than last they'd heard. A surprised expression crossed both of their faces, but they said nothing. "Before this happened, she made a blood bargain with the Demon Princess. She needed to come here to conjure the mirror to resolve her debt."

They both nodded, not asking how he knew. Blood bargains were a secret, but now I had no secrets. Closing my eyes, I pictured the black glass. When I opened them, the mirror stood in front of me with the cracked pane. I stared into the large cracked glass.

Eric stepped next to me, "You can't see yourself..."

Jenna Marie said softly, "Souls have no reflection... They aren't," she broke off looking for the right word.

Lorren added, "Tangible. Mirrors show things that are. Things that can be touched. You no longer exist as anything but a lost soul, free to roam the Underworld with infinite power." I nodded, understanding better as he spoke. I was a ghost. Sort of. "What's your debt?" He asked the question, black eyes piercing into mine.

"You know I can't say. And it doesn't matter anyway. I can't pay it. That isn't why I came here."

The tension in his shoulders eased, "Then why are you here?"

"The mirror wouldn't come to me, not without you here..." the blood bargain prevented me from saying more. "I have to pay the price. I'm not giving her what she wants. And I can't kill her. Kreturus was wrong. It would only force the debt to be paid, and she'd survive. That was what she did to him, and I won't allow her to do it to me, only to rise up again later. No one should have to do what we did." All three of us used the stone. All three of us were cursed for eternity because of it.

I raised my hand to the pane, ready to press through, when Lorren's dark sleeve darted in front of me. He pressed himself between my form and the mirror, preventing me from stepping through. It may have been possible to pass through him. I didn't know. And I wouldn't find out.

"Stop, Ivy," he said softly. His dark eyes met mine. "I know why you're here. Why you need me. Let me go. I'll take care of it. The bargain will be complete." Lorren was earnest, his jaw tense. Coldness flooded me from head to toe as he spoke. He knew. But I couldn't hear his words. I could only stare at the glass knowing that I shouldn't listen to another word. I couldn't let him do this.

"No, Lorren. It's my debt." I protested, still staring over his shoulder at the glass. Locoicia was on the other side, waiting for me—waiting to take my place.

Jenna Marie darted to his side, "What is he talking about? Go where? I thought you couldn't leave this place?"

But he didn't answer Jenna Marie. Lorren simply looked at me and said, "Out of all the angels for you to send, she would never expect me. You do know who I was? Before I was trapped in this tomb?" I had an idea, but I wasn't certain. Some of the depictions I'd seen while I searched the archives in Rome had a glaring resemblance. I nodded once. I knew who he was. "Then, let me go. This will end." If the mirror was in the Lorren, he was able to pass through it. As long as the glass stood where it was now, he could stay there. It would be like he wasn't trapped anymore. It would be a way to make his curse more bearable. That was what he said. That was how he appealed to me, but something seemed wrong.

All three of us had paid horrifically. I couldn't do anything that would cause him anymore pain. What if Locoicia won? What if she bested him? I couldn't chance it. I shook my head, and started to tell him no, but Lorren smiled at me. Pressing his back into the mirror, he said, "I love you Jenna..." And he was absorbed by the dark glass.

My eyes widened. I pressed on the glass half panicked, but it wouldn't let me through. "Eric! What happened?"

"What'd you bargain for?" he asked quickly. He stood behind me, watching Lorren disappear.

"An angel. She wanted an angel." The bargain was complete. The magic that gagged me was no more and I spilled what I knew, "Collin said she requested something I couldn't possibly deliver! She was supposed to screw me. I can't let him do this!" I turned to Jenna Marie. She was walking toward the glass with a smile across her pink lips.

"You are a vision of beauty, Ivy. You will have peace. Be patient and it will come." She stood before me and as she spoke her breath crystalized into tiny scrawling words in a language I didn't know. They circled around me, landing gently on my head like a crown. For a moment, I was warm. And I realized what she'd done - it was a blessing. Angels rarely gave blessings because they only had a handful to use over their existence. And Jenna Marie gave a blessing to me—Queen of the Damned. The words faded away as she watched me with a soft smile on her face.

I stood there, my mouth agape. Jenna Marie's inner perkiness reemerged, "We'll be fine. We're together, again. You gave him back to me. It's a price I'm glad to pay." She laughed, "Besides, you just sent the angel of death into her lair. Bet she wasn't expecting that!" Jeanna Marie continued to laugh as she dissolved into the black glass.

Eyes wide, I turned back to Eric. He laughed, "Lorren was the death angel?"

Eyebrow arched, I asked, "I knew something you didn't?"

Smiling at me, he nodded, shoving his hands into his pockets and said, "I guess so." But he could see the worry in my eyes as I glanced at the dark glass. Eric moved next to me. "Don't worry. If the Demon Princess could overpower the death angel—by some insane stroke of luck—there is no way she can best two angels."

I nodded, looking up at his face. "I would have never put them together. The perky pink princess and the death angel." I smiled to myself.

Eric mumbled to himself, following me out, "Yeah, love does weird things."

CHAPTER THRITY-TWO

I sat on my throne, my body curled into a ball to conceal myself and get warm. I was freezing. It seemed to be part of the curse. I doubted that I'd ever be warm again. My knees were pulled into my chest, and my ankles were crossed, as I attempted some form of modesty. Eric's eyes slid over me. He sat on the marble stairs in front of me, with a viewpoint that left little to the imagination. I seriously considered hiding behind draperies for the rest of my life.

T'agar, the demon who first addressed me, entered the throne room, humbly bowing as he entered. He waited for me to address him before stepping from the threshold. My voice echoed across the vast room. "Come."

The demons had left me alone for the most part. They ran the place, and continued to do so, asking my approval for things. Eric had to tell me what some if it was. I had no idea. I always thought I'd go to heaven, and now I was Queen of the Underworld. T'agar's claws scraped against the marble making a sound like a knife being sharpened as he neared us. He stopped thirteen paces from my feet, as they all did when summoned. A step closer meant death. I had no plans on killing them, but they believed they would erupt in a ball of flames if they disobeyed. Eric told me to keep my mouth shut. It would prevent anarchy, and since I wanted peace, I listened to him.

I straightened my legs, sitting up in my throne as he neared. His voice gurgled, "The portals have been secured, but we are in need of a new Guardian, Most Gracious One. The creatures that you demanded to return are here and accounted for, but this last meeassssure," he drew out the word, making it sound more sinister, "will ensure that they remain here."

I nodded. Where did the last Guardian come from? The angels made it, didn't they? Were we supposed to order another one? A smirk formed across my mouth, and quickly vanished. Eric gave me an odd expression, eyebrow raised. I didn't acknowledge him. "Is that all?"

The demon remained with his head bowed. His hesitation was uncharacteristic. I leaned forward in my seat, my hair dangling forward. There obviously was more, and from his silence, I assumed it was bad. "Speak, demon. Tell me."

He lowered his hunched back, making his neck sweep closer to the floor. His stance was nearly a grovel. I wondered how he remained upright without falling over. "The angels requested conference with your Highness. They said war is imminent. They are... coming." his great scaly head turned upward, meeting my gaze. My mouth opened in shock. The demon thought it was directed at him, and bowed lowly, "Forgive me, Beautiful Queen. We know not what to do. Directives are needed. Soon." He bowed lowly and swept from the room.

I glanced at Eric. I knew what he wanted me to do. It was the same thing the angels wanted me to do, but I couldn't. I wouldn't allow it.

Eric rolled his eyes, "I don't know why you're trying to save them. Even their makers want them gone, and you stand in the way like some sort of martyr. You're already dead, Ivy. You already paid the ultimate price. Let this go..."

I rose, stopping in front of him. His legs were clad in dark denim and sprawled in front of him. He used to smell like wholesome goodness. He used to be an angel, a Martis, and then a Valefar. He knew everything there was to know about all of them. I shivered, wrapping my arms around myself. "I can't. I can't allow them to destroy the Martis. They can't wipe out an entire race because they don't think they can change." I failed to recall the Valefar to the Underworld, as the angels thought I would when I summoned the rest of the creatures of Hell back below ground. But the Valefar remained topside.

Eric moved behind me, silent as always. His hand was raised, as if he was going to rest it on my shoulder. He held it there. I could feel the heat from his hand. I pressed my eyes closed, savoring the sensation. When he finally spoke, I turned to look up at him, "One Martis changed. It doesn't excuse the lot of them for everything they've done. In many ways, they are worse than the Valefar. Ivy, you know this." His voice softened, as his gaze slid to my lips. "You can't save them."

The way Eric looked at me sometimes made me suffer horribly. But my pain eased his. I couldn't deny him. I couldn't tell him to stop. He learned that I could sense the heat from his skin. It radiated off of him in small waves that made me melt inside. Eric was becoming more daring. Since he couldn't use force anymore, he was looking for other ways. And he'd found one.

His eyes remained fixed on my lips. I felt so hollow inside. So cold and numb. Nothing would change it, but this felt like a cheat. Like Lorren going through the glass. It was a go-around that let me feel something. Eric lifted his hand from his pocket where it'd grown warm. I thought he was going to put it by my cheek, but his gaze drifted lower to my neck. His hand remained perfectly still, slightly above the soft skin of my neck. He watched as I closed my eyes, feeling the heat from his hand, imagining his touch on my skin. Before the heat ebbed, I felt his warm breath slide across me. I shuddered, backing away. Eric's lips twisted into a wicked smile as he straightened. My mind was blank. What were we talking about?

Turning from him, I let the heartache last longer. The pain and longing for human touch fed him, easing his agony, giving him peace. Peace that alluded me. I finally said, "She did what was right. Shannon took forever to get there, but she sacrificed herself for me. They can't think that's nothing." And they didn't. It was another matter entirely that had them enraged.

CHAPTER THRITY-THREE

The Pool of Lost Souls sat silent as my entourage passed its azure depths. Eric walked a step behind me, and Legion, the demon who controlled my armies, followed. My throat tightened as we passed the spot where Collin stood last time we were here. And over there, by that stone, was where I'd realized Apryl was a Valefar. I hadn't seen her since the day she walked away from me, but I knew she didn't survive. As soon as I was queen, before I recalled the demons, I sent them to search for my sister. There was no trace of her. Finally we heard a strange story of a little girl. Someone protected her—a girl with flame red hair and wild eyes. My sister. They were attacked by Dreanoks and she wouldn't surrender the child. I pressed my eyes closed. I wasn't fast enough. Even after I sacrificed everything, I still lost her.

As if Eric could sense my thoughts, he quickened his pace, urging us to move faster. The Pool of Lost Souls was at my back, and I found I could walk no more. The stone's magic stopped me at the portal out of the Underworld and prevented me from passing into the catacombs that were under Rome. Eric stepped forward, opening the portal. When it opened, it revealed two angels. The meeting began.

The angels averted their gaze when Eric stepped back, and they saw my form. One of them sneered as if I'd chosen to arrive this way. I said evenly, "I do not look away from you in disgust. Please show the same respect for me."

The angels were uncomfortable, but they looked back. First at Eric, and then me. "So it is true," the tall one with thin blonde hair said. His light colored clothing stood in contrast to his heavy coat. I wondered if it was still snowing. Snowing in places it shouldn't have. "You used Satan's Stone, and it did this…"

Eric usually spoke for me about this matter. I found it hard to admit what I did and the result, but this time when Eric began to speak, I lifted my hand,

~ 316 ~

indicating I would answer. "Yes. I used the stone. Two others used it previously. We all paid the price for using it. This is my curse. I hide nothing from you—I conceal nothing. I cannot touch or be touched. My humanity was stripped away with my flesh. I killed Kreturus for you. I stopped his war, and recalled my creatures, as I am the one who assumed his throne. But, I will not condone the slaughter of the Martis." My arms were at my sides. The expression on my face was neutral, but confident. "One of your lowest creatures saved me, though the Martis wanted my head. I cannot ignore her actions. I cannot condemn them as you have. I will not recall the Valefar, as that is the only thing keeping you from killing the Martis."

The blonde angel's lips curled into a soft smile as I spoke. The dark-haired angel next to him remained expressionless. It appeared that my words angered him, but he did not interrupt. When I finished the blonde angel said, "That is a very compelling argument, but that is not why we are here."

Surprise lifted my eyebrows, "It's not? Then why have you come?" I glanced at Eric, but he continued to stare at them like they were threats to my safety.

Blonde-boy stepped forward, "An angel is gone. Unaccounted for. Her name was Jenna Marie. She did not die in battle, and last she was seen was with you. It is rumored that you captured her and abandoned her in the Underworld. That was construed as an attack on our race—on our people. Give her back or we will be forced to retrieve her."

I laughed. It bubbled out of my stomach, and spilled over my lips before I could stop it. "You're not going to kill the Martis?"

He shook his head. "No. They have been warned of their probation. Their hierarchy was destroyed and reformed. Those who survived the war will have to adjust to their new place. And if you will not retrieve your Valefar, we will not retrieve our Martis."

Nodding, I said, "Agreed." I didn't tell them that I commanded the Valefar to only prey on the despicable. At some point the Martis and the Valefar would realize they were working toward the same goal, though hell-servants were doing it in a more grizzly way. "About Jenna Marie... she is not dead. She is with the Death Angel—her love."

The silent angel, unfolded his arms, hissing, "The Death Angel is not her lover! And Jenna Marie is not with him. We just saw him. For all your curses, it appears you can still lie." The veins in his arms were popping up like little straws. I watched him for a moment. He hated me, that much was obvious.

Eric remained silent, but I could sense him tensing at my side. I answered, "I did not say I couldn't lie. I'm sure I can, but what's the point? To deceive you? To trick you into thinking something that isn't true?" I laughed. "You fail to see that we want the same things. That makes me an unlikely ally, but I'm not the enemy. Jenna Marie is with the original Death Angel—Lorren. He is trapped in the depths of his golden maze, and will never emerge. It is his curse. He was the first angel to use the stone. Jenna Marie is with him. I took her to him."

The angry angel looked like he was going to rupture. The blonde-boy gave him a look that appeared to diffuse him. Then he turned back and asked, "What proof do you have? We cannot simply take your word for it."

I arched an eyebrow, "Can you not tell if I am lying? Can't you use your powers and draw the truth out of me?"

"You think you are speaking the truth, I can tell. But your story is... extreme. We need verification."

Eric cleared his throat. "I remember you G'hreil. Do you remember me? Look at my face and see who I was. Remember the second time Satan's Stone was used to defeat the devil Kreturus. Remember who paid for it with his life." Eric spoke softly, and the veil that he held so tightly, lifted. I could see him as he was—part angel, part man, part demon. He was terrifying. The angel gasped. The veil slammed back into place. Eric's golden eyes burned. "I vouch for her. Jenna Marie is with Lorren—alive."

I didn't think that would be the end of it, but it was. The two angels bowed at the waist, nothing like the demon bows, more like a polite good-bye and left. Several days later, we were called to the Pool again. This time a gift waited in the catacombs.

"Eric, coming up here is..." I didn't want to be here, but I couldn't shun their gift. I hoped it was clothes, but I honestly had no idea what they would send or why.

His face had a pleasant expression, which meant my pain was calming him. "I know. I know, Ivy. Just accept the gift, and leave. I'll take care of the rest. It's formalities. We don't want to avoid one war only to cause another." I nodded.

My bare feet moved across the cold wet rock. I could feel that, but not Eric's touch. I even had a demon try to take my hand to see if they could do it—they couldn't. I was untouchable. Eric seemed restless lately. Stopping before the Pool, I said, "Eric, wait..." he stopped, turned and walked back to me. I didn't know how to say this. I could see it in his eyes. The two of us staying together, feeding off each other's misery only made it worse. I had a sincere affection for him, and I wanted him to go live his life—not mine—not my curse. It was my burden and mine alone.

"After we accept this gift, I want you to spend some time in the sun."

"What?" he whispered. Shock washed across his face. He tried to hide it, "If that's what you want." His shoulders tensed. He turned to walk away from me. Instinctively, I reached for him. My pale hand swept through his shoulder, making him shiver. He turned back to me.

"Eric, what do you want? Because I think some twisted girl might actually make you happy. And I know you aren't stupid enough to love anyone again. Your curse, and all." I smiled at him for a second, but he didn't smile back. "There's no future here … Eric, I would have let you use me. It would have helped me heal..." my gaze dropped as I thought about the way he made me feel before—when his hands were on me. "But, not now. And it does little for you. I sense the curse growing inside of you. I don't wish you to become something more sinister than you already are, trying to deal with it. You need someone else, Eric. Your life continues—apart from mine." As I spoke, his gaze remained on my face. His lips parted as if he was going to disagree, but he didn't. He simply nodded again, not sharing his thoughts. "Say something."

He pressed his lips together. Taking a deep breath, he rubbed his hair out of his face, and tilted his head, "What should I say? That you're right? That your pain can't give me what I need because I'm not the one who caused it? Ivy, I don't want to leave you right now. You seem... fragile."

I smirked, "Compared to you, I'm always fragile. You shocked me, scared me, and enraged me more than anyone else. But, seriously, I'll adapt. I've grown used to this," I gestured toward my nakedness. "It's not as horrible as it was. I'll get used to the rest. God knows I have enough time to figure it out."

He laughed, "I will never tire of all of this." His gaze slid over my body, head to toe. When his gaze returned to my face, I continued to smirk. "But if you think it's best, I'll do as you ask."

"You'll have to come back once in a while, and tell me what it's like up there," we continued walking, leaving the Pool behind. It was hard to let him go. It meant I'd be alone. My last friend would leave. But his life was somewhere else, and mine was trapped here. If I had one last chance to feel sunlight on my face, I'd take it. And I wanted him to revel in the warm beams the way I would have.

When we stopped at the portal, the lump in my throat grew bigger—until we opened the gift from the angels. Apparently, their last visit was thought of as "offensive" and grounds for me to attack them. Some of these old battle laws seemed like they were created by the mentally impaired. As if I'd attack. All the same, a huge gift sat on the threshold to the Underworld at the Roman portal.

Eric moved toward the white scaly mass, "Awh, isn't it cute, Ivy?" A baby dragon sat on its haunches, white as snow. Its miniature wings looked like they were made out of snowflakes. Eric laughed, moving closer to it. He had no fear. Maybe he knew it couldn't kill him, at least that was how he acted—like an immortal despite his quite mortal body. "I think they gave you a new Guardian." Eric walked over the threshold and up behind the beast. He spoke softly, urging it toward me. As soon as the beast saw the blue waters at my back, he bounded down the beach and jumped in the water. The creature acted like a puppy let off its leash. I laughed.

When I turned back to Eric, I saw him standing in the catacomb. His hand was on the portal seal, ready to close it. "Good-bye for now, beautiful girl."

I smiled sadly, "Until next time... And Eric?"

"Yeah?" His eyes were locked on mine.

"You were never invisible to me..." I smiled again, and wrapped my arms around myself. He grinned, and I watched the portal door seal into a mass of stone. Eric was gone.

CHAPTER THRITY-FOUR

The baby dragon played in the sand, jumping in the water, until it passed out on a rock to sleep. His sides gently expanded as he breathed. I sat watching him for hours after Eric left. The beast's joy was so pure that I couldn't look away. At one point I'd cast a spell and a ball of fire hung high on the cavern ceiling, illuminating the whole Pool like the midday sun. The dragon's scales appeared even brighter then—almost as if he were made out of light. I lay back on the sand, staring at the false sun spinning high above me. It cast shadows across the space, making it look like a

romanticized version of the white beaches at home.
The only thing that was different were the reddish
rocks that stretched into the sky and towered high
above me. Moving my arms, I could feel the soft grains
of sand under my skin and between my toes.

A memory tried to force its way into my mind
again. This was the third time I had to force it back
down. It was the day Collin found me on the beach at
home. I sat alone, like this, on the sand listening to the
sound of the waves lapping the shore. And then he was
there. It was like magic. Some form of power I didn't
understand. And now I did. Now I knew what it was,
and how he found me. But it was no less remarkable. It
was no less romantic in my mind. I clung to those
memories, hoping they wouldn't fade as time passed.
The day the memory became like a faded photograph,
and I could no longer recall the look in his eyes, I
would die inside. I was connected to Collin in a way I
didn't understand. And now that he was gone, I never
would.

Eric distracted me from my grief, and I allowed
him to. I needed the reprieve. But as time went on, I
began to think it was cruel. He needed to continue his
life. And I needed to continue mine. Our paths no
longer crossed. Pulling my arms over my head, I
dragged my fingers through the warm sand. The flame
ball hanging from the cavern roof warmed the grains,

which clung to my naked body and for once I didn't feel so cold.

Day after day, I snuck off to the Pool of Lost Souls. The demons didn't like it, but they wouldn't question me. The baby dragon grew larger, slowly. Its eyes glittered like emeralds. It was strange. In every way, it seemed like it was the opposite of the Omen. It played, bounding down the shore, following at my heels. I'd taken to tossing it sticks and the beast would spit out a ball of fire and char the stick in the air. We quickly ran out of sticks and I couldn't get anymore. I needed to have the Valefar swipe me some.

As my feet moved through the sand, the white creature and I wandered into a cove that I hadn't visited before. The blue-green water was still. It felt warmer in the small space when I lit the false sun and hung it high above us. The dragon bounded off, setting out for deeper waters to play in. Nearing the edge of the Pool, I extended my foot and tested it with my toe. The Pool was too cold to swim in, but this shallow place was warming from the flames above. I waded in, feeling the warm water slipping up my body.

Leaning back, I submerged my head and came up with my hair dripping wet. Water flowed into my eyes and I sighed in contentment. I examined my arms in the orb of light. My form was incredibly pale with a slight blue shimmer around the edges. It was deceptive how human I looked in the light. As I gazed at my hand, I saw someone between my fingers watching me in the distance. My heart lurched. I blinked once, but he was still there. Watching me from across the Pool. Watching as if I were a mirage. Which is exactly what I thought he was. A likeness of Collin. But nothing more. The boy didn't move or blink. I wasn't a fool. I knew it wasn't him. But day after day, I returned, hoping my mind would trick me again and again. And that I'd see him, if for only a second.

The baby dragon ran from the cove, as it always did. And this time I dove into the deeper water. My mirage wasn't where it usually was. As I walked around the water, I didn't see the image of Collin. I thought it would be nice to see him closer, so I moved to the spot where he always stood. Memories of Collin surged through me. It made me feel something again. The warm water lapped against my skin, as the false sun baked the sand warmer and warmer. I didn't see him that day, so I didn't leave. After I'd swam, I decided to lay on the beach. Dripping, I laid back and was instantly covered in sand. Closing my eyes, I took a deep breath when a shadow crossed my body. Startled, I glanced up. Someone was standing in front of me, their face obscured by the sun.

"It is you..." he said softly. I could barely hear him. My arm flew to my eyes as I tried to see, but he positioned himself perfectly. The false sun was too bright and I had to stare directly into it to see him. "What happened to you?" he asked. I didn't recognize the voice. It was different somehow.

Sitting up more, I pulled my dripping hair over my body, trying to cover myself. "Step out of the light." When I spoke, he startled. Turning, he ran back toward the water and disappeared below the surface. Not understanding why, I chased him, and dove in after him. He dove lower and lower, his body moving away from mine. Unlike me, I could see clothes on his body. Shame or something like it, washed over me, and I darted away, surfacing like a drowning mermaid.

I pulled myself up onto a rock, and curled my body into a ball. My wet hair hung down my back, dripping. I buried my face in my knees. I was going crazy. There was no way this was Collin. Whatever I was chasing was some sort of poltergeist screwing with my mind, but I couldn't walk away. I couldn't leave. There was a slight sound as the thing surfaced behind me. Using a spell, I uttered the incantation and arched my back, falling into the water, grabbing the boy by the throat. He gasped. And so did I.

I could touch him. He had Collin's face. Collin's body. "Who are you? Why are you tormenting me?" I shook him, and dropped the thing into the water. I expected it to flee, but he remained still, staring at me like he was seeing a ghost.

Wiping dark hair out of his eyes, he answered, "Don't you know me, Ivy? Can't you tell what I am? What I've become?" His voice was stronger, more certain. Blue eyes pierced into mine. But I couldn't believe what I was seeing. Turning, I swam away from him, and walked out of the water and onto the beach. I rang out my hair, intending to leave. He followed me, his gaze moving up and down my body like he'd seen it before. Drawing a deep breath, I stopped, watching him. Finally, I said, "Collin died. I saw it. You're not him."

He stood in front of me, exactly the way I remembered. And I could touch him. That's how I knew it couldn't be real. Nothing could touch me. I was dead, a lost soul with no body. But he reached for me, his hand pressing into mine. He tangled our fingers together, and I looked up at him. "You're right. I'm not him. Not entirely. My body died that day, but my soul didn't... because you put it here." He looked at me, still not certain. His eyes were wide as he gaped at our hands. "You were so pale, shimmering like you had flesh. But you saw me... I had to know if you could see me. And you can."

Collin looked into my eyes as I listened to him speak. His soul. The demon kiss. Shock flittered through me. I still tried to squelch my hope. "The demon kiss saved you? But the Pool was broken. Emptied. How?" As my mind melted I could only say one word at a time. I'd broken the Pool. I'd set the Lost Souls free. It was empty.

He smiled softly, touching his hand to my cheek the way he had a hundred times before. "It's not broken. At least it wasn't for me. When you reclaimed your soul with the demon kiss, what was left of mine came here. I've seen others come, but they were quickly whisked away. Their souls floated out of the Pool and out of sight. I was the only one who remained. I waited, thinking that I'd have the same fate, but it never happened. The Pool only held one soul—mine.

"I thought I'd never see you again. You look so real, you feel alive. The light, it made me think you were alive. That's why I didn't come closer. But, today, you forced me to. You moved." Slowly he backed away, waiting to see what I would do. His gaze slid down my body. My breath caught in my throat. "You look as beautiful as before. Ivy, what are you thinking?"

Tears filled the corners of my eyes and rolled down my cheeks. "I'm thinking this can't possibly be real. That it's a cruel dream and I'll wake up at any moment." But before I could say another word, he wrapped me in his arms and pulled me to him. Collin's body felt warm, pressed against mine. Every taught muscle was the same as before. The curve of his neck, the scent of his body—it was all the same. Without waiting for my brain to catch up, he lowered his lips to mine and kissed me. His hands slid down my sides, linking around the small of my back, as he pulled me down to the sand with him. I laughed when we fell.

His lips trailed down my neck, and I felt every caress of his tongue—every stroke of his hand. Gasping, he stopped and looked at me. His eyes lingering on my lips and then my breasts. His fingertips tracing along the curves of my body, playing and teasing. "Since when do you swim naked?"

Wide-eyed, I stared at him. I couldn't believe he was here. That he was in my arms. I smiled shyly, "It's the curse. I'm always naked."

He laughed and pulled me to his chest. Cradling my head, he looked into my eyes. "That is a blessing in disguise." He smiled again, and kissed me so deeply that bliss shot through me.

Jenna Marie's glittery blessing came to mind. The words she said that fell like a crown on my head before she followed Lorren into the glass. I smiled. She gave me a blessing that transformed a hideous curse. I wondered if she knew Collin was here. I wondered if she knew that he would be the only person that could touch me. Jenna Marie gave me more than I ever hoped for, and there was no way for me to thank her.

Collin pulled back, examining the expression on my face, the smile that lingered on my lips and the tears in the corners of my eyes. "What are you thinking?"

"I love you with all my soul, Collin Smith." I pressed my lips to his gently, tasting him with a flick of my tongue. Collin wrapped his arms around me tightly, deepening the kiss, and took my breath away.

Assassin: Fall of the Golden Valefar

is a Demon Kissed spin-off series that will be released Summer 2012.

STONE PRISON
Twisted Tales #1

By H.M. Ward

CHAPTER ONE

The sky was dark the night my father was killed.
The servants had just lit the nightlights, and the flames
flickered happily in our windows. I was barely two-
years-old when it happened, but I remember everything.
I remember the sticky night air that was dripping with
the scent of honeysuckle. I remember hearing the
hushed whispers of frantic servants. The noises carried
through the house making the tiny hairs on the back of

my neck stand on end. I remember the sound of my father's footfalls crossing to open the door.

An unnatural silence filled the house as the door creaked opened. Then, I heard her voice. It was sweet like honey, promising everything and asking nothing. It drew me from beneath my covers. I had to see the face that went with that voice. As I padded across my room, Father hushed her, and forced her outside our home. Dressed in a white nightgown, I stood at my window shrouded in darkness. I stood on the tips of my tiny toes to peer over the ledge.

The shadows painted a pattern of black lace across her form, but I could still tell that she was the most beautiful woman I'd ever seen. Thick golden hair fell in long waves beneath the hood of her black cloak. As she spoke, full ruby red lips shone like they were covered with dew. Her skin was like that of a fine doll's—perfectly smooth. But her eyes were angry. As they spoke, the woman became more agitated. Her beautiful face contorted with rage.

The only thing I heard my father say was, "No." He wasn't unkind. It didn't sound like he was chastising one of the servants, or rebuking her. He sounded pained, like he didn't want to say the word. But he did.

That single word shattered my world.

Before he finished speaking, the woman lunged at my father. One fist was at her waist, while the other hand grabbed my father's shoulder. She looked into his eyes, as she thrust the blade into his stomach and twisted. Scarlet poured from the wound, spattering on the dirt at his feet. The woman released him. Without a scream, my father fell to the ground, dead. Before my tiny lips could scream, the woman's gaze turned upward to my little body, watching from the window.

I disappeared from my home that night. Not a soul saw the woman pluck me from the window, and carry me to the stone tower deep in the woods. Every night since, I dreamt of a beautiful woman stabbing my father. Every night was the same. The screams that no one shrieked the night of his death rang out deafeningly loud in my dreams, waking me with my heart beating so fast that I thought it would burst. The dreams did not cease. And I grew older, alone, locked away from the rest of the world, with a murderer as my only companion.☐

CHAPTER TWO

"Blood is power," the old woman said. Her golden hair had faded long ago. The sun had been unkind, weathering her skin like an old hide. She had trudged up the long staircase to my room at the top of the stone tower. Fifteen years passed since the night her horrific shadow first crossed my path. The old woman's hunched form gasped for air, and she lowered herself into a chair.

The hag's ancient gray eyes were listless. She sat across from me like we were old friends, though were not. Staring at her gnarled hands, I remembered seeing them smooth and covered in blood. It was impossible to forget. That moment was etched into my mind, like acid burning away metal, for eternity. That dark memory crushed all happy ones. I couldn't remember Father's laughter, or the sparkle of his eyes when he spoke. I couldn't remember his warm voice and strong touch. All of that was gone, stolen by the woman who sat across from me.

The witch.

The old sorceress wrung her hands, and took a deep breath. This was the only night out of the year that I was allowed a small amount of freedom. It was my birthday, but that wasn't the reason I was allowed to venture from her side. The reason I was permitted to leave my stone prison was due to someone else's birth—the Crown Prince's. Each year the royal family held a ball to celebrate his birth. And every year the witch forced me to attend.

However, that tiny bit of freedom came at a price. The only way I was allowed to attend was if I took things from the castle, if I stole. The penalty for theft was severe in this kingdom. The guard who caught me had the right to severe my hand at the wrist. If I was caught a second time, my head would be severed at the neck. And theft from the palace was a higher risk. There were more guards to see me steal. I risked much in doing this, but it was worth the risk.

The witch taught me how to take things and evade the guard's detection. I became more than adept as I grew. No one suspected me. A governess trailed behind me, until I found what I needed. And the witch usually asked for things that wouldn't be missed—like a lock of hair, a piece of cloth, or some other discarded, worthless, item. She collected these things and stored them under lock and key in the wooden cabinet. I expected that this year would not be different. She would require me to take something that wouldn't be missed, and send a governess to trail along behind me.

But my assumption was wrong.

The witch licked her withered lips. They were so chapped that they bled in the corners, making it appear as if she had sores on her mouth. "This night is more important than the previous balls. This night you will steal the object I seek and then your future, and mine, will be secure. The item I require will bring us much. You will take it for me and return home before midnight." She paused, looking at me with her withered lips pulled into a tight smile. "If you do as I say, there will be enough endless beauty, unsurpassed riches, and power to last a lifetime."

Those things were foreign to me, though I knew she craved them. I'd been locked in a tower, shunned for a lifetime. And on the nights I was allowed out, I still had to return before midnight. The witch made certain that I was always locked in the tower by the twelfth toll of the night bells. To most people, midnight marks a new day that brings new hope. But not me. I was always acutely aware of the twelfth chime. There was a stirring within me that seemed to long for something, but I didn't know what. It only appeared at that hour and vanished instantly as I sat alone, staring at stone walls from my pillow.

Then the morning would come, and rays of sunlight would spill across the cold floor. Most days I stared out the window that was too small to throw myself through. I know because I tried. It would have been more bearable to plummet from the tower than to endure another day of confinement. I dreamed of walking among people again, and staying with them past the eleventh hour. I dreamt of a normal life, just another content peasant in a vast kingdom.

But the witch had other plans.

I glared at her. So many thoughts rushed through my mind. If I could only be free from her. I'd tried to run away several times. And each time ended with the same hard-learned lesson. No one can escape from the witch. Ever. I could tell from her posture, from the wringing of her hands, that this night mattered more to her than the others. This night was unlike the others, but a single facet remained the same.

I was to leave at the eleventh hour.

Her gray eyes seemed to come to life as she spoke. "For too long, our kind have not been welcome there, Ella. For too long we have toiled amongst the stones and forests trying to claim a life worth living, like wild animals. But no more. After tonight, things will change."

~STONE PRISON IS ON SALE NOW~

VAMPIRE APCOLYPSE

BOOK #1: BANE

The world as we know it is gone. The ice caps have melted and shifted south, devastating the northern territories and eradicating major cities such as New York and London, which are now under water and frozen. Humans died off during an epidemic prior to the ice disaster, and many more died during the floods at the start of this new ice age.

These events have forced vampires out of hiding. In order to ensure that their food source wouldn't completely die off, the vampires have sequestered the remaining humans into farms and taken control of all that remains of civilization. Over time, the humans breeding on these farms became anemic. Their blood no longer sustains the master race.

But not all of the humans were captured and sent to the farms. Some of the humans evaded the hunters, hiding in safe houses across the frozen tundra.

As decades passed, the free humans disappeared, died, or were captured, until all that remains is one.

Kahli is the last wild human. BANE is her story.

COMING APRIL 15, 2012

If you love the DEMON KISSED series and can't wait for more, visit with over 45,000 fans on facebook:

Facebook.com/DemonKissed

Visit the official website:

DemonKissed.com

Demon Kissed Series By H.M. Ward

Demon Kissed

Cursed

Torn

Satan's Stone

The 13th Prophecy

Valefar Vol. 1

Valefar Vol. 2 (Spring 2012)

Assassin: Fall of the Golden Valefar
(Summer 2012)

More Series By H.M. Ward

Vampire Apocalypse: Bane
(Spring 2012)

Twisted Tales: Stone Prison

43741277R00216

Made in the USA
Middletown, DE
17 May 2017